TIMOTHY

THE BAD-ATTITUDE BILLIONAIRES

BOOK FOUR

PRU WARREN

**QUI
LEGIT
REGIT
PRESS**

She who reads, rules

Cover design by The Killion Group

Published by Qui Legit Regit Press
Alexandria, Virginia

ISBN 978-1-969856-03-7

Discover other titles by Pru Warren at https://www.pruwarren.com/

041926wch

❀ Formatted with Vellum

Meg isn't just a romance author—she's read every romance ever written (or so it seems to me). She's a glorious beta reader and I can't thank her enough.

Lexie is my go-to beta reader for anything having to do with the four-footed animals in a story. Any horse details I screwed up in this book are my fault, not hers; she did her best to correct me!

As for the tag-team duo of Glen and Reba, they're my new beta-reading superstars. Thanks, guys!

WHO ARE ALL THESE BABCOCKS?

You don't have to know this stuff—but if you get confused, here's a guide to who is who and who's related to who.

Zaccharias Babcock III had two wives.

- With Caroline (nee Taylor), he had a son—Henry.
  - Henry married Millicent (nee Howe). They had a daughter (Melissa) and a son (Zaccharias IV, known as Fourth).
    - Melissa married James (ne Hunter). Melissa, an interior designer, has no interest in the family business. They had two daughters (Ursula and Hildegarde)
      - **Ursula** is the Babcock director of Marketing
      - **Hildy** remains foot-loose and fancy-free. She is the Babcock special events coordinator.
    - **Fourth** is the chief executive officer of

Babcock Holdings. He is unmarried and unattached.

- With Tabitha (Tabby), he had three sons—Killian III, Samuel, and Reginald V
  - Killian III married Anne (nee Olsen). They had three children—Regina, Nicholas, and Suzanne.
    - **Regina** is in love with Emmett Scowley. Regina is the chief legal counsel and director of the in-house law firm at Babcock.
    - **Nicholas** is the chief financial officer at Babcock. He is known as "the human calculator."
    - **Suzanne** married and divorced Louis Mille. With him she had one son, Skip. Suzanne is now with Benjamin (Benja) Sullivan.
      - Killian IV (Skip) is an adorable, precocious child.
  - Samuel married Patricia (nee Custer). They have one daughter, Quinn
    - **Quinn** is engaged to Andy Riggs. Quinn is the Babcock chief operating officer.
  - Reginald V married Margaret "Daisy" (nee O'Toole). They have three children—Timothy, and the twins, Delilah and Joanna.
    - **Timothy** is the Babcock government liaison in Washington, DC
    - **Delilah** is the head of Babcock's division of corporate philanthropy. She enjoys the company of several would-be Mr. Delilahs, but none has yet caught her attention.
    - **Joanna** is the chief information officer at Babcock, and the head of the IT department.

Names in bold are members of what Tabby refers to as 'The Portfolio.'

A note about maiden names: Convention dictates that women are noted in family histories with their maiden names identified by "nee [Maiden name]." The use of the word 'nee' comes from the French, meaning 'born as.' Thanks to the Babcock legacy, both brides and grooms are encouraged to take the Babcock name. That's why Melissa's husband James is noted here as 'ne Hunter,' since he took his wife's name when they married. When Andy marries Quinn, he'll be 'ne Riggs.' Only one 'e' in 'ne' for the guys; the French like to throw an extra 'e' in for the ladies, making a woman's birth name into the more familiar (to genealogists) 'nee.'

1

VAUGHN'S BAR GAME

TIMOTHY

Typical. Vaughn Cox had picked up a hottie at the bar.

Man insisted he could solve all my challenges if I flew out to Denver and meet him, and even though I was on time to the minute, he'd managed to pick up a babe while waiting for me.

Vaughn was a pig. That's my guy.

In the seconds it took me to walk from the door to where he was leaning into her, I did a rapid assessment and approved the lithe body, the mane of dark hair. If she had half a brain, I'd have to steal her from him. Obviously. That was a given. My best friend would expect no less of me than to try. And I'd succeed.

On the other hand, if she was one of Vaughn's bimbos, unable to string two sentences together. I'd just mock him and leave her alone. How he put up with some of his hookups was beyond me.

Vaughn spotted me in the mirror behind the bar and turned

to greet me at a volume that would make a deaf person wince. "Timothy Baby-cock! Here at last!"

I sneered, but if he was going to resurrect eighth-grade nicknames, I could match him. "Vaughn Coxless! How do you even piss without a penis?" He stood and gave me the one-arm embrace, banging me on the back, and we grinned at each other. "What the hell are we doing in Denver?" I asked. "We couldn't have done this in Manhattan?"

"Fuck you, you lazy bastard. I wanted you to meet Frank. My problem solver."

The hot brunette watched us calmly. I tossed her a smile as the start of my campaign to steal her—then I did a double-take because her eyes were so arresting. Pale blue with a dark blue ring. Highly unusual. "Hi," I said, caught staring. "Timothy Babcock."

She shook my hand, hers cool and firm and delicious in mine. "Not actually Baby-cock, then?"

She had a good voice. Low and a little gravelly. Long brown hair worn in loose waves. Slim body, decent tits, endless legs stretching for miles in tight jeans. I gave her a grin and answered. "Not since I was a tiny, tiny tot. Which I'm not anymore." I locked an elbow around Vaughn's throat. "Coxless is just jealous. Ever since the boys' locker room at the Browning School. Poor guy."

"Yeah," he grinned. "Like *I* was jealous of *you*. I am not Coxless," he said helpfully to the babe.

Vaughn and I were both thirty-two. Far too old to actually wrestle in a crowded bar. Probably. So he used the alternate method of breaking my grip, which was to flick my balls. Naturally, I expected this and swiveled, so he flicked his fingers hard against my hip. We both snorted, being far too manly to giggle, and I let go of him.

I flagged the bartender and ordered a Macallan—whichever was their oldest.

"And we'll take another...what is that, Vaughn? Are you drinking a martini? Pussy. Another martini for my friend. Honey, Coxless and I have a meeting with someone named Frank, but before we leave, can I buy you another"—I picked up her lowball and sniffed—"tequila? Are you drinking tequila, honey?"

She took the glass from my hand and arched a fine eyebrow. "I am, *honey*, but I'll be buying my own drinks this evening." She dismissed the bartender with a quick "I'm good."

Interesting. Paying for her own drinks. Vaughn was going to have a hard time with this one. She seemed intelligent. And feisty.

"Of course," I said. "Perhaps you'll change your mind after we meet with this Frank."

Vaughn laughed, and the girl offered a quick twist of a smile. Vaughn held his hand out to the brunette. "Timothy Babcock, meet Frank Robinson."

Oh, shit. She wasn't a pickup. She was who we were meeting. The evening had gotten more interesting. "Frank Robinson? Like the Major League coach?" I asked.

"Not unless his real name is Francesca too," she said. "Frank is a nickname."

"And a lovely one at that," I tried gallantly, but she rolled her eyes. "Vaughn, I'm a little confused."

"I know," he said happily. "And I enjoyed it. Ma'am?" He flagged down the hostess and told her we were ready for a booth now. She pointed to an open space in the back, and the bartender arrived with our drinks. Vaughn handed me mine and took his and Frank's. "Come with me," he said. "I'm about to solve some serious problems. Like a fucking wizard."

Hm. We'd see. I dropped a bill on the bar and gestured to Frank for her to precede me. Pure politeness, of course. Not at all so I could check out a nicely toned ass.

Whatever else Vaughn thought he was doing, I decided I

was definitely going to steal the girl. Gonna get my Baby-Cock wet tonight.

2

THE USED CAR SALESMAN

FRANK

Timothy Babcock had a practiced oiliness to him. He was smooth. No, not just smooth—he was slick. The guy knew he was handsome, and he used it. Close-cropped ginger hair, pale skin that at least implied he was a natural redhead. Manly jawline, fit body wearing well-cut clothes that emphasized broad shoulders and a narrow waist. Every woman in the place checked him out when he strode in like the king of Denver.

As far as I was concerned, they could have him. The minute he opened his mouth, I knew he had a used car salesman vibe. Clearly, this was a guy who was watching to match the energy of everyone around him. He was a grown-up adolescent around Vaughn, he was a serious player when he was laying the groundwork to pick me up, he was magnanimous with the bartender. Definitely had the "you're one of the little people, barkeep, but I'm not so snobby that I won't address you" air about him. Tossing down the hundred-dollar bill like it was nothing.

I was pretty sure I knew exactly who I was dealing with—until we got to our booth and he reached out a hand to stop me from sitting.

"Hang on a minute." He set his drink on the table and wheeled back to the bar. He clapped his hands together, and the bartender looked to the sound. "Bar rag?" Timothy asked, holding up his hands. Shrugging, the bartender found a cloth and tossed it to Timothy, who came back to the table and brushed off the vinyl seat. French fries hit the floor, and he nudged them aside with one expensive shoe. "Yeah. Okay. After you."

I slid into the seat, Vaughn following me, and I worked to hide my frown.

It was a tiny thing. Nothing to be mentioned. He just cleaned off the seat. Right?

But...it didn't fit with the salesman persona.

Timothy tossed the rag back on the bar and sat opposite us. Vaughn didn't say anything, either, so I kept mute. But inside, I was thinking that maybe I needed to reassess the guy.

He didn't even sit on the side that had the fries.

Was he a neat freak? He couldn't actually be solicitous, could he?

"So, tell me about yourself, Frank," Timothy said with a patently fake smile. "Like, how do you know this guy?"

He gestured with his chin to Vaughn, who was not, I was glad to note, jammed up against me. He'd given me some room. I approved.

"I've probably known Vaughn longer than you have, Timothy." I turned to Vaughn. "How old were you when you first came to the ranch?"

Vaughn considered the question. Dark hair, an easy grin, a good mustache, and a nicely groomed beard—there were times when I wondered why I was so determined to keep Vaughn at arm's length. The guy was every bit as handsome as the glad-hander across from us.

"I guess I was ten? Or eleven?" Vaughn said.

"Hang on." Timothy cocked his head. "The ranch? Are you talking about the Circle B? The dude ranch Vaughn's family always went to?" Vaughn and I both nodded and understanding raised Timothy's red eyebrows. "Oh, shit! Are you Ranch Girl? Is this Ranch Girl?"

I looked to Vaughn, who now had hectic patches of pink over his high cheekbones. The guy was blushing. "Ranch Girl?" I asked. "Is that what you called me?"

Vaughn tucked his head into his neck, and Timothy laughed out loud. "Oh man! He's loved you since the dawn of time!" I felt Vaughn's thigh move as he attempted to kick Timothy under the table, but Timothy, now howling, managed to move long legs out of the path of attack. "Shit, Frank! He planned on losing his virginity to you!"

"Jesus, man! Shut the hell up!" Vaughn grabbed Timothy's arm and I had to rescue all three drinks as they began fighting over the table, Vaughn growling and Timothy laughing.

The waitress arrived, took one look, and backed away.

"It's okay, Frank," Timothy said to me, one hand wrapped around the fist on his forearm and the other attempting to brace against Vaughn's throat. "He's had sex since then. At least, I think he has."

"Oh, you cunt." Not my favorite word, but Vaughn was in distress. He broke free and sat back. "See if I'm going to help either of you now."

"Oh, like you could help me." Timothy leaned back with an air of victory and rescued his drink from me. "Frank, it's a pleasure to meet you. What the hell is this guy talking about?"

3

YEAH. WHAT'S THE STORY?

TIMOTHY

I watched the lustrous Frank insist she didn't know why Vaughn wanted us to meet, and I saw her with new eyes. Vaughn must have been fourteen when he first told me about the beauty at the dude ranch. She was, he'd insisted, the only reason he'd been willing to give up sailing around the Caribbean with me and my Uncle Samuel that summer.

The following summer, when my sisters nagged my mother into a family safari to Kenya, Vaughn had begged off again, insisting that he was going to "bag" the ranch girl. He'd missed an amazing trip but had managed to actually have sex with one of the cabin girls. Couldn't get Ranch Girl, settled for what he *could* get.

Which he lorded over me until I scored at last with Betsey, who'd worked at the local lobster shack by the Cox family vacation home in Newport. Betsey had been a legendary beauty, and losing my cherry to her the summer between tenth and eleventh grades had been enough to shut Vaughn up about Chita.

But he'd never lost the crush he had on Ranch Girl. And here she was.

I could see it. She had beautiful, quick eyes and an expressive mouth. Long face, high cheekbones. Like a movie elf. A strong movie elf. The adolescent version of Frank must have driven teenage boys insane.

"I'm not going to help either of you now," Vaughn said, pouting.

Frank rounded on him. "Me? What did I do? Nothing. I'm just sitting here."

Vaughn put on his I Have Been Wronged face. "You've made it perfectly clear that you don't want *my* help."

The Hurt Puppy look didn't work on Frank at all, which made me like her. "Please. At your prices, I can't afford the favor." She turned from him and pointedly consulted the notebook on the table that listed hundreds of trendy beers.

"Would it be so horrible?" Vaughn was now pleading.

She answered with the sound of a scoff, which made Vaughn frown.

"Would you two like to be alone?" Even if he'd taken me up on it, I wouldn't have gone far. To the bar, perhaps, where I could enjoy the sight of Vaughn actually being shot down for once.

Frank rolled her eyes. "*Please* stay."

"Crap," Vaughn said briefly, and then ordered from the waitress, who'd bravely returned. "Yeah, let me get a platter of those fries. Put some cheese and bacon on them. Are we eating dinner here?"

He looked from Frank to me, and I suppressed the urge to say, *I hope fucking not.* Good thing I stayed quiet because Frank shrugged and asked for a burger. There were several excellent restaurants in Denver and I had reservations at two of them, but never mind. "I'll have the spinach salad. Dressing on the side."

"Who's the pussy now?" Vaughn asked. "You didn't even look at the menu. How'd you know they had a spinach salad?"

"A place like this always has a spinach salad."

He greeted my absolutely correct assumption with a mocking sneer and added cheese to his burger order. He sent the waitress on her way and turned back to the table, his previous bad mood cleared by the promise of beef and grease. Vaughn was as slim as when he was our high school quarterback, and I secretly hated him for it.

He banged on the table with both hands to redirect our attention. "All right! Let's get down to this."

"Finally," Frank and I muttered together and then exchanged a grin.

"Sorry to keep you waiting," Vaughn said, annoyed. "But the parallels here are just too good to ignore." He flicked his hand back and forth between me and Frank.

I returned the move with a gesture of my own—the rolling hand that meant *Please—after you.*

"All right. You both have problems, and your solutions are sitting across the table from you. But"—he held up a hand to stop us when we both opened our mouths to protest—"you don't know each other. And you don't trust each other. That's fair. However, you do trust me. That's right, isn't it?"

He eyed me first. Grudgingly, I nodded. I did trust Vaughn. He'd been my best friend since three days after we met in seventh grade. (For the first two days, we'd hated each other but quickly realized how much more damage we could do if we teamed up. After that? Inseparable.)

Next, he gave Frank the Determined Eyebrow. She winced but agreed. "If this plan doesn't require me to sleep with you, *or* with anyone"—she glared at me—"then yes. I basically trust you, Vaughn. You're as close as I get to a brother. You've been a good friend."

"Yes I have. Good. This is good. Okay. Timothy, Frank here is totally out of money."

She didn't like the statement. "Hey! Shut the hell up!"

I flicked an eyebrow of my own. I liked the way the conversation was going. Frank needed money, and I had plenty of it. It's been my experience that the liberal application of a great deal of cash could smooth over just about all of life's potholes. Whatever it was Vaughn thought Frank could do for me, I was going to be able to buy her.

Good.

"Did you not just tell me," Vaughn said, "that you ran out of money after just one semester in engineering school?"

"Yeah, but I didn't tell you so you could share it with the world!"

Curious. Vaughn had never displayed pedophilic tendencies, so Ranch Girl couldn't be much younger than we were. That meant she was thirty. Thirty-one at the most. A perfectly fine age for a woman, but a little long in the tooth to be in college.

Vaughn ignored her protests and filled me in. "Frank went to technical school out of high school. She's a plumber by trade."

"A mason," she corrected with irritation. "A damned mason, not a plumber."

"A mason, then. She's a mason."

This was a surprising choice for a slim, beautiful woman, but now that I looked, I clocked the callouses on her long fingers. Girl worked for a living. How interesting.

She saw me looking and put her hands in her lap.

Vaughn went on. "And now she wants an engineering degree." He turned to clarify a point with her. "Chemical engineer? Electrical?"

Her mouth was twisted. She was unhappy but eventually gave up the answer. "Mechanical."

"Right. Mechanical. She saved up all her money from the construction jobs she was working, and she applied for grants and scholarships, but one semester in and they all fell through."

"Does he need to know all this?" Frank was squirming.

"Yeah." Vaughn dismissed her concerns, which was rude of him. But I was enjoying the recitation, so I nodded at him to continue. Which he did. "So she had to bail on her roommate, who is now totally pissed."

"Totally. And I can't blame her."

"Right. And Cal Buckley hired her to work the Christmas season at the ranch, but now it's March. Most of the construction jobs in Denver are on hold until the weather clears up or the money starts flowing again, and dude ranch season doesn't start until June. And Frank here refuses to become my mistress, which would be a very pleasurable way to earn an engineering degree, but what do I know?"

"I can't be bought, Vaughn. I will not be owned." Frank was very firm, even though my every experience proved that she was completely wrong. Everyone had a price.

"I get it," he said. "You're the queen of virtue. Congratulations. But if you won't let me help you one way, then stand back and let me help you another way."

The frown lines between her eyebrows were deep and long, but she cocked her head at Vaughn, listening.

He waved a hand to me as if he was a showgirl introducing the latest-model Ferrari. "Allow me to tell you about my friend Timothy Babcock."

4

OH NO YOU DIDN'T

FRANK

My flesh was crawling. To have my financial incompetence autopsied before this smug son of privilege—this arrogant man who I just knew had never worried about money ever ever ever —was galling. I never should have banked on scholarships and grants. I should have deferred until I had my funding lined up.

But I needed that degree, damn it. And now I was further behind than ever.

So if Mr. Moneybags would just stop waving around the offer to be his mistress, I'd listen to what he had to say.

Timothy sat back and crossed his arms over his chest, waiting calmly for Vaughn to speak.

"So, Frank," Vaughn said to me, "I want to tell you that my buddy Timothy here was talking to a friend at the U.S. Patent and Trademark Office."

The response to those words startled the hell out of me. Timothy unfolded from the booth like he'd been electrocuted.

He grabbed Vaughn by the lapels of his jacket and hauled him bodily off the seat.

"Can I speak to you," he ground out, although it was clear this was not a question.

Vaughn, off-balance, would have stumbled if Timothy hadn't caught him. He dragged Vaughn with him, passing out of my sight. I had to kneel on the seat to spot them in a corner of the crowded bar, hissing at each other.

While I watched, I felt pretty sure that, in addition to making some overblown gestures, Timothy was saying some highly curious words, including *prison* and *illegal*.

Yeah. This evening had just gotten a lot more interesting.

I was back in my seat, innocently swirling the ice in my glass, when they returned. Timothy fixed me with a large, fake smile, displaying an orthodontist's wet dream in terms of perfect teeth.

"What Vaughn misunderstood," he said, "is that I was talking to my friend Patton. Who certainly does not work at the U.S. Patent and Trademark Office. It's a silly mistake but an easy one to make. It was my friend Patton. Not Patent."

"That's right," Vaughn said, his voice lacking any expression. "A silly mistake. His friend Patton."

"Patton Oswald?" I asked innocently. "The comedian?"

"Yes," Timothy confirmed smoothly. "Patton Oswald. A dear friend of the family."

"How nice for you," I said. "He seems like a wonderful guy."

"Wonderful guy. Wonderful guy."

These lies seemed to have shut them both up entirely, so I nudged the conversation onward. "And what did your dear friend Patton say to you?"

"Nothing at all." Timothy was eager to bring the conversation to a close. Expensive shoe's on the other foot now, huh, buddy?

"Well, something." Vaughn was hedging. Timothy glared at

him, and Vaughn held up a hand. "She can help. I'm sure of it. Trust me."

Anger and horror were warring in Timothy's dark blue eyes, but he jutted out his jaw and nodded. HIs hands were fists, and he noticed me looking. He put them in his lap.

Yeah, I knew what it is to not want to be quite so blatantly presented for review.

"This friend *Patton*," Vaughn said to me, emphasizing the name, "has a theory—only a theory—about a brand-new battery that might or might not be released in, you know, some months. If it exists at all."

"A new battery," I clarified, trying to decipher this insidious code. "I see."

"Yes. A battery dependent on a... some substance that has never been harnessed for such a thing before."

This evening was going to take a long time if we were going to have to camouflage every statement with such keen cunning. "What substance would that be?"

Timothy interjected. "Doesn't matter. Doesn't matter at all." He glared at Vaughn. "Just something that can be extracted from stone."

"Like cadmium?" I theorized.

"Cadmium." Vaughn smiled. "This is going to make the nickel cadmium battery look like one of those clocks that runs on a potato. Sorry. Sorry, guy. Right—like cadmium. Exactly."

Timothy looked like he was inches away from leaving the bar entirely, except he must have known he'd have to drag Vaughn with him—and here came a spinach salad and two burgers.

Vaughn's fries were laden with heart disease. They looked really good.

We addressed ourselves to the food for a moment, and then I led us back into our stumbling conversation. "So, Timothy knows of a...a substance that might prove to be more valuable in a few months."

"Very well put. Very well put." Vaughn's mouth was full of bacon and cheese and potato, but he was a polite guy and hid his food behind a discreetly raised napkin until he swallowed audibly. "And now he's wondering how to access, well, a part of the nation that might, um—"

"—include some of the mysterious substance. Which Patton Oswald told him about."

"Right. Exactly." Vaughn nodded, and Timothy studied the salad he was slowly moving around with his fork.

"Is this something I can help him with?" I guessed.

"That's it exactly. You've got it in one. Well done, Frank." Vaughn beamed at me and offered me a fry. I demurred politely.

"How?" I asked.

Vaughn looked to Timothy, who didn't nod. He also didn't shake his head. The gesture he made conveyed his sentiment clearly, which was *You've gone this far. Might as well bring it home. Asshole.*

"The Circle B," Vaughn said.

"The ranch?" Timothy thought there was something on the ranch property he could profit from? Doubtful. "You want to...I don't get it. What is it exactly that you want?" I skipped Vaughn and asked Timothy directly.

He sighed and put down his fork. He leaned in, and I did the same, creating a little pocket of intimacy in this noisy bar. "If I can sample the rocks on the ranch and have them assayed, then I could make an offer for the mining rights. Or buy the ranch outright."

I shook my head. "It's over twenty-seven thousand acres. Almost all of it inaccessible and all of it wild."

He considered and then flicked an eyebrow. "I need a place to start. And I need to do it very quietly."

He didn't say the words *prison* or *illegal* again, but I heard them just the same. "Uh-huh," I said. "I see." I didn't. "Is there a reason why you're starting with the Circle B?"

Timothy huffed an unwilling laugh. "Yeah. Because of *him*." He threw a thumb at Vaughn, who this time was caught with a huge mouthful of burger. "Because he knew I needed a path in, and he clearly thinks you're it."

Vaughn nodded, unable to speak around his mouthful. I bit my lip. "And what am I supposed to do, exactly? Get you rock samples or something?"

"Grail guibe," Vaughn said, and then swallowed. "You're a trail guide. Since we were kids, you've taken people on camping treks into the backcountry. Take Timothy. That's it. Easy. Right?"

I was confused. "I don't get it. Anyone can take him trekking. What do I have to do with this?"

Vaughn mopped his mouth and sat straighter. Timothy looked for the answer to this one as well.

"You have to take him, because drilling out rock samples isn't exactly something he can do quietly while no one is looking. You can take him all over the ranch. Get him where he needs to go. Help him find good places to drill. And, in return, he can pay for your next semester of school." He sat back and smiled. "Brilliant. Right?"

5

OH YES HE DID

TIMOTHY

It's not that guys like me have a horrible time in jail. After all, I knew enough people to get sent to one of those country-club–like, minimum-security prisons. But that didn't mean I wanted to go. A prison sentence would play hell on my polo game.

"It's an interesting theoretical question," I said, attempting to steamroll Vaughn into finally shutting up.

He gave me a "quit fucking around" eyebrow, and the woman just rolled her eyes at me. "Oh, please," she said, irritated.

She was irritated?

I sat back, annoyance now fizzing up my horror. "I said theoretical and I meant it."

She pushed her plate away and crossed her arms on the table with an air of determination. "There is no gold left on the property. It was mined out over a century ago."

"Fascinating. Thanks for that," I said.

"He's not looking for gold," Vaughn said.

I wanted to kill him. Martha Stewart was only the most visible example of powerful people serving time for insider trading. I never should have told Vaughn what I was up to.

"Silver either. There's no silver on the property. There's no evidence of anything valuable. People have tried. The land is good for timber and for recreation, and that's about it." She was eyeing me with suspicion. "If you're looking for the Comstock Lode, you're barking up the wrong tree."

I was going to divert the conversation with more uses of the word *theoretical*, but Vaughn had other plans. "He doesn't need gold or silver. Gold and silver he's got." He waved a hand at me as if making an amusing witticism based on my net worth, but Frank, the Queen of Disrespect, wasn't paying attention.

"Anyway," she said, "all the trekking expeditions at the Circle B are booked for the season already. Maybe I can fit you in next year. I'd have to check with Cal."

I inhaled but again was too slow. Vaughn was right there. "No, Frank. The clock is ticking. Timothy needs to go now. Like, this week."

I glared at him, but he was right. If I was going to buy mining rights (or buy the ranch) before the news broke, I needed to get the whole thing done in the next month. Six weeks would be pressing it. After that, everyone was going to reevaluate what their land was worth.

Frank shook her head. "It's March. You city boys have no idea what Montana's backcountry is like during early spring. Every stream is a raging river from the snowmelt. You can go from trails a foot deep in mud to a whiteout blizzard in the course of ten minutes. Not to mention various animals, hungry from a long winter, getting more active and interested in large, slow-moving protein sources."

She waved a hand at me, and I was offended. "I'm not slow moving," I said, angered.

"Oh, please," she said again, dismissively. "There's no way you could make it."

I found my nose was curling up in scorn. Vaughn laughed. "He's tougher than he looks," he said.

"He certainly would have to be," she sneered.

Deliberately, I parroted her. "Oh, please," I sneered back.

"Look," Vaughn said. "Do you want to get your degree or not?" He focused his intensity on her. "Because if you're not going to let me pay for it, then this is a good opportunity." She tucked her head in and looked like a stubborn child. I was enjoying the petulance until Vaughn turned to me. "And if you want to pursue this latest crazy scheme of yours, then stop looking so smug. Because this is a good opportunity for you too."

Now it was my turn to pout. "Huh."

Vaughn shifted in his seat. "Okay. What's your biggest objection?"

He cocked his head at me in irritating fashion. Like he'd understood an assignment in French class that I'd missed entirely. It made me want to beat on him a little. When he didn't relent, I had to sick up an answer. "How about trust?" I said. "How the hell do I know if I can trust her?"

Frank erupted. "My question entirely! I'm supposed to trust this guy?"

Vaughn held out a hand to her. "Hang on. Tim, you can trust her because I vouch for her. Same goes for you, Frank. I know you both. I know you're safe to trust the other. Frank, is that your biggest obstacle too?"

Her petulance was on full display. She shifted on the bench in a huff. "How about the fact that I'm supposed to shaft two people who have been like family to me for my entire life?"

"How would I be shafting them?" I asked, disgusted. "I said I'd pay them for the mining rights. Or buy the ranch at whatever price they set."

"Sure—you're just not going to tell them they're sitting on a load of some mysterious substance that is about to change the world. And I'm supposed to let you do it."

"Honey, I haven't said I'd let you do anything at all yet." I got chilly with her to counter her hot anger. This annoyed her every bit as much as I hoped it would.

Vaughn touched her arm to draw her attention back. "Look, I've known Timothy since we were kids. He acts like he's totally amoral, but there is a sense of fair play in him, deep down."

"No, there is not!" I protested, but he ignored me.

"He'll do the right thing in the end. Frank, this is your next semester. I'm telling you—don't dismiss this so quickly."

She swallowed. She glared. She tried to assassinate me with those alien eyes. "Let me out," she said. Neither Vaughn nor I understood what she wanted until she raised her eyebrows at Vaughn and nodded past the end of the booth. "Let me out. I need a minute."

"A minute?" he said stupidly.

"I get a minute to think about this," she said as if he was slow.

"Go ahead," he tried. "Think about it."

"Let. Me. Out. Of. The. Booth. Get out of my way." When he remained immobile, she shook her head. "I have to pee. Can I go to the ladies' room, please?"

"Oh!" Vaughn leaped up and cleared the way for her exit. She stomped away, and he sat to regard me with a grin. "Well?" he said. "Am I right? Isn't she perfection?"

I was tall enough to see over the back of the booth. "You'd better hope the ladies' room is in the parking lot, because perfection just stalked out the door."

6. SHOULD I, SHOULD I NOT

FRANK

I wasn't going to stay out here for long. I'd left my jacket in the bar, and although it wasn't yet below freezing, there was a pretty determined wind blowing my hair around.

But I couldn't go back in just yet. I could shiver in my T-shirt for a while. Maybe it would cool off my temper. Because there was no doubt that Vaughn had found me a lifeline.

I hadn't been exaggerating. Wilderness treks in early spring weren't for the faint of heart. I could do it—and had, many times—but it was going to challenge the pretty boy. And there was no saying I had to take him by the easiest paths either. I could make him miserable if I wanted to.

And did I want to?

Well...yes.

Guys generally assumed ownership on the slightest pretext, and I was done with it. Every guy I'd ever dated believed I wanted to be their property. To be owned. Sleeping with a guy was a guaranteed path to acquiring a stalker. And a man like

Timothy Baby-cock already had an I Am The Master Of All I Survey vibe going pretty hard. If I ever slipped up and smiled at the man, he would assume I was auditioning to be the future Mrs. Arrogant Millions.

But...

An engineering degree was the path out for me. I couldn't see another way around that. And this guy—this holder of The World's Most Astronomical FICO Score—was the ticket in I needed.

So, okay. I'd do it. But there would have to be some provisions included.

Vaughn stood as if I was going to meekly slide back into my seat. "Oh no no," I said. "I'm going to sit on the outside. Push over." He did, and I sat. "All right. I'll do it. But I have three conditions."

Timothy gave me a patronizing smile. The mouth meant *amused* while the eyes said *cold hard calculations*. Smug bastard. "I see. We've gotten to the negotiations. I love this phase. Let's hear your conditions."

If I was going to put up with this guy, I was going to get something for it. "First, I'll spend the next month in the backcountry with you, dragging you from mountain to mountain. But I negotiate the trip with Cal and Eliza, you buy all the equipment I say we need, and you pay for *two* semesters of my college, not one."

Again, the eyes didn't match the smile. "I have appointments I can't miss this month. We'll need to take several trips into your wilderness."

The arrogance of the man. "You want to survey the backcountry immediately, but you can't take the time needed to do it in one trip? You're going to go out, come back, go out, come back?"

"And go out again and come back again. I have at least three events I'll be leaving for."

"That's astonishingly inefficient," I said.

He shrugged. "Should you care? You'll get your two semesters. And I'll buy all the dehydrated camp dinners. So, move on. What's the next condition?"

I refused to look away from his navy-blue eyes. Refused to clear my throat nervously, although I wanted to. "If you buy the mining rights, or the ranch outright, I get 10 percent of your profits."

Timothy laughed. Threw back his arrogant head and exposed his naked throat as if I didn't have a pocketknife on me. "You're hysterical. What's the third provision? Come on, spit it out now so I know what I'm dealing with."

He was patronizing me. Making me feel like a child in the boardroom. My anger, disgust, even some shame, tried to choke me...but fuck that. "The third condition is I get to draw a circle around part of the ranch, and you promise to leave it alone. About seven hundred acres. Not even a tenth of the property. And I get to go there for the rest of my life."

He snorted, and his stupid ginger eyebrows went up. "Why?"

I sat back and crossed my arms. "I like it there. Don't want it disturbed."

He leaned in, matching my retreat. "Why?" he asked again.

Vaughn was watching me too. "Yeah, Frank. Which property? What's out there?"

I tried to shut them down with a raised eyebrow, but they outlasted me. "It's pretty there. I like it. I don't want to see a huge strip-mining destruction in just this one damned valley. Okay? Is that all right with the two of you?"

Timothy leaned back and laced his fingers together. He eyed me, and I just knew he was about to condescendingly call me "honey" again. My assumption was wrong, though.

"No," he said succinctly.

God, I hated this man. So fucking sure he held every card. I glared at him, trying to figure out a way to make him give me what I wanted. What I needed.

Since I didn't speak, Vaughn did. He eyed his buddy. "No? Just like that?"

"Yeah. Just like that."

His eyes got small as he squinted at me, daring me to object. Well, to hell with that.

"Fine," I said. "I'm out."

"I am too," he countered quickly.

Vaughn threw his hands in the air. "Then *I'm* out. Jesus, you two. I come up with this brilliant plan. *You* get your education paid for, and *you* get access to land that might get you what you want, and you're both too fucking stubborn to get out of your own way. Well, I tried. Christ, I need another martini."

He tried to flag down the waitress. I glanced up at Timothy, side-eye. I *did* want tuition for the next semester, at least. He was eyeing me from lowered brows in turn.

Vaughn was still craned around in the booth, looking for his next drink, when Timothy spoke. "Half of one percent. For five years."

A jolt of adrenaline burned through me. We weren't done after all. Vaughn whipped around. "What, now?"

I put a chilly hand on Vaughn's forearm. "Nice try," I said, trying to sound as if my pulse was steady as a clock. "You won't have shit done in the first five years. I'll take one percent for a decade."

Timothy sneered. "One percent of nothing is still nothing, you know."

"I still get two semesters out of the deal, whether you find what you're looking for or not."

He dismissed my comment with a gesture. "We've already agreed on that."

"Have we?" I glared at him. "I don't think we have."

"Sweetie. Really." His arrogance was infuriating. "How

about I get you a credit card? My comptroller will approve any expenses necessary for the expeditions, plus two semesters at Wherever University."

I eyed him suspiciously. "Housing and food too? Or just tuition?"

"Like I'd notice. Or care. Whatever. Honey."

He called me that again to prove he knew I hated it. But he was offering far more money than I ever could have expected. I felt my grasp on good sense slipping. "Huh," I said, trying to buy some time to make sure I wasn't selling my soul to the devil or something.

"See?" Vaughn nudged me. "It's a good deal, right?"

I shushed him absently. "And all I have to do to get this magical credit card is take you on multiple treks in the back-country."

"That's all I'm asking." He spread his hands out to the ends of the table. I just knew that if he were on a sofa, he would have done the eagle's wings thing along the back. Expansive and magnanimous and clearly satanic.

"And I get one percent for ten years if you go into business there."

One of his hands made a *but of course* gesture, but I was going to need to see a contract that my lawyer would have to approve.

I was going to need to find a lawyer.

Fuck. A lawyer would want a retainer.

"And what about the seven hundred acres?" I asked.

"Absolutely not." He didn't even raise his voice as if it mattered. He was matter-of-fact. Totally icy about it. Just a flat-out denial.

I had to regroup. Weigh whether I could proceed without it. "What if I asked for just five hundred acres?"

His chuckle made the muscles around my eyes tighten, like

I was getting ready for an attack. "Honey, you get no acres. Not now, not later, not until you die. None."

I sat back, stumped. Redheaded Beelzebub was offering me almost everything I needed.

Almost.

"You won't last a day without me back there," I said, considering. "I could make your life miserable, or I could make it easier. Wouldn't it be smarter to give me what I want? It's not even a tenth of the property. You won't notice for decades."

His lip curled in a sneer. "I barely need you as it is," he said. "I can send out drones to chart the best route. I know my way around horses, and I've been camping plenty of times."

I shook my head, working to keep my poker face in place. "Not one day. That's my world out there, *honey*. I'd like to see you try."

He sneered. "You must be so proud. Total control over *your world*. Must feel great. Meanwhile, you wouldn't survive one *hour* in my world."

I huffed a laugh, ignoring the jittery need to move that was running like quicksilver through my veins. "You think I'm just a country bumpkin, huh? That I couldn't do just fine at one of your billionaire gatherings? I'm so sure."

I let him see my contempt. Vaughn tried to correct me. "He's a lobbyist in Washington, D.C., Frank. His world is national politics."

"Oh my!" I feigned sarcastic awe. "Gosh golly, a lobbyist! Why, I bet you even take your Stetson off when you go inside, don't you? Gee!"

Timothy shook his head at me, his lips pursed in thought. He leaned in again. "I'll give you your five hundred acres, free and clear"—my heart jumped up against my breastbone, but he went on—"*if* you can persuade someone from my world to do something they don't want to do."

"What the hell does that mean, Satan? Could you be any more vague?"

He liked that I'd given him the nickname. He grinned. "I have a luncheon next week, a board meeting after that, and a black-tie gala in three weeks. You come with me. I'll say you're my new assistant. I'm thinking of a person—no, two. Okay, there are four people I'm thinking of. If you can persuade even one of them to do something they don't want to do, you've got your five hundred acres."

My brain was spinning. My hands were red from being clenched. "Of course I can't do that in your circles. I don't have the money to compete."

I watched him. Eagles eyeing rabbits couldn't watch more closely—especially if the rabbit was likely to suddenly morph into a demon. "No problem," he said. "You'll have the credit card. Buy whatever you need to level the playing field."

Silent, in my soul, I gasped. Did this guy really not care at all about money? "Anything?"

He sneered. "Honey, I'll never even see the bill. I could not care less."

God, this guy made me sick.

Where was the catch? There had to be a catch. "And if I fail? Do I have to pay everything back?"

He scoffed again. "You *will* fail. And the money is not the issue. So no, you don't have to pay it back. But you do have to..." His eyes scanned the bar, looking for something he wanted that he couldn't buy. Satan plotting chaos. As I watched, my lips hurting because I was biting them so hard, I saw the idea come to him. It washed over his face in a vicious grin. He gestured to Vaughn. "You have to date this guy."

"What?" I was hopelessly off-balance. Date the guy who I regarded as a big brother? Wasn't that kind of disgusting?

"Yeah," Timothy said, reading my reluctance with an evil

grin. "Date him. At least three times. Long enough for him to have a real chance with you."

Vaughn's eyes were so wide, the eyeballs were at risk of falling out. "Oh, damn!" he breathed.

"Oh, damn," I echoed.

Paralysis locked me in place until Timothy spoke with a tone that both challenged and belittled me. "Do you want the five hundred acres or not?"

Oh, fuck you, I thought. The pulse slamming in my ears was damned close to blowing my skull to pieces, but I wasn't going to fold here. *I'll see your bet and raise it. Show your cards, cowboy.* "Seven hundred," I countered.

"Seven hundred," he said and banged the table. "Done."

Holy shit. Holy crap.

Holy moly.

What the hell had I just gotten myself into?

"What did I tell you!" Vaughn cheered, the sudden noise making me jump in a hot flash of terror. "This is awesome! My god, I don't even know who to root for! What happens now?"

7

ALICE THROUGH
THE LOOKING GLASS

TIMOTHY

I called my guy at the U.S. Patent and Trademark Office from the plane, far too overstimulated to wait for a face-to-face.

"Hello?" Even his voice was timid.

"Alice!" I gave him a hearty greeting, relishing the chance to blow off a little energy by teasing him a bit.

"Mr. Babcock, why are you calling me? You shouldn't call me!"

"Now, Alice, who's going to care?"

"Mr. Babcock!"

"Alice!"

"Mr. Babcock, please! My name is Aleister. It's a family name. Don't call me Alice."

The poor bastard. Entertainingly, his last name was Darling, which meant I could legitimately refer to him as Alice Darling. Never failed to give me a snort. "Don't feel bad, Alice. I just met a woman named Frank. It's a day for gender-bending. I wanted to give you an update."

"No! Not on the phone!"

"Alice, life isn't like the movies, you know." I stretched out, propping my feet on the ottoman. The corporate fleet had planes that could hold more people, but I liked my little Learjet for personal travel. This new one had a gorgeous cabin upholstered in dark leather and hunter green. It looked like a British gentlemen's club. The perfect place to talk to a man named Aleister Darling. "No one is bugging your phone."

"You don't know that! Meet me tomorrow. The usual place. Please, Mr. Babcock!"

Alice thought it was the height of cleverness to have casual, surprised-to-see-you-here meetings at the sea lion enclosure at the National Zoo. In March, it was the kind of place only determined amateur spies would possibly want to go. "That doesn't work for me. I thought you'd like to hear about my visit to Aunt Molly."

His reaction was to freeze. Alice Darling was a rabbit of a man. At the first sign of a predator, he went absolutely still, apparently under the kindergarten belief that, like the T. rex in that movie, if you didn't move, nothing bad would find you.

"Alice?" I questioned his silence. "About Aunt Molly?"

I figured Aleister would like this question. He might not want anyone to hear him discussing the mineral molybdenum in any form, but calling it Aunt Molly would appeal to him. We'd have our own code. "Yes?" he finally breathed. "And how is...Aunt Molly?"

I muffled my snigger. If anyone really did decide to eavesdrop on a low-level patent examiner, Aleister couldn't have been more obvious.

"Well, I'd say the old girl is in very good shape." I thought with satisfaction about my negotiations with the lovely if annoying Frank Robinson. She wanted one percent of the first decade's profits, without any clarification at all about what *profits* could mean. At the very least, I could pay myself a whopping huge salary. She'd be getting one percent of whatever I cared to pay her. "We should be able to start the mills up in two months."

"Two months! So soon!" I assumed the man was faintly quivering. His voice certainly was. "We—I don't—I think—two months is moving, um, very fast!"

"No harm in it. We can get Aunt Molly ground up and ready right off, and stockpile her until she's needed."

"Oh dear." As if I were a mind reader, I knew Alice had just replayed the discussion in his head as if Aunt Molly were a real person, in which case he and I were potentially discussing her gruesome dismemberment. "Oh dear. Aunt Molly!"

"Yes," I said heartily. "Aunt Molly is ready to get off the ground. I assume you still want to help pay for her plane tickets?"

"Her plane tickets?" Alice was sweating. I could hear it over my cell.

"You said you had thirty-seven thousand you wanted to invest in the plane tickets."

"Oh yes! The plane tickets! Yes, of course! And that will ensure me a share in the...the vacation? For Aunt Molly?"

He was a real James Bond, this guy. "Yes, indeed. I think probably ten percent of the vacation." Aleister thought I was buying a grinding mill to process molybdenum from rock. And of course, I might do that. More importantly, though, I was going to secure the rock itself, which was where the true profit would come.

Not to mention the massive satisfaction of being ahead of the curve. Of looking modestly brilliant when the Patent Office approved the new battery, and I was right there with the materials. The gross increase in my net worth would never be as important to me as the chance to flaunt my foresight in the faces of my cousin Nicholas, the math nerd.

And my smarty-pants sister, Joanna.

And Zaccharias "I'm the CEO" Babcock IV, who was too damned cool to be happy.

My entire family, of course, although those three cousins were the richest. They represented the net worth I was chasing.

I'd show them who was the best. I might end up as rich as Tabby—the grandmother who ruled the Babcock Holdings empire.

My toes curled in my fine shoes in anticipation. "Aunt Molly is going to do right by you, Aleister."

"I see, I see. And how shall I get the funds to you, Mr. Babcock?"

He'd want a drop somewhere. Small, nonsequential bills. Grocery store bag. "Bank draft will do."

"Oh no!"

"Relax, Alice. I'll have my guy take care of it. Aunt Molly will never be able to figure out who's paying for her pulverization." Alice yipped. "I mean, her vacation." My valet, who acted as steward when I flew, handed me my highball. Now, *that* was a Macallan. Smoky, mellow, laid down before the Second World War and aged to perfection for eighty-four years. Ah. "I'll be in touch, Alice."

I ended the call while he was still sputtering his thanks and fears. How he'd had the courage to approach me in the first place, I could not work out. But that momentary aberration from life as a prey species was going to change his retirement. I felt good about that.

Not as good, of course, as I felt about what was going to happen next.

8

THE OLD PERCOLATOR

FRANK

"Sweetie, we're booked right through the summer. Even for a friend of yours, we can't fit anyone else in. You know that." Maria Buckley poured a cup of coffee from her ancient percolator and set it in front of her husband at the table. He reached for the sugar bowl, and she swatted his hand away. "Use the mannitol, Cal. You know what your doctor said."

His under-the-breath mutters gave me a smile. Similar scenes had played out in this kitchen throughout my childhood. Uncle Red should have been sitting across from me.

"I know we're booked," I said, "but—"

Cal interrupted me. "Still time to get in for next summer, though. Tell this guy to come back."

Maria shot Cal a significant look that I didn't understand, and Cal raised his eyebrows in response and amended his sentence. "Or we've got room to book for the Christmas season. Always plenty of room then."

Maria nodded at him and turned back to pour me a mug.

Their silent exchange raised alarm bells in my head. They'd been treating me like a granddaughter since my great-uncle Red let me tag after him when I was six. Red and Cal were best friends from childhood, even did a stint in the Army together. Any child of Red's was a child of Cal's. Usually, I could read the unspoken language just fine. But maybe I'd been in Denver too long.

"He doesn't want to go this summer," I corrected their misunderstanding. "He wants to leave this weekend."

Maria slid my coffee to me and took her place at the table. "This weekend? He wants to go *now*?"

"Is he crazy?" Cal asked.

Sunlight was pouring into the kitchen, showing every crack in the peeling linoleum, but there was no guarantee the afternoon would remain clear. The water dripping constantly from the roof provided the springtime backbeat of The Thaw as snow and ice surrendered—temporarily—in the face of all the solar energy. But once the sun set, everything would freeze up again, coating the world in treacherous ice over gluey mud.

"He might be crazy," I said, "but he's willing to pay. And I've got the time to take him out. If you'll let me."

Cal leaned back to consider. "I'm not saying it would be impossible, and we could damn sure use the money."

Maria's laugh was scornful. They were still recovering from two years ago, when they renovated the guest cabins. Industry standards for dude ranches had gone crazy in recent years, as the only people who could afford "Wild West" vacations no longer embraced the primitive that had been thought to be charming to the last generation.

"New bathrooms," Maria said in disgust. "Single faucets." She rolled her eyes, still frustrated because guests couldn't figure out how to wash with warm water when the two taps on either side of the sink gushed icy cold or boiling hot. "Like they can't figure out how to put the stopper in the basin. It's like they're all four years old."

"Now, Mother." Cal spoke automatically, laying a gentle hand over hers. We'd all heard her rant before. "Frank, what's your plan for this trek?"

I breathed in, gathering myself to come to grips with the situation. "Not trek, Cal. *Treks*. The guy thinks he's going to go out and come back several times."

The crease between Cal's eyebrows got deeper. "Why?"

I threw my hands in the air dramatically to cover my lie. "I don't know. Because he's got too much money? He told me he wants to spend time in the natural world, but he has all these fancy appointments he can't miss back East. So he wants to go out, come back, go out, come back." The three of us exchanged looks of confusion. "I know it's crazy, but we can charge him a fortune."

They were perplexed, but the mention of money paved over a lot of questions. "I like that part," Cal said thoughtfully.

"Me too." Maria drank her coffee and winced. The 1950s percolator she used made the worst coffee, but neither of them seemed to realize there were alternatives.

"I thought for the first trip out, we'd take the snowcats. There will still be enough snow on the high trails to make it possible. I'm making him do a test run first. One overnight up to the old trapper's cabin, and I can see if this guy is capable of actually exploring the backcountry."

Cal slapped a hand down on the dinged-up table. "Now you're talking! Snowcats! I don't want to ruin a good horse if this guy doesn't know what he's doing. Not even," he added to the comment Maria hadn't made yet, "if he's willing to buy the horse."

She sat back, her lips lightly pursed in response.

"My thoughts exactly," I said. "And if he can handle one night, then I'd be willing to do a longer trek."

"On horseback, you'll take the low trails," Cal agreed. "Stay away from the higher elevations until all this melts." He waved a hand in the direction of the window, where sunlight was bouncing off last night's snow.

"Right." Wrong. If smug, handsome Timothy could even get his fine ass into a saddle, I was going to take him up the toughest trails I knew. Thought playing polo—polo!—was enough to be safe in my world.

You wish.

"If anyone could keep him safe out there," Maria said loyally, "it would be you, sweetheart."

"Or Red," Cal added. "Red could have done it too."

It had been three years since my great-uncle's lungs had given out, but his place at the table was still glaringly empty. I nodded. "He knew the backcountry better than anyone."

The sting of his death hit me right in the tear ducts and I blinked away the evidence. It came out of nowhere sometimes.

"He trained you right, Frank." Cal slapped a callused palm against my shoulder, which was as close as he got to hugs. "You can handle this."

I nodded. He was right—but Maria wasn't convinced. "Still, I'm not sure I like it. You going out there alone with just one man. What if he decides to...get fresh?"

I bit back my smile. Twice I'd been stalked by hungry pumas—once without my uncle to help. I'd discovered people illegally running herds of cattle over Cal's property without permission. I'd been caught in a rockslide and avoided two more. I'd endured the worst weather possible, handled lame horses, guided a party of seven when all of them came down with horrific cases of diarrhea...and she thought one prissy billionaire would do me in?

"I can take care of myself, Maria. I promise. I'll have the rifle. And you can be damned sure Red taught me how to defend myself."

She patted my arm. "I know he did. I just worry. And watch your language, dear."

It was the *damned sure* she didn't like. Any male within earshot could say it—or worse—and she wouldn't bat an eye. Ladies, she'd often assured me, had to be better than men. And despite my boyish nickname—despite spending every non-school hour with Red in the corral, on the fence line, across the backcountry—Maria still had hopes that I could be a lady.

"Sorry, ma'am."

"Who're you taking with you? I'm guessing you'll be on Swan."

"Yes, sir. If you're okay with it." My mare, Swan, wasn't really mine. She was the property of the Circle B Ranch, but I'd trained her (and she'd trained me) and we were inseparable.

"Of course. And who do you want for Mr. Fancy-Pants? Smoky? Big Red?"

"I was thinking Whistler."

Cal rocked back in laughter. "So, you really don't like this guy, huh?"

Whistler was a perfectly good choice for the backcountry. Trail-wise and sure-footed. Big enough to carry a large man all day without injury. But the horse got his name because he whistled like a teakettle whenever he went uphill. It drove guests up the wall. "I don't know what you mean," I replied primly, which made Cal slap his thigh in appreciation.

"Sure you don't. Pack mule?"

"Can I take Daisy?"

He nodded. "Good choice. You've got the heavy-weather gear you need?"

"For me, I do. I'm supposed to buy supplies for the guy. On his dime."

Cal and I both snorted. Left to his own devices, Timothy would go into REI or some other outdoor store, and some salesman would see him coming. He'd leave equipped with every wrong thing, all of which would cost four times what it should.

"You'll need a second pack mule, then," Cal opined. "How much can we get out of this guy?"

I flipped an eyebrow up. "Plenty. I'm thinking we can double our regular rates." That should have earned me a smile at least, but instead Cal and Maria exchanged a look. "All right," I said firmly. "What's going on?"

9

THE VIEW FROM HERE

TIMOTHY

For once, Vaughn hadn't exaggerated. The Circle B Ranch looked like a movie set.

The road along the Gallatin River was on mostly flat land, but that was just about the only territory that was. Most of this part of Montana looked like mountain-goat territory, with soaring slabs of rock reaching over the road far overhead and every little view capped by another mountain.

I came around a rock outcropping at seventy miles an hour and almost missed the driveway tucked up against a cliff. No worries about slamming on the brakes. I hadn't seen another vehicle in twenty minutes. So, I reversed back up the road and turned in.

Someone had lashed rough-cut tree limbs together to form an Old West-style arch over the drive. An equally primitive circle hung from the top with a *B* inside it, formed of smaller sticks.

Welcome to the Circle B.

The land opened up as I eased along the track. A natural valley had formed between mountains, most of the space dark with pines or showing the bare branches of a forest before the spring leaves emerged. Cabins dotted the upper slopes, and a long, low ranch house had pride of place at the top of the drive.

And across the valley pastures? Horses.

There's nothing better-looking than a horse. The design was so elegant, so powerful, that even I—as big an atheist as they came, as long as I wasn't trying to appeal to some powerful person of faith—thought that whoever designed the horse must have been divinely inspired.

The Circle B's livestock was enjoying the sunny morning. Some clustered around dried bales of sweet hay, but most were wandering across the fields, nosing hopefully under the melting snow for the first sweetgrass. They looked delightfully disreputable, their heavy winter coats shedding in uneven patches as the weather warmed. Some groom would be brushing the hell out of those coats.

Thirty horses.

No, forty.

I passed a large barn and amended my numbers upward. There were another ten or fifteen idling in a paddock on the sunny side.

The Circle B was paradise for horsemen. Why hadn't I come sooner? It's not like Vaughn hadn't tried to get me here.

A tall old man waited at the top of the driveway. He waved me into a muddy parking place next to a tough-looking Jeep with fans of dirt up its sides.

"Son," he said as I got out, "what the hell did you do to that truck?"

I turned back, surprised, to examine my ride through his eyes. "It's a Ford," I said. "An F-150 Raptor."

He chuckled. "Maybe when it was born. It's not no 150 now." We walked around the truck together, and he saw the

Hennessey badge. "That's those guys in Texas, huh? They upgraded this monster, I see. Must go like a storm."

"I guess."

The old guy turned to watch me with as much curiosity as he'd shown the truck. "You guess?"

I shrugged. "I told my guy to get me a good car for the terrain. This is what he delivered."

He made a sound in the back of his throat that might have been humor or disgust. "You've got to be the billionaire."

His directness took me aback. Most people weren't quite so blatant. I pulled my eyebrows out of my hairline and offered my hand. "Timothy Babcock."

"Calhoun Buckley," he offered back, shaking mine. "Call me Cal. We've been expecting you, of course. Frank's not here yet, but she'll be along. You come into the office. I've got a disclaimer for you to sign. Standard stuff, of course."

"Of course." My response was dry. Everyone wanted disclaimers from me. Promises that I wouldn't sue them back to the primordial ooze for real or imagined slights. It was assumed that I kept a fleet of predatory lawyers on retainer.

Of course, I *did* keep a fleet of predatory lawyers on retainer, so who could blame them?

The form handed to me by Calhoun Buckley would prove no impediment if I wanted to drag him to court. It had been downloaded from the internet, and my suits would howl with laughter if I let them read it first.

I didn't let them read it, of course. What they didn't know wouldn't cause me any delays. Same as when I went skydiving in a wingsuit in Australia. Ice climbing in Nepal. Diving on the SS *Andrea Doria* with a helium fill in my scuba tanks to reach the full two hundred and forty feet. My life, my choices.

"So, you want to commune with the natural world," Calhoun said, watching me with the same sharp eyes.

I smiled back, rolling with whatever lie Frank had told him.

"Absolutely." I fanned my hands out expansively. "My life is all skyscrapers and sycophants. Mergers and acquisitions. Time I got back to Mother Nature."

My smile was warm and natural, but I felt a slight shiver down my spine. I'd unwittingly stumbled into a truth while playing a role. Not the mergers and acquisitions part—that was more the remit of my cousins and sisters—but I spent most of my life cozying up to elected officials. Getting them what they wanted, so my family could get what we wanted.

I loved my job as a lobbyist on Capitol Hill. Loved the thrill. Often, the risks and excitement were as pure as the extreme sports I preferred...but the sycophants and skyscrapers part? The endless lies and unreliable deals? Assuming the patsy was going to betray an agreement and figuring out what to do when that happened in an endless tangle of high-stakes what-ifs?

Yeah. The idea of getting back to good old Mama Nature didn't suck.

"Well, this is a good place for that. Here comes Frank."

A baby-blue truck, more rust than paint, rumbled past the window. By the time we made it out, Frank had popped the door on her truck and was standing on her seat to peer over the top at my Ford.

"Jesus and Mary and all the Apostles," she said, climbing into the bed of her truck without touching the ground so she could fist her hands on her hips as she continued her survey.

"It's an F-150," I said, feeling a touch defensive at their response. "A Raptor."

She scoffed audibly. "Hennessey calls that thing a Veloci-raptor. Must have cost you, what, an extra eighty thou? A hundred?" She didn't wait for my answer but climbed back into her truck. "Come on." She gestured with her chin to the passenger seat beside her.

"I can take my ride," I said.

"Leave the keys with Cal." She rolled up the window, ending our conversation.

"Oh, you're going to have a great time," Cal said sarcastically, apparently enjoying my confusion.

"She's a good guide, though, right?" I handed him the keys.

"The best. Really. Have fun, billionaire. We'll watch for your return."

His chuckles didn't soothe my unease. I had to lift the door slightly before it would open, but Frank's heater was going and the cracked vinyl of the bench seat held up under my weight.

She regarded me dispassionately. "Need anything before we head to the barn?" she asked. "Hand lotion? A complimentary chocolate?"

"Do you have those things?"

She dismissed me and backed her truck around to point downhill. "Hope you're ready."

"I hope *you're* ready," I replied. "Why aren't we taking my truck?"

The flip of her head somehow indicated the bed of her truck. "Because I've got all the supplies."

She didn't actually say *duh*, but I heard it all the same. "So you got the credit card, then."

I caught a little side-eye as she navigated the ruts in the drive. "You didn't notice?"

I leaned back to survey the horse pastures below us. "I told you. I'd never notice. I'm sure my comptroller did."

"I bought a lot," she admitted.

"That's fine. You got what we need, though, right? Not just for this overnight, but for the longer treks next week?"

She nodded, but her eyebrows were up. Even with her frosty attitude, Lovely Frank the Cowgirl had never before spent all the money she'd wanted to. She might mock me, but at least part of her was now being consumed by jealousy.

Good. My job here was well-begun.

She pulled around the barn and parked on the side still in shadow. No horses to enjoy, although a high-stepping bay mare at the fence called for attention. Frank ignored the supplies she'd packed and walked swiftly to the rail to caress the long nose begging her for attention.

"A beauty," I said as I joined them. I ran a hand down the graceful, strong neck, admiring her lines.

"She is, indeed. This is Swan." Frank was nuzzling the horse, who looked as if Frank hung the sun. If the cowgirl had sat, the horse would have tried to become a lap pony.

"You're friends, I see."

"We are." Her smile was soft, gentle, and a surprise to me. I didn't realize Frank had a loving side.

"She coming with us today?"

"Oh." Frank looked away from the horse with what I thought was regret. "Not this time. It's still a little early for her. No, we're doing our overnight with those."

She gestured over her shoulder with a thumb, and I turned to see the snowcats parked under an open-sided shed. "Snowmobiles? Hang on." I turned to protest, but Frank held up a hand.

"This short trip is so I can assess your experience on the trail. I already know you can ride. Now I need to know how you handle being outside of cell phone range. How you survive where roads aren't paved and there's no turndown service. So, we'll be riding the snowcats. Up and back, one night in camp. Any problems?"

This wasn't what we'd agreed, and I'd been looking forward to spending the day on horseback, but her attitude now had enough fight in it that I refused to give her the satisfaction. "No problem at all. Lead the way."

I think I surprised her by acquiescing. She kissed the horse's nose to say goodbye and directed me to fill the stowage areas in the cats with our supplies. "I'm assuming you can drive one of these, but if you can't, you can ride bitch behind me."

She wanted to mock and humiliate me. "If it's like a motor-cycle, I think I can manage."

We went through an annoyingly long safety briefing, which I submitted to meekly. We talked about how to cross the bare parts of the trail where the snow had already melted, so Cal and his team wouldn't have too much repair to endure before the summer season if our treads chewed up the earth. We considered the various conditions we would meet, and the care we would take to avoid frostbite or other obvious issues.

And I let her go through the entire thing. I made no objections. And eventually, she ran out of lectures.

"All right. Follow me."

10

THE OTHER KIND OF HORSEPOWER

FRANK

Timothy Babcock was deeply annoying.

After arriving in that arrogant Big Swinging Dick of a truck, I couldn't help but be rude to him. That Ford was worth more than my mother's trailer, and it quickly became clear that its owner had no idea of its cost. Nor cared.

I let my temper get the better of me, and it wasn't until I got to commune with Swan that I was able to get a grip. My horse had a far kinder nature than I did, and she reminded me that life didn't have to be filled with anger and resentment. I could let it go.

Which I tried to do.

Sort of.

Forcing the billionaire Babcock into the most rigid and detailed safety lectures was hardly kind. On the other hand, Uncle Red always said *Safety first. You don't dare assume some tenderfoot is going to know his ass from his elbow, Frank.*

Annoyingly, Babcock took it. He listened politely. He

correctly answered the questions I fired at him to make sure he was paying attention. When we finally headed out, he hung back the prescribed distance, maintained the safe speed, offered no complaints.

So annoying.

We took the west trail, past the summer turnout paddock and up the old logging road, until I turned us into the north fork trail. The higher we went, the deeper the snow got. It had been a year since I'd been even here, the shallowest part of the deep backcountry. My autumn months had been taken up by the fascination of my lone semester of engineering school, and I'd stayed in Denver for the remaining months, trying to pick up jobs and begging friends for one more week on their sofas, so this trip up the mountain felt like coming home.

Better than coming home. It felt like if I went far enough, Uncle Red would be waiting. His dented coffeepot on the cooking grate. Stars beginning to be visible behind the setting sun, and freedom all around.

My eyes blurred and I blinked hard. The snowcats made too much noise to enjoy the sounds of the forests in winter—the soft plop of snow falling from a branch, the peculiar sound-deadening properties of deep snow in shadow, the occasional and sudden angry chatter of a flying squirrel or the high-pitched *eep* of big-eared pikas, alarmed in the rocks.

But I could still refresh my sight with the trunks of trees, black against the snow. The flash of cinnamon from the paper-bark maple. The deep green of conifers and the outcroppings of stone, shaping the landscape from below.

Under the sharp tang of the diesel fuel, the air was chilled and sweet. Air in the mountains must hold more oxygen than in the lowlands. I often felt mildly drunk until I got used to it. My nose would get cold, but the thick band of my knitted cap warmed me to my eyebrows. Eventually, the sweat would cause more trouble for me than the cold.

Not that the cold was much of a challenge. Spring was definitely springing, and we had to slow down to a crawl across each muddy patch. But Entitled Timothy was obedient and even understood that he had to gain momentum *before* hitting a hill, lest he hit an icy patch and slide backward in humiliation.

Or into a ditch.

Or a ravine.

Not that I took him on a route that was particularly dangerous.

Mostly.

We made it to the top of Seaforth Mountain in pretty good time. I led him to the lookout and dug out the lunch.

"Soup and sandwiches," he said neutrally. "Thanks."

"Sorry. The five-star chef had the day off."

"I'm not being sarcastic. This is really good. Thank you."

I eyed him suspiciously. He sipped from his thermos, filled with black bean soup from the Riverway Diner, and ate his pastrami on rye without further comment. "It's gorgeous up here. Is that the Gallatin?"

We were still in sight of the road, although far above it. "Yep. Down that way is Yellowstone. Go the other way, you get to Big Sky. Should look familiar. That's where you flew into, huh?"

"Huh," he said. Again, a very neutral comment. Since he clearly wanted me to ask, I refused. I gathered up our trash and stowed it. "Cookies in here." I slapped a baggie against his coat and he took it automatically. "Eat them on the trail if you get hungry. Need a pit stop or anything? No? Okay, let's keep going."

Once we crested the mountain and were facing south, I saw something that made me smile: Here came a storm.

Of course it did. It was March in the Rockies. The weather would reliably change every fifteen minutes.

I waved Timothy over and called to him over the rumble of the snowcats, "You got a rain cover for that fancy lid?"

He looked up and fingered the expensive cowboy hat he was wearing—chosen, I suspected, because he knew he looked handsome in it. "Rain cover? This hat can handle the rain."

"Sure it can. Put your rain shell over your coat."

"My rain shell?"

That gave me satisfaction. It was a moment of victory for me to cut my engine and go back to fish in my storage area. And then in his when mine didn't have that bag. "Here. I got you one. Put the pants on too. Sorry, I didn't know about your hat. Put the hood up under it."

His was a navy color, a fancy material that would keep water out while still being breathable. My foul-weather gear was coated red plastic and I looked like a kindergartener in it, but it worked. My cap was wool and would keep me warm even when wet. His hat was felt, and while it would look good for a while, his scalp was going to get damp and then wet. What price fashion, handsome?

"Ready?"

"You think it's going to rain, I'm guessing."

I nodded at the sky ahead of us. "Chances are."

"Okay then."

Again annoying, just being so obedient and showing no resistance, even though he was clearly a man who thought he knew better than anyone around him.

Halfway down the back of Seaforth, we got to the saddle of land that carried us on a curve to Sangster Peak. Most of Red's log bridges had held and were in good shape. The ones that hadn't survived the winter weren't so far gone that I couldn't put them back together myself.

We made it to my chosen campsite just as the rain hit.

"Damn," Timothy said as he pulled his cat in next to mine and shut off the engine. "You were right. I'm really glad we didn't have to drive into this."

I offered him a big fake smile. I was sort of disappointed by that fact myself. "We'll camp here tonight. Let's get a look at your camp craft, Timothy. Go ahead and set up."

"Set up?" He looked around, perhaps looking for the butler. "Set what up?"

"I'm guessing you'd like a fire."

"In this rain? Well, if you think we can keep it going."

Wait until he found out I'd refused to bring a lighter, and he was going to have to fight his way through flint and steel.

"I think you're going to want to keep it going. We don't have tents."

He came to a halt and stared at me. "What?"

"What, what? I told you. We don't have tents."

"What kind of—you're crazy. You said you had the supplies we'd need."

"I *have* the supplies we'd need. You have a sleeping bag and a drop cloth. Surely you can fashion something appropriate out of that?"

"Motherfucker." Timothy began to pace. He couldn't go far. The heavy clouds blocked most of the sun, which was just about out of sight anyway. In minutes, this clearing was going to be as black as the inside of Timothy's soggy hat. "Are you serious?"

"I'd suggest putting together a firepit as soon as you can. A three-stone ring ought to do it if you clear away these needles."

"Are you shitting me?"

"We'll need enough fuel to cook dinner, too, so maybe you should be looking for some deadfall under the trees."

"Are you going to do nothing? You're in charge here."

"Oh, I could." I sat on the cat's seat, exuding enough patience to drive a saint up the wall. "But this is supposed to be your chance to show me how capable you are at camping. Isn't that right? Aren't you showing me how easily you can survive in my world?"

He was little more than a silhouette against a darker sky,

but his fury and frustration glowed like a searchlight. "You're killing me. You never told me you were going to drop me in the middle of nowhere with nothing."

"Not nothing. You have a sleeping bag. And a drop cloth. And flint and steel too. But that could be tricky. I can barely see you now."

He cursed again and then must have hit his foot against a rock or something because I heard him lose his footing. Fell to his knees, by the sound. The cursing got louder, and then a bright light ruined my night vision. He'd found the flashlight attachment on his phone and was using it to glare at me. "You are fired," he said succinctly.

"Oh, don't be such a baby. Up that path right there. Go on. Jesus, what a whiner. Well, go on. It's a cabin, for chrissakes. Hang on—you're going to want that sleeping bag, Jungle Jim."

When he flashed the light on the storage compartment of the cat, I saw that his rain pants were black with mud from the knees down. It was wrong to feel pleased with that. Swan would be disappointed in my lack of kindness. But I'd found the guy a cabin that would at least keep him dry. If he remembered he had cookies in his pocket, he wouldn't go too hungry.

He found the sleeping bag and set off up the clearing to find the path. He turned back. "You're not coming?"

"*I* have the supplies I need to do just fine right here," I said smugly. "Go ahead, city mouse. Go find your shelter before your phone runs out of batteries."

I didn't need to see the glare to feel it. It felt good.

I heard him fumble with the door to the old logging cabin and then slam it once he was inside. Chuckling, I pulled my tent and pad from my cat. I already had a firepit under the trees, but the night was so balmy, I wouldn't need it. Tomorrow morning I was going to make up some line about a nearby Starbucks when I presented him with a cup of coffee and pretended to be sorry I'd forgotten to send him to his luxury accommodations with his dinner. *Call me* girl *and honey, will you?*

So sure you could handle my world and I couldn't handle yours.

Insist that I date Vaughn. Poor, moose-in-the-headlights Vaughn, whose crush I'd been carefully ignoring since I was thirteen. Right, Timothy Babcock. You think you're in charge and I'm nothing, huh?

How you feeling now?

Just before I zipped myself into my tent, I smelled woodsmoke. Clever man. He'd brought his own lighter and found the stove in the cabin—not to mention the only dry wood for miles around—in the niche where Red kept it.

So, not entirely miserable, then.

Not yet anyway. Tomorrow was another day.

11

ALL NEW TERRAIN

TIMOTHY

First thing I did once the plane hit cruising altitude was take a hot shower. My Learjet was a small craft, but I'd insisted on proper bathing facilities. Max, my valet, served as my steward on my plane. Max ruled my home world, taking care of my D.C. townhouse as well as my Manhattan apartment, and he liked things tidy. He'd *tsk*ed in despair when Frank and I boarded, covered as we were in mud, and he willingly laid out my change of clothes.

By the time I came back into the main cabin, Max had served Frank a light lunch, which she was regarding with deep suspicion.

I dropped into the seat across from her and she jumped in surprise. "Something wrong with your food?" I asked.

She looked down at the tray, which held a beautiful array of nigiri. "I'm not much of a fan of sushi," she said uneasily.

How fun—how delicious—that the hiking boot was now on

the other foot. "Oh, come on. You're telling me you haven't pulled a huge, fighting salmon out of a river with your own two capable hands?" I looked at her with mock suspicion.

"I've been fishing," she said guardedly.

"Well, you won't find fish much fresher than you're getting right here." I picked up the oblong sticky rice with its strip of salmon, pink as a perfect rose, and held it to her lips. "Open up. Here comes the choo-choo. Just a little nibble. Go on. You'll love it."

Her strange eyes, dark blue rings circling the pale blue center, watched me from under drawn brows, but she eventually opened her mouth. White teeth attempted a small nibble, but I *tch*ed and she finally bit off a third.

I sat back, smiling. Chances were good she hadn't gotten far enough up the nigiri to find the pale green wasabi that waited to flash fire across her sinuses and then vanish, but at least she'd tried it.

She chewed slowly and swallowed. Then she nodded. "It's okay."

I popped the rest in my mouth. Perfect. "Shall we ask Max for pastrami on rye? I bet he could rustle up some soup."

"This is fine." She picked up the next offering and regarded it sternly.

"Yellowtail," I said helpfully. "Mild and perfect. Go ahead. Sooner or later you're going to get to the horseradish, and that's going to light up your brain for four or five seconds. Wait—give a little dip into the soy sauce. There you go."

This time, she popped the entire thing in her mouth and chewed, waiting. I knew the minute the wasabi hit her because her eyes went wide and she began smacking the heel of her hand against her forehead. By the time the fire faded, she was laughing. "What the hell was that?!"

Since she was reaching for the next piece, I assumed she'd

become a sushi fan and sat back. "That's wasabi. You can take a shower when you're ready."

Her mouth full, she looked around. The cabin, although small, was beautifully appointed. I'd had the walls and ceiling upholstered in dark green. It gave the plane an intimacy that was so lacking in those white-leather-and-chrome planes in the Babcock fleet. "We're in a plane," she said.

"To state the painfully obvious. How astute of you."

"There's a shower?"

"Well, yeah. How do you think I got so clean?" I gestured to myself, enjoying her astonishment.

"I didn't think about it," she said quickly. "I make it a point not to look at you if I can help it."

I shouted my laughter. She was entertaining, at the very least. "If you have nothing to wear, Max will get you a robe."

She sneered and nodded at the backpack on the seat across the aisle. "I have clean clothes."

"Well, please. Be my guest."

Her look was suddenly guarded. "Why? Do you have peepholes into your shower or something?"

I arched an arrogant eyebrow. "Please. I make it a point not to look at you if I can help it."

She snorted and stood. She grabbed her backpack and then came back for the rest of the sushi, which she took with her into the bathroom.

Thought she'd be able to make it in my world, huh? Oh, this was going to be fun. Revenge was a dish best served to a woman who thought she could attend a hearing in a Senate Office Building dressed in clothes that came out of a backpack.

My turn.

Gilbert met us at the front of the private terminal. He took my bags and tried to take Frank's backpack, but she held on suspiciously. Gilbert chatted incomprehensibly to her, and he put us both in the sedan.

The door shut behind me, and Frank whispered her confusion. "What did he say?"

"I dunno." Gilbert's Jamaican accent was sometimes so pronounced that I had no idea what he was saying, but he was a good driver and, after some specialized classes, had managed to pass inspection with my grandmother as a bodyguard. Not that I needed one. "I rarely catch anything he says."

Frank was perplexed. "But...he works for you? This isn't a car for hire?"

"Nope. Gilbert's my guy. I love him. Did you see that grin? He's happy all the time." And he paid attention when I texted him. Masking my evil grin, I gathered the supplies he'd left in the hidden bar. "Need anything? I have some hand lotion here. And some complimentary chocolates."

Frank was startled when I parroted her words back to her. *The first of many*, I thought with fierce satisfaction. "You literally have lotion and chocolates in here."

"Cookies too." I handed her the small pink box from Washington, D.C.'s finest patisserie. "Eat them on the way if you get hungry."

I gave her my most innocent smile, and she growled. She also took the box from me and stuffed it into her backpack. "I guess I'd better keep these." I'd made her grumpy. "Probably the only thing you're giving me for dinner."

"Oh, no." My point had been made, but why let up now? "The five-star chef does *not* have the day off. He'll have dinner for us at the end of our afternoon."

"All right," she conceded. "I was a dick to you. Do I assume you're going to make me equally as miserable?"

I relaxed into the supple leather. "Oh, were you trying to make me miserable? I didn't notice."

She tried to bluff me but then was surprised by her own laughter. "I guess I'm in for it, huh?"

Game, set, and match to Timothy. I win. "How bad could it be? All you have to do is sit next to me at a Senate hearing. It's hardly a three-stone campfire in a rainstorm."

"I'm sure it's going to be that simple." Her tone of suspicion was obvious. "What is the hearing about anyway?"

"Honey, trust me. You don't want to know."

I'd forgotten how much she hated being called *honey*. Stupid of me. She shifted in the seat, putting her back to the door and facing me.

"Look. I'm not your honey and I'm not an idiot. I can follow the basics of governance, so stop patronizing me."

Okay. She was right. My remark was insulting. But we weren't done yet proving who was the victor here. "Sure," I said. "Let me explain."

Then the poor dear had to listen to me unveil all the details of S. 413, which sought to increase the state's abilities to tax properties held for resale—a nightmare for a nationwide realty like Babcock Holdings, with properties in all fifty states and most of the territories. I bored my naïve little cowgirl into passivity by sharing every arcane detail and legislative proceeding.

Slowly, she slumped against the door and then settled back against the seat, eyes glazing over. And I kept it up for the entire ride.

"And that's why," I said as Gilbert pulled up to the front of the Russell Office Building, "I'm here to make sure my senators remember what we've agreed. Death to S. 413. Got it now?"

"Huh?" She was startled when Gilbert popped her door and handed her out onto the sidewalk. "Jeesh."

Jeesh was right. I let myself out of the Mercedes, not bothering to mask my swagger. "Leave your pack in the car. Thanks, Gilbert. We'll be a few hours."

His response featured a massive grin and a string of near-understandable syllables, but I knew he meant he'd head to the reserved lot, where he and the other drivers would hang out while waiting for important people to be done shaping the world.

I held a hand behind Frank's back to usher her forward—nothing as bold as actually touching her, of course. The line for security screening wasn't impossibly long. I scanned faces as usual to see who I needed to talk to (or snub), but the crowd was mostly low-level office drones.

Frank looked like she fit in with that crowd. She wore dark trousers that did not properly honor her excellent ass and a jacket that I felt sure had been sold to her because "it will never wrinkle." Must have appealed to a woman who lived out of a backpack. She probably thought she looked appropriate for my world.

And she did. If she wanted to be a receptionist.

Looking at Frank's outfit made me aware of how well-tailored my suit was. How it fit across my shoulders. If I casually took off the jacket and rolled up my sleeves, anyone in the room would be treated to the artwork of my ass in perfectly fitted trousers. My shoes were Italian, my cuff links understated platinum, the fountain pen in my inside chest pocket a Namiki Yukari. Maybe I hadn't known to buy a rain cover for my new Stetson, but I was perfectly appointed here.

Frank, as it turned out, was not.

An alarm went off as she passed through the metal detector.

"You brought a pocketknife into a Senate Office Building?" I asked her, astonished, as three security guards crossed their arms and glared at her while the fourth stood behind her, ready to tackle her if the occasion warranted.

"I never even thought." She looked as alarmed as they did and protested far too vehemently when the guards confiscated the blade. "No! That was my uncle's—I've got to have it back!"

"You can have it back," the captain said. "But you're not coming in here."

The look of panic Frank shot me gave me the chance for a hero moment. "Give her back the knife. We'll get rid of it and be back." This time, I did grab her elbow. We fought our way back up the line while I texted Gilbert, and then we waited outside until he pulled up. Grinning, he took possession of the pocketknife and said something to her that was obviously both funny and admiring that neither of us caught.

Frank blinked and smiled uncertainly, and I waved Gilbert on. "Did I just give him Uncle Red's knife?" she asked me.

"I'm not sure. Come on. Oh, quit worrying. I'll get it back for you." Damn it—if only I could remember what she'd said to me when I was stomping to that cabin the night before. She'd told me not to be a wimp, hadn't she? Shit, I should have flung it in her face. But the moment had passed. I'd missed my chance.

Frank got the full pat-down from the security guards (and who could blame them?) while I took the time to come up with a zinger. I led her down the marble hall and commented "This was supposed to be your chance to show me your camp craft. O —or, I should say, your lobbyist craft." She made no answer, but I heard the growl in the back of her throat. "I thought you were going to try to win this bet. Now I see you've really been trying to date my buddy Vaughn all along, and this is your convenient excuse, huh?"

I needled and tormented her (and her growls and frowns became more pronounced) until we made it to the hearing room. Johnston, my assistant, fluttered around me. I ushered Frank to two good seats in full view of where my senators could see me, and I scanned the room.

Mostly people I knew. Some interesting discussions I wouldn't mind eavesdropping on. Senator Starmer holding court among an admiring throng. He needed to remember on which side his senatorial bread was buttered this afternoon.

And there was Ursula. Shit. I was supposed to meet her before this. I was about to come up with some clever excuse when I saw trouble walking in the door.

Oh, hell no.

12

THE RINGER

FRANK

Obnoxious Timothy bolted away, leaving me sitting on a fancy leather chair and watching the gorgeous blonde he was apparently running away from, his weaselly assistant trailing after him.

"Timothy!" Her voice was outraged.

He looked back long enough to flap a hand from her to me and back again, and then he ducked through the growing crowd.

She looked back to me. We studied each other, equally confused.

"Are you with Timothy?" she asked me.

"Well," I replied, not sure how to answer. "I'm with him, but I'm not *with* him. You know?"

She perched on his empty seat. "Yeah. I know."

She was slim and stunning. Honey-blonde hair cut to swing just under her jaw. Dressed in some impossible dress that looked like a man's shirt but made of superheavy ivory silk that came to her knees. It was totally casual and alarmingly formal at the same time, and it moved with her like a lover. The thin, tan leather belt around her small waist probably cost as much as a new car. "Are you?" I asked. "With him, I mean?"

Her eyebrows shot up and she barked out a laugh. "Oh, hell no. I'm his cousin." Ah. That explained the fact that she looked like she'd never sweated out a minimum payment on any credit card. "Ursula Babcock." She held out her hand to me, and I shook it automatically.

"Frank Robinson."

Her firm grip tightened and then she let go, watching me quizzically. "Like the baseball player?"

"Sorry—it's Francesca. People call me Frank."

"I see." She eyed me. "I should have known you're not with Timothy. He definitely has a type, and you are not...I mean...I am now realizing that I have said the wrong thing, and I really regret it."

Her thought process, spoken out loud without any filter, made me chuckle. "Don't worry about it. Let me guess Timothy's type. Let's start with big boobs? And big hair?"

Ursula's eyes got big, and she bit her lip to hold back a smile. "Maybe."

"And an attitude? I'll bet he likes women who can coo 'Ooh, Daddy' to him and make him believe it's sincere."

Now she was giggling. "That does sound sort of familiar."

"And I'm guessing they wear the highest possible heels without actually being taller than he is?"

In trying to smother her laughter, Ursula uttered a snort, which made her look around guiltily and then laugh even harder. "How well you know my cousin!"

I liked her. Plus, she wasn't wearing high heels. In fact, she was wearing a pair of low boots in tan suede that I longed for. "It was just a guess."

"A good guess. I've always thought that Timothy liked

women who—" She cut herself off and looked at me instead. "I'm sorry. How do you know my cousin? I mean, are you a fan of his, or what?"

I ducked my head, not sure of what I should say. Certainly not about Timothy's possible prison sentence for hunting some mystery element...but Ursula and I were simpatico right off. I wanted her to like me. "I'm here because he and I have a bet."

She crossed her arms and turned to me, settling fully into his seat. "Go on," she intoned comically. "You must tell me all."

I craned my head, wondering where Timothy had gotten to. "Um, well..." I hedged, not sure of my next play here.

"Oh, he's schmoozing someone. You can tell me. He's all the way over—oh, fuck." Her expression darkened.

"What?" I asked. I'd spotted Timothy. He was grinning in manic fashion at two older men. One had a head of hair like a silver lion, and I felt like I'd seen him on TV before. The other was unhealthily plump and red-faced and looked like he could probably throw pizza dough in the air pretty competently.

"Goddamn it," Ursula said. "Fred Rose, trying to get in good with Senator Starmer. No wonder Timothy took off." She turned back to me. "Look, is there a reason why you have to be here? I mean, can you come with me now?"

I gaped at her. "I don't—I mean, Timothy—"

"Oh, he's going to be tied up with that mess. Rose Realty only has offices in two states. They're fighting to get this bill passed just to fuck with Babcock. Believe me, Timothy isn't even going to notice you're gone. Come on, let's get out of here." She stood and gestured to the door. I was paralyzed with indecision, and my delay made her sigh. "Fine. Hang on."

She pulled out her phone and typed. Across the room, Timothy pulled out his phone and read it. He looked to see us and nodded when he saw Ursula. He waved to the door impatiently.

"See? He doesn't care. Come on. I want to hear all about this bet." I was caught in the wake of Hurricane Ursula. She pulled me after her out of the room and down the hall. "You don't have Gilbert's number, do you?"

I shook my head. She was already summoning an Uber. "Tabby would shit if she knew. She likes us all to have body-guards at all times." She was weaving through the massive building as if she'd grown up there. I almost volunteered to be her bodyguard, but Gilbert had my knife somewhere. We emerged, blinking, into the afternoon sunlight. "There's the car. Come on."

Ursula had wizarding skills. We were somehow ensconced at a swank pub called Barmini in what seemed like a blink to me. She told me she'd order for me and then demanded the full lowdown.

So I told her. Even before my hollowed-out apple arrived (it was full of the most mellow bourbon I'd ever tasted), I dumped the entire bet in her lap. Her cousin would help me protect seven hundred acres of pristine Montana wildland if I could persuade someone from his circle to do something they didn't want to do.

"Let's skip over how Timothy can protect wildland as being less interesting than understanding what it is you're supposed to persuade someone to do. And who you're supposed to persuade."

"That's been left up in the air," I admitted. "He said he'd give me four targets but hasn't yet specified who. But he did give me a credit card so I could compete on his level."

She perked up. "What's the credit limit?"

I shrugged. "I have no idea."

"Let's find out." She got the card from me and began placing phone calls, ignoring her color-changing cocktail. "Oh, we're doing this," she announced happily. "Unlimited credit. I'm about to be your fairy godmother, Frank. This is going to be fun."

"What is?" Ursula's excitement was confusing me.

"Winning the bet, of course. On Timothy's dime."

"You're going to help me?"

"Of course I'm going to help you! He totally stood me up today. He was supposed to introduce me to the head of the National Historic Preservation Society and he completely forgot about me. Not that this is so surprising. Once he hits Capitol Hill, Timothy becomes uni-focused. It's all legislation, all the time. But he's fucking with the first project I've had in years that I'm actually interested in. I'm looking for a way to get back at him, and you are definitely it."

"I am?"

"You are. You say he's got you going to three events, with this totally boring hearing being one of them. What are the other two?"

I tried to remember the details. "One is a board meeting and dinner," I said uncertainly, "and one is some black-tie event."

"When are those happening? That soon? Okay, the board meeting and dinner is probably the annual Babcock sharehold- ers' meeting. He's got to go to that anyway. And the other is... hang on..." Her fingers were flying on her phone. "Here it is. The Beckford Department Stores Gala to Benefit Young Designers."

"How do you know it's that one?"

"Because it's being held in the Babcock Riverfront Events Center and I can see the RSVP list here. See? You're already on the list. I do marketing and publicity for Babcock, so I've got access to all kinds of things. It's terribly boring. But that gala is going to be very star-studded. We're going to have to get to work on your gown right away."

She signaled the bartender and passed over her credit card before pulling it back and getting me to hand over Timothy's instead. "Drink up," she said. "On my cousin."

"We're leaving?"

"Well, yeah. Did you hear me? We're months late on your dress. I'm going to call in a few favors."

The hurricane was moving again, and I was drawn along. This time, the Uber took us back to the airport, where, to my astonishment, Ursula led me onto a gleaming plane all dressed in pure white and chrome.

"I can't leave," I protested.

"Why not? I'll have you back before the hearing ends. Probably." She buckled herself into a plush armchair and gestured to me to do the same. Helpless, I did.

"Where are we going?" I asked.

She looked up, astonished. "New York City, of course. Where else? Oh, you poor dear. It's okay that you don't know where to go. You have come to the right place."

I was caught in a whirlwind. Abducted by a charming witch. Dropped into the middle of Manhattan via an eye-popping helicopter ride from the airport and taken by a tall driver named Kennet in a town car to a designer named Cormac Heggerty. The name sounded Irish, which showed why I should never assume. She was a small Asian woman with a bare workshop that nevertheless featured a selection of the most beautiful and utterly simple dresses I'd ever seen.

"She's lovely," Cormac said thoughtfully to Ursula, as if I wasn't in the room.

"She is," Ursula agreed. "Under all the ugly clothes. Oh, sorry, Frank."

My clothes were ugly? Well, all right. Now that I saw what she was comparing things to, my sensible black slacks and unpretentious white shirt were a little...plain.

"May I take your measurements?" Cormac asked me. Since I was suddenly visible to them again, I agreed and was astonished anew when she wanted to ply her tape measure against my bare skin.

"Of course you must be naked," Ursula said consolingly. "Cormac is going to work a miracle in just three weeks. She can't guess at your sizes."

I was at least allowed to go behind a screen with Cormac, and she politely asked me to remove my bra and panties, as well as my clothes—but this indignity became worth it when she brought The Dress.

She actually brought four dresses, but once I saw The Dress, I was blind to the others. She nodded and held it out for me to slip into. "Show Miss Ursula," she advised.

I walked from behind the screen as if I'd been drugged.

"Oh," Ursula said. "Oh, *yes*."

The fabric shone like liquid. So supple and shiny that I felt I'd been dipped in a lake of satin. It was utterly simple—slim spaghetti straps pulling to a plunging neckline. The dress fell to the floor, the whole thing made of a steel gray that edged toward blue. It was the color of a mountain lake under a stormy sky. There was no ornamentation to it. No frills.

It was perfect.

"Stunning with her eyes," Cormac said. "I've been waiting for the right person to wear this. I'm glad to meet you at last, Miss Frank."

I would have said something appropriate, something polite in return, but I could only stare at the dress in the mirror. "Oh," I said. Had I always been this kind of girl and just never realized?

"I will pin it. You'll come back for a fitting in...how long? Ten days? Yes, I can make it work. And the final fitting will be the Saturday of the gala. I'll note these dates."

"It isn't perfect now?" I asked meekly.

They both looked at me. "Like your skin," Cormac said. "This will fit you like your skin. Look."

She turned me back to the mirror and, with gentle fingers, gathered the cloth at my waist. With an experienced twitch of her hand, she moved the liquid silk until it framed my hips and gave me curves I'd never had before. "See? You will be so lovely."

I gazed at my reflection as if at a stranger until the click from Ursula's camera app broke my reverie. "This is outstanding. Get dressed. We've got so much to get done."

She wasn't kidding. After we embraced Cormac as the savior she was, Ursula took me to a hole-in-the-wall that turned out to be a bespoke shoemaker. He promised to have the right evening sandals ready on time. Next we traveled through a maze of streets that made no sense at all and climbed up four flights to find a small woman with a thick Slavic accent who took Timothy's credit card in exchange for lingerie so exquisite, so beautiful, that it should have been worn outside my clothes. Ursula was so caught up in the frenzy that she arranged for five sets to be made for herself, too, and persuaded Madame Magda to replace the plain, serviceable cotton I was wearing with the nicest "everyday" underwear I could imagine. Didn't ride up, didn't pinch, didn't bind. Since I'd already charged a fortune to Timothy, I drunkenly added three more sets to the credit card. *Never even look at the bill, will you? Try this!*

We emerged onto the sidewalk as the sun was setting. Ursula's driver, Kennet, a Middle Eastern man whose muscles looked like he threw the shot put on the East German team, took our packages. I was expecting a trip back to the heliport and the sleek company jet—but Ursula wasn't done.

"I'll text Timothy. You'll stay with me tonight. You still need something to wear to the board meeting, not to mention some ready-to-wear for now. And I've got just the person you need to teach you to do your makeup."

"My makeup? I don't do that right?"

"Oh, sure. The lipstick and mascara are fine. You're gorgeous, really. But wouldn't you love to learn how to really enhance your beauty? And if you stay tonight, I can get the hair team together tomorrow to plan your updo for the gala."

"My—my—"

"God, you look so overwhelmed. You need food. Carla, we're heading home. Let François know we're coming and that there will be two for dinner. Comfort food, I think. It's been a long time since the bourbon apple, hm? Don't lose faith, Frank, It's all going to be worth it."

I was Cinderella. How was I going to go back to being a trail guide without my fairy godmother in attendance?

And what the hell was Timothy going to say when he saw the bill?

13

INTO THE WILD

TIMOTHY

If there was any justice in this life, Fred Rose would rot in hell.

Thinking he could buy Baldrick Starmer when that was clearly my senator. Who really needed to remember all the great times we'd had together—and I had the video proof too.

I sent Frank back to Montana on her own while I cleaned up the mess on Capitol Hill. Ursula had absconded with Frank, anyway, and I had to send my Learjet to Manhattan to collect Frank. It took me another three days and a private meeting with the senator to bring him back in line, but I finally got my way. Rose Realty ought to tremble when they thought of going up against Babcock.

I delayed just long enough to nip up to Manhattan to play with my nephew. My cousin Suzanne's son, Skip, was four and already down for all kinds of entertaining amusement. Skip's male nanny, Benjamin, was a good guy, though, and let me wire Skip up on sour candies and tales of exploring the wilds on horseback. I'd forgotten that Suzanne had taken Skip (and

Benjamin) to the Circle B over New Year's. I had my suspicions that this was where Suzanne's romance with Ben had begun. He shared no news on the subject, but Skip was thrilled that I was going to the same place.

"Unca Timofee, I think me and Benja need to go with you."

"Maybe next time, little man. You'd miss your mom."

"She can come too!"

That kid delighted me, and I was happy that Suzanne had found a guy as good as Benjamin to make up for the shit she used to be married to.

It was a short visit but worth the time. I was finally grinning again by the time I got back to my Lear. I checked before we took off—thanks to several days of my thoughtful phone calls, the luggage compartment was now much fuller than the first time we'd headed west. This time, I was prepared for any tricks Frank might pull.

She was working in the paddock by the barn. Two horses were saddled (one of which was her lovely Swan), and a mule was wearing the panniers we'd pack our gear into.

Not enough, I thought. *We're going to need two mules.*

Frank's eyes bugged when I flipped back the cover on my truck bed. "What the hell is all that?"

I eyed her coolly. "I'm not getting trapped by you again." I thumped the assorted lumps. "This is my tent. This is the equipment I need for...samples. These are food supplies. And this," I said, holding up a tough canvas tote, "holds the hand lotion and complimentary chocolates without which I simply cannot continue."

She blinked, and then an unwitting chuckle erupted. She fought it valiantly but lost, eventually snorting because she was laughing so hard. "All right. I admit I was a jerk, and I apologize." I smiled in satisfaction, and she fisted a hand on her hip. "And you? You can't say you were kind of a dick when we got to D.C.?"

"A dick?" I feigned shock, one hand protectively against my chest. "Me?"

She snorted, but the laughter was still lingering in her eyes. Her unusual, arresting eyes. "Are there really chocolates in there?" she asked.

I tucked the case closer. "That's for me to know."

An older woman stuck her head out of the barn. She had a weathered look, like she'd been here since the Civil War. "What are you up to out here, Frank?"

Frank waved her over. "Maria, have you met Timothy Babcock yet? Timothy, Maria and Cal own the Circle B, and it's their horses and mules we'll be using. So behave, please."

She was still smiling, and the vibe was trending positive. I turned my back secretively, opened my tote, and pulled out one of the small boxes. "Then this is for *you*, Mrs. Buckley."

Surprised, she took the box and peered at the logo. "Vig-dis Rosen-kilde," she sounded out. "What am I holding, Timothy Babcock?"

I took the box back gently and untied the ribbon. Lifting the lid, I held the box back to her. "He's Norwegian, but he sources his chocolate in Peru. Smell that."

Maria's eyes widened as she inhaled, and Frank leaned in for a sniff. I turned to exclude the younger woman. "For *you*," I said sternly to Maria and gave her back the box.

Maria was now sniffing like a bloodhound. "Can I taste one?"

"By all means," I said. "They're yours. But we're going to need another pack animal."

"Whatever," she said, distracted. I grinned at Frank.

"I surrender," Frank said. "You win."

"I usually do," I said smugly.

Frank shook her head in mock annoyance and led me into the barn. "Come on. I'll show you where we're going on a map."

I'd already studied the combined parcels of land that made

up the Circle B (it had quite a history of sales and acquisitions on the fringes, but the core property had been owned by generations of Buckleys since before Montana was a state) and had reviewed topographic maps and aerial views, but I pretended ignorance when Frank stopped in front of a massive map pinned to the rough walls of an office.

"My plan," she said, "was to start you out on the trail to Charla Lake up here." Her finger reached high to stab the blue blob near the far border.

"Charla Lake," Maria murmured, sitting at the desk and distracted by her chocolates. "That's a good expedition."

"Why there?" I asked. I had no ulterior destinations. One path was as good as another to me, but I wondered if Frank would have a good reason.

"Well, it's a reasonably easy trek, which will be good in this uncertain weather. Takes two days to go up the Wild River... here." Her finger traced a wandering blue line. "Think of this as Main Street, fed by all these other creeks and streams coming out from the mountains. We can follow any of these streams if you want, although some of them won't have been ridden in a while, so I can't promise they'll be in good shape."

"Good shape meaning...?"

"Oh my god," Maria moaned. We turned. She was holding the box cupped in one hand, a finger just touching her lips. "Oh my god."

"Give me one of those chocolates," Frank tried, but Maria wheeled in her ancient desk chair and refused. "You're so greedy, Maria. God."

"Oh my god." Maria's only response. I loved it.

"Go on about trails in good shape," I prodded.

Frank scowled at Maria and then at me. We both ignored her frown, so she went on. "There could have been rockslides. Or riverbanks can erode," she said, "which we either need to clear by hand or find a way around. When the log bridges over creeks get washed out or rotted, that takes just as much time. We either have to find the missing bridge downstream or we have to make another one. So all these tributaries to the Wild River are possible, but we might not get as far as you'd like before your board meeting or gala."

Her reasoning was sound. "So, Charla Lake."

"Charla Lake. The trail has been used every summer and it's in good shape. There's a bunkhouse up there in case you get tired of sleeping in a tent, and if you like to fish, you won't find a better spot."

I studied the map as if I'd never examined the property before. "There are other lakes. Bigger ones. What's this one?"

"Daughtry Lake," she said. "Named for my family, actually. My great-uncle Red was a Daughtry."

"Good family friend, if Cal and Maria named a lake after him."

She huffed a laugh. "It was named by some ancestor of mine who used to own that valley. Then he lost it in a poker game to some ancestor of Cal's. Can you imagine?"

I could. "How very Old West."

"Yeah. We can go there if you'd like. I'd like to see how things are doing up there. But it's been since before Red's death that anyone's been up the Second Fork. Five years, maybe. I'd save that for a later trip." She turned to face me, her expression studiously neutral. "Up to you, of course. It's your party. Your dime."

I knew Frank wanted to wall off some seven hundred acres and I thought she might be just a little too casual about Daughtry Lake, but she was a mystery I would need time to solve. "Charla Lake it is," I said.

Frank nodded, still so neutral that my instincts were pinging. She rapped on Maria's desk to get the woman's attention. "Hey. Log it in, please. We're going up to Charla Lake."

"Of course you are," Maria said dreamily.

"Write it down, please. Five days." She turned back to me. "Or six? Do you want a day to fish while we're up there?"

I calculated. "The board meeting is on the twenty-seventh. We need to fly out on the twenty-sixth, so six days should be fine."

Frank nodded. "Are you writing it down, Maria? Today is March twenty-first, and we'll be back on Thursday. That's the twenty-sixth. Damn. Those chocolates have narcotized you."

"I've got it, I've got it," Maria grumbled.

"And we're going to need to pack in more food for us and the animals. We really will need another mule. Besides Daisy, who are we taking?"

Maria was actually writing in a logbook by hand. If it was good enough for the Civil War era, it was good enough for the Circle B. "You can take Clop. He's in the west paddock."

"Clop?" I asked as Frank led me out.

"Full name is Clippity-Clop. That's what you get when you let the summer kids vote on the new mule's name, but old Clop is a good guy. We'll do fine with him."

For the next hour, we worked companionably as Frank explained why she was loading the mules as she did and we fit my supplies and hers into the panniers.

My gelding, a big black named Whistler, greeted me politely. He lacked the unconscious grace of my polo mounts, but he looked strong and intelligent. There would be no changing out of mounts if I wore this one out, so his powerful hindquarters and strong neck spoke of endurance over speed. As we neared the time for departure, I checked his girth before mounting. Then I had to stand back and shrug at Frank. "What's this rig?" I asked.

She came around Swan to see what I was looking at. "Oh— you're used to an English saddle. Watch. This is the cinch. It's wider than the girth of an English. Here's how you tighten it... this is the latigo strap...goes to these rings on this side..."

She was enjoying the fact that I needed instruction, and I chafed under the irritation. But she'd apologized for being a jerk and I had not apologized for teasing her in turn, so I was still ahead in this competition. I smothered my annoyance and listened.

Frank expressed surprise when I said I could lead Clop, acting as if I were a delicate little flower and laughing when I rolled my eyes. She took Daisy's lead, and at last we were ready to move out. She waved to Maria, who was now defending her chocolates from Cal and another woman who'd come to watch us off.

"Maria, don't be greedy," Frank called. "Bye, Cal. Bye, Chita."

I did a double-take when I heard the name. Chita? As in the Chita who'd taken Vaughn's virginity when he was sixteen? I bit back my grin. She was an attractive woman. *Way to go, Vaughn.*

We followed the ranch driveway until we crossed over the bridge and then headed up a trail that followed the water.

Whistler and I got used to each other. There's a rightness to the feeling of horse and man moving together. It's music and lyrics coming into sync. Tempo and dynamics. I felt the horse in my tailbone, in my rump. My legs got used to his responsiveness. I tried the neck reining and found it pleasingly simple, since my other hand held Clop's lead.

It took a little while for my spine to adapt to Whistler's rolling gait, and I knew he was waiting to see if he could simply follow Swan's attractive butt or if I was actually going to be in charge, so we had a few brief but significant conversations on the subject of grazing on the branches we were passing. I knew he didn't actually want to eat the brown, withered leaves he was trying to nip. He just wanted to know if he could get away with it. When I objected, he settled and stopped trying.

Very nice.

Clop came along willingly. He was a soft gray mule with

long ears and a slightly jumpy nature, but we did just fine. I didn't need to drag him. He seemed to want to keep up with Daisy. *Have a little crush, do you, Clop?* I could understand. Daisy was a white mule with a delicate step. *Best of luck to you, old man.*

The footpath we were on crossed the open area behind the main lodge. The gentle hill turned into a real slope as we crossed under the trees.

And Whistler began...whistling.

I watched him, surprised. His ears were still relaxed, and his pace hadn't slowed. He obviously wasn't tired, and his breathing wasn't labored. So why was he whistling?

And whistling?

And whistling?

The path wound between trees that had blocked most of the snow. We were generally on bare earth, winding up between massive trunks. Most were bare, but some pine trees added color to a black-and-white scene. Whistler and I avoided the worst of the roots, navigated easily around rocks and stones. He was content. But still whistling.

It wasn't until I looked ahead to make sure we hadn't fallen too far behind Frank that I noticed her shoulders shaking.

Was she laughing?

"Is this funny to you?" I called.

As if I'd broken a spell, her laughter bubbled out of her. "I love that horse," she called back, grinning.

"Is he going to whistle like this the whole time?"

"Oh, no," she said, flashing a grin over her shoulder at me. "Only when he goes uphill."

"Jesus. I have never heard of such a thing."

"Me either." Her glee seemed unseemly. "He's one of a kind, Whistler."

I tried to lean over to watch him. "He's not actually whistling, though...is he?"

"Seems to be something he's doing with his lungs. Or his throat."

"Not unhappy, though?"

"He's fine."

"You chose this horse for me on purpose, didn't you?"

She laughed again.

The air was balmy. Chilled, of course, but the sun filtering through the bare trees had warmth in it. My Gore-Tex expedition jacket protected me from the occasional breeze, and I was able to unzip it as we drew to the top of the incline and emerged onto a stony spur of land that fell away to both sides. The view was astonishing. Below on both sides, forest crowded against the ridgeline, and I could hear the sound of rushing water below us. Across the immensity of clear, cold air was a vista ringed with mountain peaks. They were clear and detailed on the opposite side of the valley and faded to gray sawtooth shapes as they receded into the distance.

I reined Whistler to a stop so I could take it all in. Swan and Frank waited patiently. 'It's just one mountain after another," I noted. "All the way to the curve of the earth. Do they ever come to an end?"

"You're looking pretty much due south, so no. This range goes all the way down to the bottom of South America, really. Baring a few gaps in the Central American lowlands." She gestured. "Over that way is Yellowstone, but ahead of us? About all you can see is Circle B land."

I'd grown up in the real estate industry. I appreciated the scope of land. Its permanence. Its value. Its finite nature. (After all, no one is making more land.) But I realized I'd never truly come to grips with the truth that there were people who could own...mountains.

Not just mountains, but mountain ranges.

How could such a thing be possible?

Frank nudged Swan into motion and Whistler and I

followed, each trailing our amiable mule. Over the years, I'd heard the same old saws about some unnamed tribal leader from the American West who made some poetic statement about how they didn't own the land, they held it in trust for their children.

Or they didn't own the land—the land owned them.

Pretty words. Looked nice on the decorative burned-wood signs of liberal do-gooders.

But for the first time, I wondered if there wasn't something to the concept. Suzanne's little boy, Skip—would this view still be here when he grew up?

The trail crossed back into the woods, and Whistler began his signature song as we rose along the cresting land. I shook myself mentally. Was I really supposed to change my attitude because of the view from the very first ridge? Shit, this was going to be a long trip.

Deliberately, I spent the next hour thinking about the molybdenum plan. The timing, of course, was crucial. I needed to find a supply of molybdenum, mine it from solid rock, crush it, and have it ready in a storehouse before the new battery patent was approved. Somewhere in there would be negotiating ownership of the land.

As a method of reorienting my values away from the "noble savage" nonsense, this was inefficient, as I did not yet have enough information—or molybdenum—to plan properly. Therefore, I checked emails and messages on my sat phone as we rode along and turned my thinking to plotting new ways to drag Senator Starmer's more weak-willed colleagues into my thrall. The dinners I could host. The supermodels I could introduce them to. There were two women in Starmer's coalition. Would *my* charm be enough? Did I need to scout out some likely male escorts? There was nothing wrong with my look, but I'd noticed that the older females in the Senate tended to melt a little in the presence of big gym muscles.

Huh. No panoramic view was going to make me question *my* priorities.

The trail crested a slope and dipped downward. We entered a thin valley that bent out of sight. The Wise River burbled and chuckled over rocks as it followed the contours of the valley. Perfect trout waters, fast and clear and very cold.

"This would be a nice place for a canter," I called to Frank.

Her scorn was audible. She didn't bother turning but raised her voice to be heard over the river.

"First time since last summer on this trail and you think it's a good time for a lope. I thought you were a horseman."

The worst thing about her scorn was that it was justified. I'd gotten so comfortable following my trail guide that I didn't even think about what she was doing. What she was seeing. We'd veered around some mud slicks and ridden through others. We'd stepped over some downed trees and bushwhacked around others. She was making choices as we went along that I was ignoring, and I was the fool who wanted to run the horses.

"Besides," she called back, "there's no cantering in Western. Say *lope*. Greenhorn."

Lope. I rolled my eyes. The gait was the same.

Possibly she felt bad about mocking me because she slowed Swan, allowing me to come alongside. "You can tie Clop's lead to your saddle. Hand it here."

With a few efficient tugs, she secured the mule. Her hair fell forward as she worked, brushing against my arm, and I had a flashing moment when I regretted the tough shell of my coat. That hair probably felt pretty soft. It looked soft.

"Thanks," I said when she was finished. I must have been successful at hiding my grudging tone because she walked along beside me instead of taking the lead.

"I guess I should thank you," she said.

I liked it when people thanked me, so I sharpened my attention. "Yeah? For what?"

She looked uneasy. "For the credit card. I mean, I spent some of your money with Ursula."

I huffed a laugh. "Ursula. She's okay, huh?"

"I like her. I don't guess she's afraid of anything at all."

I raised an eyebrow, considering, as Frank nudged us away from a sludgy pool of meltwater on the trail. "I guess I never thought about it. Is she particularly fearless?"

Frank pursed her lips in thought. "Well, she sure isn't afraid of spending money." She shot me a glance side-eye. "Spending *your* money," she edited.

I grinned. "Ursula," I said fondly. She was my most skeptical cousin and perhaps my most discriminating. Throughout our childhoods, Ursula was the hardest to impress—but if I could get her on my side, there was no better ally. "I guess she is kind of fearless at that. She's all right."

Frank was silent as we rounded a near-blind corner in the valley. The new view was much the same: a long, skinny valley made by a fast-moving river, although this new vista included a hill too steep for trees, which the trail traversed. We fell back into a follow-the-leader format as we climbed out of the valley. Whistler continued to whistle. It began to give me some very unmanly giggles.

At the top, we entered the woods again. A low rumble of sound grew slowly until, after about twenty minutes, we came to a view of the reason we had to leave the valley. The Wild River was making a sudden and startling descent down about forty feet in a series of gorgeous waterfalls, the thunder generated making conversation challenging. I had to stop and gasp at the sight. The air was warm enough that the mist generated hadn't frozen on the surrounding trees, but there were enough downed limbs lying half in the water to tell a winter story.

Frank waited patiently while I stared.

And I did. I stared. And thought about hydroelectric properties. If you could harness all that free energy, what couldn't you accomplish?

"You should put in a waterwheel," I called to Frank. I had to repeat myself when she didn't understand, but when she heard me, she gave me a grin.

"Now," she shouted, "you're thinking like a mechanical engineer!"

She ducked her head down the trail, asking silently if I was ready to move on, and we continued our journey. Mechanical engineer. That's right—that's what she was studying

Now that I thought about it, I had to wonder. Why?

Why did this unusual woman want to be a mechanical engineer?

How did she figure she could fit into my plans to extract molybdenum?

What did she see when she looked at this landscape?

14

WELL, IF YOU'RE GOING TO BE NICE

FRANK

Timothy's easygoing nature was confusing me.

I much preferred him to stay neatly in the pigeonhole where I put him. He was arrogant and pushy and thought that money was the same thing as honor. He was a dick.

Even flirting so adroitly with Maria was no less than I would expect from him.

With one strange exception (him gallantly wiping fries off my seat at the Denver bar before he let Vaughn and me sit), I had Timothy Babcock sussed out. I knew what to expect. The kinds of private planes that only Arab sheiks could afford and credit cards with no limits. Right. Got it.

But when we crossed over the first saddleback—the stretch of land Uncle Red had referred to as the Welcome View— cocky, obnoxious Timothy Babcock was...moved.

I didn't want to believe it. He was an acquisitive, irksome man who'd been indulged at every turn from birth. If he saw anything and wanted it, he got it. He had no humility and no humanity.

Until he saw the view.

That small stretch of trail gave me happy shivers. It was the gateway to the lands that I loved, and I never crossed it without breathing more deeply, without stretching like a long, hard day was, at last, coming to an end.

I hadn't expected Timothy to feel the same way.

It confused me. But I had to confess that it made me think differently about the man.

Yes, he was handsome. Yes, he could be charming. Yes, his teasing on our trip to Washington had been more lighthearted —kinder—than my version.

Now I was left wondering if he could be someone I...liked.

I flicked a look over my shoulder, ostensibly checking on Daisy. He sat a horse like he was born to it. He probably *could* play polo. His posture was tall but not rigid. He was adapting to Whistler's stride through the hips. There was a case to be made for lust, but so what? No big deal. I lusted after a lot of guys. Didn't mean I slept with them.

But liking a guy...that was trickier. Someday, I'd find a guy who inspired both lust *and* like, and then what was going to happen?

We came to the first big falls on the Wild and Timothy came to a halt again, staring open-mouthed at the beauty. Damn it. I didn't want to like this guy.

And where did his mind go? To hydroelectricity. To a power supply. I got a little zing of adrenaline from the back of my neck. It warmed me across my shoulder blades like an embrace and laced down my spine. If he thought that was a good idea, what would he think about my projects?

The thought snapped me back from fantasy. This guy was not my partner. I didn't need to impress him or get his advice. He was a means to an end.

I let him draw alongside me when we got back to the river valley.

"I'm not kidding," I said. "I spent a lot of your money. A lot."

He didn't seem interested. "Oh yeah?"

"You honestly don't care?"

"Sorry. Sure I care." He didn't. He was humoring me. "Why? What did Ursula talk you into buying? Did I get her a new Lamborghini or something?"

I goggled at him. "Wouldn't that bother you?"

"A car? I guess. No, not really. Depends. What color was the Lambo?"

I laughed. "We didn't buy a car. I got a dress for the gala."

"Oh. Good idea."

"And some shoes."

"Have to have shoes. Can't go barefoot."

"And some, um, underwear."

"Oh yeah?" This was the most interested he'd been and he leered at me. "Do I get to see it?"

I scoffed, hiding the giggle that would not have seemed strong. "Maybe in the bag, when I get them."

"Ah, I see. You're not talking about underwear. You're talking about lingerie. Custom-made lingerie. I bet you'll be gorgeous in them."

This conversation was not helping my confusion. "I don't even dare tell you how much it all cost."

He tossed his head, indifferent. "I've bought some of that underwear for various, um, friends." I bet he had. "I know what it costs."

"And you don't care. What about the suit for the board meeting? And the boots? And so much makeup. And these people are going to do my hair. I mean, it's so much money!" I felt like I was in a confessional, laying my sins bare.

But my sense of guilt had no effect on Timothy. "That was the deal, wasn't it? You get the credit card to level our playing field. And if you persuade someone to do something they don't want to do, then you'll protect some hunk of land out here in the nowhere. Where is your land, by the way?"

I waved a hand vaguely. "I'll show you." Eventually. If I couldn't figure out how to keep him away. "Charla Lake first."

"Right. That reminds me. Hold up."

He reined Whistler to a stop and dismounted, almost popping Clop in the nose. The mule didn't expect the stop and had come right up on Whistler's butt. Well-behaved, Whistler didn't register any objections.

Timothy fumbled in Daisy's panniers and then in Clop's, finally unearthing a chisel and hammer. He picked his way across the melting snow to the bare rock by the river and started banging away.

I blinked. "I thought you'd have a drill. You know...to extract a core."

He shrugged and kept chipping away at the stone until a large fragment flew off and landed at his feet. He gathered it and weighed it in his hands. Then he pulled out his phone.

"There's no signal up here," I said triumphantly. "You see a cell tower around here somewhere?"

He didn't even look up. "You see a satellite up there? This isn't a cell phone."

Shit. Every time he checked his phone, he really was staying in touch?

How...horrible.

He read something off his screen and used a marker to write on the stone fragment. "There. Now I know exactly where this one comes from." He came back to the mule and stowed his supplies and rock sample. "And I can't use a drill for a core sample. No power source. And no hand-cranked auger is going to do the job. If we had some hydroelectric, now, *that* would work!"

He'd thought this out. I had to approve. "How often will we

stop? How many rock samples do you hope to shove into Clop's baskets?"

He looked up and shrugged. "Not sure. At least one per mountain, but it's surprisingly hard to figure out where one mountain stops and the next one starts, you know? I guess I'll take a sample whenever we stop. Which, if you'll excuse me..."

He headed for a thicket of bushes. They were mostly bare branches, but they'd serve for a guy in need of a whiz. I ground-tied Swan and found my own rock outcropping to hide behind. We were back up moments later, much relieved.

"There's a good lunch spot over the next rise. You good to go on for another half an hour or so?"

He was agreeable, so we pushed on.

The rest of the day followed in this pattern. In conversation, Timothy was entirely too casual about money. When confronted with epic views, he was brought to stillness. Yes, he constantly checked his stupid sat phone, but he didn't keep his focus on the tiny screen for long. He particularly liked the sight of waterfalls coming over cliffs.

Was he admiring beauty? Was he imagining power sources for the mining operations that would scar the landscape and destroy the rivers? Did I like him, or did I hate him?

I wanted to hate him. That was simpler. He was making it hard, though.

Until we reached the first campsite and he proved that he might have been a skilled horseman, but he had no idea how to care for his mount.

He ground-tied Whistler and then started unpacking the panniers. "Excuse me," I said. "What are you doing?"

He turned, surprised. "Dinner? Tent? You've got some hidden servants who are going to take care of that?"

Thank you for irritating me. "You've got some hidden groom who's going to take care of Whistler? Saddle off, please."

"Oh. Shit. Sorry. Sorry, Whistler."

I'd shown him how to tighten the cinch at the beginning of the day. Could he figure out how to get the saddle off?

He could—and then stood there with the sweaty saddle pad hanging down, looking for the wooden post in every tack room.

"That log will do. Lay the saddle pad out separately to dry. Can you get Clop's panniers off without unpacking them?"

Embarrassingly, I couldn't get Daisy's panniers off alone and Timothy had to help me. Very annoying. If I'd been alone, I would have just unpacked her and handled it myself, and now I had to express grudging thanks for Man Muscles owned by a guy who, it turned out, had never brushed a horse.

I pulled the halters out of Daisy's baskets, and we secured all four animals. We brushed the horses, and I forced Timothy to check and pick all eight hooves he was responsible for. Last, I walked him through setting out dinner for the animals before he got to even think about his own. We hobbled the horses for the night.

And he did not complain.

I wished he would, but he didn't.

"Do we have to worry about predators?" he asked, and I gave him credit for the question.

"I've got a rifle, and the horses should let us know if something is after them. They're not defenseless, and I think we'll be okay. We're going to hoist our food into a tree far from camp, though, because we are not idiots. Got it?"

He got it.

When we finally unpacked our gear, Timothy committed the unpardonable sin of having consistently higher-quality gear than I did. He brought fuel-soaked fire starters. His cooking gear was undented and beautiful. His food was more flavorful and easier to prepare than mine. He shared all willingly, and I hated him. Imagine hauling full-strength chowder to a backcountry trek, rather than something concentrated and in need only of water and rehydration.

Not that the chowder wasn't absolutely delicious. Once the sun set, the air grew colder and the breeze felt more aggressive, and that mug of corn chowder felt like paradise.

Damn him.

His lantern was significantly brighter than mine. I felt sure his camp shovel and biodegradable toilet paper were nicer than mine. The entire thing was making me grumpy, and when he set up his elegant two-man tent with barely any effort, I had to suppress low growls.

He had room for me in his tent, but I was not a beggar. I set up Red's tent as usual, staking it to the thin layer of soil over the bedrock. I found the pine needles to fill my mattress and watched as Timothy used a powerful foot pump to blow up a large air mattress.

"Not too late," he said, catching me watching. "Big enough for two."

"I'm fine," I said shortly. Thank god he was so annoying. My confusion had cleared right up.

I didn't know when he did it—perhaps when I headed to the stream to brush my teeth—but when we left our campfire safely banked and crawled into our respective tents, I found a damned box on my pillow.

"Vigdis Rosenkilde!" My shout of irritation was involuntary.

From his tent, I heard his chuckle. "Complimentary choco-lates," he called. "For sweet dreams."

"Asshole," I muttered.

I sat there in the shabby tent that was so often home for me and Uncle Red and looked at that box as if it was betrayal. This was not how backcountry treks were supposed to go.

On the other hand...

The chocolate was a revelation. Fruity with no fruit in it. Deep as night in just a nibble. Creamy but magnificently firm under my tongue. I suppressed my groan, knowing he'd hear it. A total sensual experience. What a bastard.

"I have a heater in my tent," he called. "If you get cold."

I rolled my eyes. "Good night," I said firmly.

"Night, *honey*," he called back.

Growl.

Fine. You think you're in charge here? Tomorrow's trek just got a great deal harder. I had some plans for the man.

15

COMING EAST

TIMOTHY

Frank tried. She really did what she could to piss me off.

Little did she know her attempts to wear me out had the reverse effect. The more log bridges I had to help her pull out of creeks, the more rockfalls we had to route around, the more short-handled axes she handed me, the more determined I got.

And everywhere we went, I shaved off more granite in hunks big enough to bear the GPS coordinates that would tell me where I'd taken the sample.

The unexpected delight to this trek was my growing competence. At caring for Whistler and Clop. At reading the terrain for mud slicks versus deep sinks. At coming up with a song I could sing with every hill ascended. The big black horse whistled my accompaniment while I sent my voice echoing to the mountains with a song that made Frank hide her sniggers:

> I'm climbing and climbing with Whistler
> We're going up and on and on.

Following my handsome horsey sister
Lead us onward, Lady Swan

Of course, I couldn't admit to the blisters coming up on my hands from axe, chisel, camp shovel. I couldn't confess to muscle aches or the stupid headaches when I forgot to drink enough water. I doctored those ills alone at night in my lovely, warm tent and never breathed a word, since Frank would have counted each blister as the weakness of a *greenhorn*.

So, I did my bandaging out of my excellent first aid kit and then slept every night more deeply than I'd ever slept at home. It took until we were on the return trip—four nights into the journey—to realize I hadn't laid awake at all, plotting against Starmer, or considering Aleister Darling, or calculating how much more success I'd need to achieve before Nicholas and Joanna and Fourth would consider me worthy of respect.

No, I'd slept. Deep and hard and efficient. And woken up looking forward to another day of whatever Frank had to dish out.

We made it back to the Circle B on schedule. When I bid a temporary farewell to Whistler, I knew I was looking forward to the return trip. "Back in just three days, boy. We'll come up with a second verse to our song next time." Whistler shook his head at me, which I assumed was an equal expression of enthusiasm to my own. "Bye, Clop. You're a good sort." Clop liked to be scratched between his long, soft ears. We had a moment of mutual delight until Frank was done checking everything in.

She pulled her day pack out of her truck and announced she was ready. Maria looked longingly after me as I walked to my Ford, so I timed it perfectly and ducked back to her with my last box of chocolates.

"Ever tried Guido Castagna?" I whispered when I put the box into her grasping hands.

"What's that?" Her eyes were wide as she pulled the chocolates to her bosom.

"Next time." I winked. She giggled like a schoolgirl, and her husband glared at me. "Box for you, too, sir?"

He was appeased. "I don't eat that sweet stuff," he said, but that was a lie. Or rather, it was the truth—but only because his wife refused to share.

I lay my finger against my nose and winked. "I got you."

He did his best to look stern in return, but we understood each other. Cal was probably a whiskey man. I had another bottle of the Macallan 84 that ought to make me his favorite.

Frank and I headed to the airstrip, and she thought to question why we weren't going all the way to the commercial airport in Big Sky.

"Because John's strip is big enough for a little plane like mine."

"John?" she asked. His house was far above on the mountainside, the airstrip being placed on the only level ground around for miles.

"John. My buddy, John. That's his private strip."

She thought about it, undoubtedly reviewing all the wealthy men in the neighborhood named John. It didn't take her long.

"John Mayer?" she asked. "We're using John Mayer's airstrip?"

"You know him? Great guy, right?"

I'd annoyed her. "No, I don't know John Mayer!" Her voice rose in irritation. "I live in my mother's trailer and drive a truck made before catalytic converters existed. Where the hell do you think I'd come across a rock star?"

"Well, don't get mad at me. He owns a bar around here, doesn't he?"

"In Livingston. Like I spend my time there."

"How was I to know?"

She crossed her arms and studied the road out the window in a huff. *Didn't mean to upset you, princess.* We were working our usual pattern. The person in charge of the world we found ourselves in was the one who got to piss the other one off, and we were heading for my Learjet. My turn.

This time, Max was waiting for us on the tarmac with a stiff wire brush. Relentless, he made us stand still while he briskly worked at least some of the mud off our pants and boots. "I'm being currycombed," I said to Frank, who didn't want to smile at my observation and so turned away so I wouldn't see. But I did. I was getting addicted to her reluctant amusement.

Once Max let us onboard, I felt the satisfaction of being home. The backcountry was glorious. Better than I expected. But nothing beat a hot shower, clean clothes, and the attentions of a man who cared deeply about how much mud he'd have to clean out of my Persian rugs.

Once Frank and I scraped almost a week of hard living off our bodies, she faced me across the table. "Board meeting tomorrow?" she asked.

Assuming she wanted clarification, I nodded and offered some context. "We'll be at the Babcock Tower in Lower Manhattan. That's a word you'll get used to here—Babcock. All the attendees, with a few exceptions, are Babcocks because only Babcocks are allowed on the board. All the significant positions in the firm are expected to attend, which is why I'll be there. All of us Babcocks. The meeting will be on the eighty-first floor, and the reception and dinner afterwards will be upstairs in the Sky Lounge."

Her eyes were narrowed in concentration. "Everyone's a Babcock?"

"Well, principals can bring a second, which is how I'm getting you in there. But no one's going to invite you to venture an opinion. Mostly it's Babcocks only who talk at the annual."

"Wow. You've got a pretty exclusive company going there, huh?"

"You have no idea. You'll meet Tabby. She's the biggest dog at the board meeting—our board chair. And my grandmother. Scary lady."

"She's a scary grandmother?" One of Frank's eyebrows was down. She thought I was exaggerating.

"You can form your own opinion. What are your grandmothers like?"

She shrugged. "My mom's mother was pretty cool. She was Uncle Red's sister. He was actually my great-uncle."

"And your father's mother?"

The face she made seemed an unconscious moue of dislike. "Never met her."

My internal radar pinged. "Why is that?"

Her quick eyes caught me studying her. She spoke clearly. "Because she died before my father was sent to prison, where he remains to this day, for vehicular homicide. I'm sure you'll be interested to know that he was blind drunk at the time. Can I answer any questions about this, Mr. Babcock?"

She probably thought she was being direct and honest. Frank was unaware of the pain and defensiveness showing up in her posture, in the strength of her neck, in the hands on her thighs that might have looked relaxed if each finger wasn't digging in so deeply, they were dimpling the fabric.

I could read a "Keep Out" sign as clearly as anyone else. Not that I wouldn't attempt a little trespassing later. I had a digital detective on retainer. I'd have Frank's entire history before we landed.

"No questions." I continued explaining who she'd be meeting. "Tabby has three sons and one stepson. They all had high-level jobs with the company, but they've persuaded their sons and daughters to take over their roles. Except my father, who would love to retire, but I refuse to become the head of all sales, and neither of my sisters want the job either."

"You have sisters?"

"Delilah and Joanna. Delilah is in charge of philanthropy, and Joanna's the massive brain who runs our IT department."

"I might need to take notes," she said apologetically.

"Hang on—I'll draw you a family tree."

She thought I was kidding, but Max brought me paper. "Look. I have two sisters and seven cousins. Tabby refers to us as her Portfolio. At the top of the pyramid is Fourth—that is, Zaccharias Babcock IV. He answers only to Tabby and definitely believes his shit doesn't stink."

I ran through the major players she'd meet, and Frank's eyes went wide.

"Am I supposed to memorize all of this?" she asked. I hadn't even gotten to the more far-flung cousins and other Babcock relatives.

I gave her a half shrug. "I don't know. Maybe if you want to win the bet, you'll want to know who you'll have to persuade."

I saw her eyes flash to where I'd written Ursula's name. Frank had just found someone who would help her win the bet. "Nuh-uh," I said firmly, palm flat over Ursula's name. "Not her. If you want to persuade someone to do something they don't want to do, you have to focus on..." I considered the map of my relatives I'd created. They stood out like neon—the people who had never given me the credit I was due for my work. I'd chosen four to test her against, and I boxed their names on the page as I went along. "Fourth," I said firmly. "He's the CEO. Number two is Nicholas, the chief financial officer. Good luck with him. Your third potential target to persuade is my sister Joanna, who really really does not suffer fools, so watch your step."

Her brows drew in over her nose. "If I can persuade one of those people to do something they don't want to do, I'll get seven hundred acres protected?"

"Or Tabby," I added. "She's the fourth option. And you have to tell me which seven hundred acres you're fighting for."

"Sure," she said so easily I knew she was lying. "Sure. When we get back, I'll take you there." Liar. "So my targets are the CEO, the CFO, the head of IT, and the chair of the board. Right?"

"Well, unless you want to add some senators to the list?"

She shot a look at me. "This list of four will do just fine."

I did some texting on the plane. Even with my sat phone, being out of touch for almost a week had left residue. So I answered messages. Alerted my actual assistant, Johnston, that he wouldn't be coming to the board meeting. Ensured my board reports were in order—always a delicate task, since I could never say (and the board would definitely not want to hear) how many senators I had control with or influence over.

That taken care of, I then set up delivery of supplies for the next trip West. Ordered the Guido Castagno chocolates to be flown in from Italy; must arrive by Sunday. Set my investigator on Frank's digital history.

It was a busy plane ride.

Frank was doing a lot of texting too. I should have been more suspicious of that.

16

WHOA. GIRL POWER

FRANK

Timothy was astonished when I wouldn't get into his power-hungry Mercedes.

"That's okay," I said to the grinning Gilbert. "I'll grab a cab."

Astonished, Gilbert looked to Timothy, who gaped at me. "Sorry?"

"I'm just going to get a cab," I repeated, trying to look cool. The idiot grin would definitely get in the way of an excellent departure.

"...To where?" Timothy asked. "Just ride with me. I have a perfectly nice apartment in Manhattan. You'll have your own guest suite."

Guest suite. Not even a guest room—I'd have a guest suite. I adjusted my pack on my shoulder. "Oh, I'm staying with a friend."

"A friend?" His rust-colored eyebrows all but disappeared into his hairline. "What friend? Who do you know in...oh. Well, pardon me."

Now he looked annoyed, and I just shrugged. "She invited. I accepted."

Gilbert said something incomprehensible to Timothy, who watched his driver blankly before saying, "Ursula. She wants to stay with Ursula."

That was true, so I smiled at both of them. Gilbert said something that Timothy didn't bother attempting to interpret. "Get in. We'll drive you there."

I backed away, liking the freedom. "I'll get a cab," I repeated. "Thanks, though. I'll see you at Babcock Tower tomorrow at four."

There was a moment when I thought Gilbert might have rushed me. The guy looked big enough to put me over his shoulder. But Timothy held up a hand, restraining his body-guard. "It's going to cost a few pennies to take a cab out to Darien."

I smiled sweetly. "Fortunately, I have a credit card." Happily, a cab was idling on the curb, and I slipped into the back seat.

"Lady," the driver said, "if you want me to take you to the commercial terminal after I waited in that line for the last two hours, then I don't want the five-dollar fare."

I was still trying to avoid a goofy grin as I watched confused Timothy and Gilbert stand on the curb by their open back door. "Nope," I said. "How about a fare to Darien?"

"Connecticut? Fuck yeah. All right, lady. For once, the private terminal pays off. Sit back and relax. I'll get you there."

We pulled out, and I waved to Timothy as we slid into traffic.

Not in his car. Not being led through the Big City by the hand, forced to play the Country Mouse to his urban sophisticate.

FRANK ROBINSON

Got a cab

On my way to you now

URSULA BABCOCK

I know

Timothy just called

He's very annoyed

I absolutely love it

Thanks for helping me

You're the most interesting thing to happen to me in months

How long until you get here?

I checked the driver's name on the hack license in front of me. Fortescue M. Buffet. Great name.

"Mr. Buffet, how soon will we get there?"

He plugged the address into his phone. "On a Thursday afternoon?" he said happily. "Oh, we'll be lucky to get there in under two hours. You can afford this, right?"

I found Timothy's credit card and waved it at the cabbie in the rearview. "Unlimited. We're good."

"Want to stop off and get something for the trip?" he asked. "I know a great sub shop in Hackensack."

So, Timothy bought great big dripping Italian subs for me and Fortescue M. Buffet. They tasted of In Your Face, Mr. Guest Suite. Absolutely delicious.

I've summoned the cavalry

What cavalry?

You'll meet them soon

Fortescue kept me entertained by telling me impossible

New York cabbie stories, and I was still enjoying him when we pulled into a driveway through massive hedges. The house that appeared made me and Fortescue both curse. I went with "Holy shit," and he preferred, "Motherfucker, Frank! That's a classic Queen Anne cottage. If you can call a place this big a cottage."

"What's a Queen Anne cottage?" I asked, distracted by the view.

"That," he said. "Like, all that fancy detailing around the porch and turret. That's some serious carpentry right there."

Ursula appeared at the front door and ran down the ornate steps, waving as if we'd been best friends since childhood. Even unnerved by the beauty of her home, I was thrilled to see her.

"Who's the babe?" Fortescue asked.

I ran Timothy's card through the reader. Reckless, I gave him a hundred percent tip. If I spent enough, maybe Timothy would actually notice. "I hope I meet you again some day, Fortescue. Nice riding with you."

"You, too, Frank. Best fucking wishes, man. Call me if you ever need a lift out here again."

Ursula pulled me from the car and into a hug. She smelled like sunshine and pine trees and was dressed in a sweater so soft, I hated to let go of her. "Come in, come in! Where are your bags? That's it? You came in nothing but a backpack? Frank, Frank, Frank. You still have Timothy's card, right? We'll go shopping again."

She drew me into her gingerbread house and I was assaulted by what turned out to be a bubbly woman, all dark, curly hair and laughing eyes.

"Frank!" this little pixie cried. "This is Frank! I know all about you! I want to play, too, okay?"

I pulled back from her, blinking, and Ursula laughed. "Meet my sister Hildy." They looked nothing alike. Hildy had none of Ursula's cool sophistication. "She and I are the babies of the family, and we are ready to slap some people around, I can tell you!"

"Um...slap some people around?" Their combined enthusiasm was a little overwhelming.

"Metaphorically, of course. Come on, let me show you where you're staying." Ursula led me up the sunny staircase, Hildy on our heels and babbling about my hair, my eyes, my bet with Timothy.

"You know about the bet," I said to Hildy, who nodded with shining eyes.

"I told her," Ursula said. "There are only three boys in the Portfolio and seven girls, and we're all still expected to bow down to the boys, which...come on!"

"You know about the Portfolio?" Hildy thought to ask.

Suddenly grateful to Timothy's lesson, I gave my guarded response. "You're the ten grandchildren of...Tammy?"

"Tabby," they both said.

Ursula went on. "It's short for Tabitha. A force to be reckoned with."

"Oh, she's a pussycat," Hildy corrected. "I just love her."

Ursula took my arm and drew me into a light-filled bedroom with white lace curtains, like in a movie. "Hildy really is the baby," she mock-whispered. "She has no idea."

"Yes, I do!" Hildy was irate but was soon distracted when I eased my pack off a shoulder. "Want me to take that? Ursula, is Mrs. Worth going to unpack this?"

I pulled the pack closer, unnerved by the thought of these beautiful birds of paradise having to touch my ancient T-shirts and jeans. "No one should unpack for me."

"Mrs. Worth is making dinner," Ursula said. She opened the door to a closet, where a garment bag hung. "Here's your outfit for the board meeting, and Magda sent all the lingerie. You've got a fitting with Cormac tomorrow at eleven, and then the board meeting is at four." She pointed out the attached bathroom—larger than my entire room in my mom's trailer—and sat on the bed on a soft quilt. Ursula waved me into the plump armchair, and Hildy perched in the window seat. "If all that's okay with you, of course."

She looked at me, as did Hildy. Realizing they were expecting an answer, I came up with, "This room is beautiful."

That made them laugh. "Thanks," Ursula said. "I love my old house, even if it does occasionally leak."

"I know what that's like," I said honestly.

She grinned at me. "Overwhelmed?"

I tried to measure the depths of her understatement. "A little," I confessed.

"Take heart. You've found a whole army of allies."

"An...an army?" I gulped, and a horn sounded from the driveway.

Hildy whirled. "It's Joanna and 'Lilah! Come on!"

She raced from the room, and Ursula stood to gesture me before her. "I know this is a lot, but your situation has kind of interested us. Come meet Timothy's sisters."

Lilah, whose name turned out to be Delilah, was one of the most beautiful women I'd ever seen. She was the kind of blonde most women asked for at the beauty salon, with an honest and beaming smile and eyes that looked like sapphires.

She arrived with her sister Joanna, who was perfectly nice looking...but we all looked dowdy standing in a room with Delilah. "Joanna Babcock," she said directly, shaking my hand. "Timothy's sister and Delilah's twin. Fraternal, obviously." We exchanged little pouts of understanding. No sense hoping to be attractive with Delilah beaming at us all like a benevolent goddess.

"Joanna," I said, recognizing the name. "You're one of the ones I need to persuade."

"Persuade? What do you mean?" Joanna's focus was alarming. I was suddenly being studied by all four women.

I inhaled, longing for a pause to figure out what to tell these people.

"No, wait!" Ursula held up her hand. "Wait until we're all here. We don't want to go through this twice."

Amid a general grumbling, I asked, "How many more are coming?"

"The rest of the Portfolio, of course," Hildy said.

"Well, not the guys." Ursula crossed her arms belligerently.

"Certainly not the guys," beautiful Delilah agreed.

Joanna, watching me, took my arm and led me to the living room sofa. "Sit. You look terrified, and who can blame you. We're waiting for Regina, who is our legal counsel, and her sister, Suzanne. And then we'll definitely need Quinn, who we call the Queen Bee. She's the COO of Babcock. How much information would you like to have?"

"Well," I tried, trying to think.

Joanna waved her hand when the others tried to add their thoughts. "She's drowning. Shut up, you guys. Let her take a breath."

I decided I was in love with Joanna.

She let me process without talking at me, and things got even better when wine appeared. It was a measure of how off-balance I was that I didn't even blink when the wine was served by an older woman called Mrs. Worth, who was dressed in a maid's uniform.

Because of course she was.

The wine helped, and the crispy, cheesy little nibbles that came with it absorbed some of my tension.

I stood to shake hands with the final trio to arrive: two blondes and a brunette. The blonde, who turned out to be Quinn, took me under her wing immediately. Joanna was like the dragon at the gate who kept me safe; Quinn was a mother. When she finally shushed everyone else, she asked me what was going on with such sincerity that the entire story spilled out of me.

The entire story.

"Timothy is trying to corner the market on some battery," Joanna said.

"Illegally." That was the dark-haired lawyer. Whose name was...

"He is totally amoral," Ursula said. "We've seen it over and over again."

"It does make him good at his job," the lawyer said. "Do any of *us* want to take on legislative affairs?"

Most of them scoffed, but I thought Ursula looked interested.

"Regina is right," Quinn said. (Oh, good. Lawyer Lady was Regina.) "Timothy is really good at his job. But this business about Frank having to persuade one of us? That feels more like he's dragging someone into doing something against their best interests."

"I know," Hildy said, wide-eyed. "Does he expect you to sleep with Fourth or Nicholas?"

There were cries of protest at the thought, and I waved them quiet. "I think he knows that's not going to happen." My voice was firm, and several of them nodded back to me in solidarity.

"What about the land you want to protect?" Ursula asked. "Is there something special about it?"

I shook my head, tired and overwhelmed enough to succumb to a sudden wave of nostalgia that threatened to make me cry. "It's special to me. My Uncle Red and I went there every year. It's my home, really, and I don't want to see it ruined by mining."

Quinn put her arm around me, and Hildy's big eyes grew shiny from unshed sympathy tears. Joanna, at least, eyed me with suspicion, no doubt wondering what the full story was—but she let it go.

"And you can protect that land," Quinn clarified, "if you persuade Fourth, Nicholas, Tabby, or Joanna to do something they don't want to do."

"That's right."

"Like what?" Delilah asked.

I shrugged, helpless. "I don't actually know."

Joanna sat up straight. "Well, we're done here, then," she said. "I'll agree to whatever you want." She tapped her empty glass with a finger, looking at Suzanne significantly. Suzanne obediently made the rounds with the bottle.

"Not good enough!" Ursula was adamant. "He'll figure I got to you. No, Frank has to go after Fourth. Or Nicholas."

"I don't mind the help," I said hopefully, nodding to Joanna. But she deserted me.

"Ursula is right. Let's figure out how you can wrap Fourth or Nicholas around your finger."

"Or Tabby," I added nervously.

Universally, they shook their heads. "Leave Tabby out of this," Ursula said. "Trust me."

They had the home field advantage. I'd be led by them. But this grandmother...she must really be something.

"Who's Fourth dating now?" Regina asked.

There were general shrugs. Various models and socialites were mentioned, but ultimately they agreed that their cousin Fourth wasn't seeing anyone regularly.

"And Nicholas?" Hildy asked. "Reggie, he's your brother. Who's he seeing?"

Regina and Suzanne both laughed. "Who—the human calculator? No worries there. He'd drive any woman mad in ten minutes. He's free."

"So, Frank can seduce either one of them," Delilah said.

This statement caused me to protest. "Hey. I don't want to seduce anyone."

"Ew," Ursula said. "Of course not. Not really. But both of those guys are notoriously hard to pin down. Socially, I mean. Get one of them to ask you out. That ought to do it. Don't you all think?"

Nods and smiles greeted this plan. "Just...just get one of them to ask me out? I don't have to, you know, date him?"

They looked at each other, concerned. "It would be better if Fourth or Nicholas asked you out publicly," Quinn said, "where Timothy can hear them. How's that sound to you guys?" They agreed, and she turned back to me. "And if you go out with him, that's up to you. Neither of them are beasts or anything. I suppose you might even have fun."

"With Fourth," Suzanne said. "Not my brother, though. He's a stick in the mud."

That was greeted with recognition from all present.

This hive mind decided that I would attract attention at the board meeting and dinner tomorrow, and inspire the invitation at the gala on April eleventh.

"In the meantime," Delilah said happily, "total makeover!"

I must have looked alarmed because Ursula waved them quiet. "Already in hand. She's got a great suit for tomorrow— and wait until you see the gala gown." She looked at Quinn and Delilah and said significantly, "Cormac Heggerty. Already working on it."

This name inspired cheers (remembering my liquid dress, I understood why) and another round of wine.

"Dinner is served," Mrs. Worth said from the door.

The beautiful dining room was lit entirely by candles, and the crown of lamb was a triumph. The red wine somehow became several bottles of champagne, and the all-female evening took on a wonderful, rosy hue. How long had it been since I'd been so comfortable with women my own age?

Ursula raised a glass before the citrus pavlova was served. "A toast! To Frank, for bringing us the method to teach those boys a lesson!"

"To Frank!" they all called.

I was pretty tipsy by that point, but I think I would have been touched even if stone-cold sober.

"And to all of you, for helping me!" I called in my turn.

We drank again. Then we toasted to the board meeting, and finally to the gala.

"And we'll work on your behalf while you're out riding the range in Montana," Delilah said happily. "Do you really work as a cowgirl?"

And that, of course, inspired a whole new round of questions.

17

ON THE EIGHTY-FIRST FLOOR

TIMOTHY

It annoyed me that Ursula hadn't gotten Frank to the board meeting early enough. Half an hour before the start was exactly the right time to mingle and be seen and watch the power dynamics play out—and here I was, dividing my attention between the ever-moving scrum of Babcocks and the *ting* of the arriving elevator.

Then I heard Ursula's laugh. She was with her mother and grandfather, theoretically engaged in familial chat...but in fact, she was staring at me.

Staring and laughing.

I shot her a look across the room. *Where?*

She shrugged and gave me a Mona Lisa smile that made me want to shake her.

Damn it.

I scanned the crowd more slowly, moving slightly to scan the thicker clusters of aunts, uncles, cousins. Nowhere to be seen.

My eyes jerked back of their own accord. Who was at the windows? Staring out at the view as if she'd never looked down on the world's most impressive city?

Casually, I moved toward her, taking a moment to assess. No surprise I hadn't recognized her. Ursula had her all dolled up. That wavy head of dark hair had been tamed and twisted into one of those fancy braids girls used on their horse's mane and then clubbed under in a little bun. She was dressed in a two-piece suit that I could tell was brutally expensive because it was brutally simple—a soft, belted jacket in some supple wool in a toasty caramel color. The matching skirt had flares, or gores, or whatever they were called, so the fabric hugged her trim ass and moved gracefully around her knees. The top of the skirt brushed a low pair of lace-up boots that would have spiked the blood pressure of a foot fetishist.

And other things.

She turned, started by my arrival, and I saw the silk blouse that perfectly matched the blue of her eyes—the light, inner ring. "Timothy!"

Someone had perched a pair of gold eyeglasses on that sun-kissed nose. She looked like the world's sexiest librarian. I was caught staring, slack-jawed, and opened with a stupid line.

"Do you even need those glasses?"

The eyebrows went up, and then she relaxed into the familiar grin. "Nope. Ursula says they look good. What do you think?"

I made a *hm* face in consideration and didn't give her the satisfaction of admitting she'd inspired half a chub in my trousers. I looked to the view instead. "Down that way is Yellowstone," I said, gesturing along the East River. "And we're facing pretty much due south, so these huge buildings pretty much stretch all the way to the tip of South America."

She chuckled. "We're facing east, so Yellowstone is that

way." She threw a thumb over her shoulder and grinned at me. "But I appreciate the touchback."

"You look good," I admitted at last.

She smoothed a hand down her jacket. "It's okay? Ursula said this would work for today and the dinner tonight."

"It works." I might have said more if one of my second cousins didn't butt in.

"Timmo! And who's this lovely creature?"

I was forced to introduce him, which was the signal for an avalanche of unmarried (and some married) family members to come nosing around like she was a mare in heat. I got a little irked at their presumption, although Frank handled them with a calm smile. Still, there was such a thing as being too polite. *Stop flirting.*

It was a relief when Tabby arrived, the signal for us to take our places. "This is your seat here," I whispered to Frank, putting her in the front row behind my seat. I had to glare at the cousins to get them to back off, and when I turned back, I found that Quinn's fiancé, Andy, had taken the seat next to Frank. He was introducing himself, and I turned back to the table, mollified. Andy was crazy in love with my cousin Quinn. He'd take care of Frank without breathing deeply at her.

I usually enjoyed these meetings. The fiscal year for Babcock Holdings ended on March thirty-first, so this was the time to provide our year-end reports in person, as well as in writing. Babcock's boardroom wasn't as powerful as a Senate hearing room, but it was pretty close. Tabby, at the age of six hundred and thirty-five, was as sharp-minded as ever and put her Portfolio through their paces.

Joanna's request for new servers—to the tune of forty-seven million dollars—was considered with a frown. Suzanne gave the final numbers for corporate sales. Hildy gave her report on special events, including a final tally on how much we were being paid for renting the Babcock Riverfront Events Center to the upcoming Beckford Department Stores fundraiser gala in two weeks.

Ursula, back to being bored as usual, tried to make a pitch for her historic preservation pipe dream but got shouted down as not being relevant to the year-end. Delilah stood to report on the Babcock philanthropic efforts over the past year, and the whole room sighed in appreciation. I couldn't understand why. She wasn't even the best-looking woman in the room.

My father, still in the traces, gave the overview of residential sales for the year. He glared at me, and I knew why. He wanted to go sit with his brothers, kicked back on the board members' side of the immense table. *Too bad, Pops. I like my job. I'm good at my job.* (He was glaring at Joanna and Delilah, too, but that was their problem.)

All the little people disposed of, Tabby called on me to give my legislative report, which I did with my standard ease and assurance. I knew I looked good. Of course I did. Too bad the meeting was too formal to casually slip out of my jacket, since my trousers were nicely tailored to my ass and the view behind me might have impressed...someone.

Tabby cut me off before I got halfway through my report. "Yes, Timothy, we know you've got all of Washington in your pocket. Any news on S. 413?"

"Working on it," I said. "There was a surprise visitor at the last hearing, though. Fred Rose showed up."

The name created a ripple in the room full of Babcocks. There were a few hisses. Older relatives forked the sign of the evil eye. Rose Realty was the Antichrist in this room.

"To what effect?" Tabby asked sharply.

"No surprise. He supports the bill."

"Of course he does. The toad." Her disgust was impressive. She wore a jet-black suit, severely tailored, with a crimson silk blouse because she liked to draw every eye to her. The dragon brooch on her lapel was set in platinum, the diamonds like fire.

Tabby regularly wore jewelry that justified the female body-guard standing against the wall behind her, a martial arts master named Livvy who could kick multiple asses at the same time. "Do you have the situation in hand, or don't you? Because we can allocate more funds if you need them."

That was as close as she could get to admitting that we bribed members of Congress—even though everyone else did, too, so where was the crime? But I was able to reassure her. "It'll work in our favor."

She eyed me shrewdly, possibly attempting her new shrink-ray eyeballs on me. When I didn't shrink, she nodded. "Thank you. Regina?"

It wasn't the attention I felt I deserved, but it was enough. I sat while Regina explained about the more serious legal cases against Babcock, or that Babcock was pursuing.

Tabby finished with the big three—Quinn as chief oper-ating officer, my officious cousin Nicholas as chief smug asshole (official title of chief financial officer) and finally the wrap-up from Fourth, a man with an unmoving spine. Fourth never smiled. Never got along. Never joined the guys for a whiskey and lied about his golf game. Fourth was unnatural.

His report summed up what we all knew: Babcock was making money hand over fist. We practically had a license to print cash from our office jets. Everyone was getting richer. Obviously. Duh. What have you done for us lately?

I spent a pleasurable few moments as he droned on, thinking about next year's board meeting, when I would be receiving admiring looks and handshakes for the astute busi-ness acumen that led me to be ready with a supply of molybde-num, acquired just before the per-ton price quadrupled. Joanna would have to admit I knew about something before she did.

Nicholas would estimate my net worth and nod in grudging admiration.

Fourth would open the bottle of Macallan I would be giving

him and we'd have a drink together, two titans of the world considering our universe.

Tabby crisply clapped her hands together. I wasn't the only one who jumped. "Very good. That's more than enough. You all are boring me. It's time for cocktails and dinner. In conclusion, *familia ante omnia*—family before all else. Remember it. Who will motion that we adjourn? Thank you, Samuel. Second? Delphine, put the second as my son Killian. All opposed? Hearing no objections, you are all invited upstairs, where I hope your conversations will be a good deal more interesting. Meeting adjourned."

By the time I got to Frank, she was surrounded again. I pulled her out of the scrum and tucked her hand under my elbow. "I'll walk you upstairs," I said firmly, glowering at the assembled masses. It was like fighting Jell-O. I could push them back and they'd just flow forward again.

We moved up to the Sky Lounge. Slowly, the question of *Who is that woman with Timothy?* filtered up through the ranks. The women of the Portfolio came by to shake her hand and make girly noises about her outfit. Nicholas and Fourth stopped by to give her the chilly nod of acknowledgment. The most interesting encounter came when Tabby beckoned me forward.

I kissed my grandmother on her papery cheek and held a hand out. "Tabitha Babcock, I would like to introduce Francesca Robinson."

Tabby, seated in her accustomed booth, beckoned us both to sit. This displaced my Uncle Killian and his wife, Aunt Anne, but they didn't seem to mind. They headed to the bar. Frank slid into the booth and I followed, careful not to sit on her skirt.

"I was told your name was Frank, young lady," Tabby said.

"Yes, ma'am. I mean, it's a nickname my Uncle Red gave me. It just stuck."

"Hm." Tabby could be elegantly charming when it suited

her, so I knew her calculating stare was deliberate. "And what are you doing with my grandson here? Please don't tell me you work for him. I know the kind of person he hires, and you are not it."

Frank, who'd been sitting as if she wished she were smaller, sat up at this. "Are you complimenting me and insulting Timothy? Or are you just insulting me?"

The apples of Tabby's cheeks popped. I knew the sign. She was biting back a smile, and I relaxed marginally. Tabby did like a fighter.

"Undetermined as yet," Tabby answered. "Perhaps you would tell me how you know my grandson?"

Framed as a request, the question was now polite enough to avoid triggering Frank's pride. "We have a common friend," she replied. Honest enough.

"How charming. And do I know this friend, Timothy?"

Those quick, dark eyes flicked to me. "Vaughn, Tabby. Vaughn Cox introduced us."

"Vaughn." Tabby nodded. As a reference, that wasn't a bad one. Tabby knew Vaughn and I had gotten into a lot of trouble in our youth, but he'd always been able to make her laugh. She liked him. Her gaze turned back to Frank. "And are you dating my grandson?"

I objected. "Gran," I tried, but she flicked an imperious finger at me and waited for Frank's reply.

"I'm his trail guide," she said. "In Montana. We aren't dating."

Tabby tucked her head back, still rudely staring at Frank. Finally, she said, "Pity." My eyebrows hit the roof. "Timothy, I would like another vodka, please. Take Frank with you."

We were dismissed and slid out of the booth. I turned to help Frank stand when Tabby's hand shot out and touched Frank's forearm. "The name suits you, my dear. Enjoy your evening."

I walked to the bar in a daze, Frank at my side. I told the bartender I needed another vodka for Tabby, which made him drop whatever he was doing. While we waited, I looked down at Frank, who was equally floored.

"Um," she said, "what just happened?"

I shook my head. "I think you got the Tabby Babcock seal of approval."

She blanched. "What does that *mean*, though?" She looked at me, her focus suddenly clearing. "Does this count as persuading her to do something she didn't want to do?"

What—I was supposed to let Frank off the hook? Just for that? "No way," I said. You didn't do any persuading. The bet is still on."

Her peculiar eyes narrowed. "You're just making up these rules as you go along," she said.

We were interrupted by two more cousins and an uncle who wanted Frank's attention. I collected Tabby's drink and left Frank momentarily to deliver it. On the way back, I saw her laughing, her head thrown back at some stupid witticism, the light catching on those fake Sexy Librarian glasses. *Making up the rules as I go? Hell yes, I am. How else am I going to keep you around?*

18

EYEING THE TARGETS

FRANK

Ursula and Hildy took me by elevator from the reception to some subterranean parking garage, where a valet brought a large hybrid SUV in an improbable pink. Hildy pushed me into the passenger seat and got in the back while Ursula slid behind the wheel.

"You don't have a driver?" I asked. "I thought all the Babcocks had driver-bodyguards."

"He's behind us." Ursula flipped a hand over her shoulder, where only Hildy sat, grinning.

The youngest Babcock shook her head at me and repeated the gesture. "Kennet's in the sedan behind us, with Mr. Lowinsky. That's my guy."

I faced front again. "You have two separate guys?"

"I don't live with Ursula." Hildy giggled. "I'm just spending the night with you guys tonight so we can strategize. Right, Urse?"

"Right." She was winding down multiple levels of the

garage, proving wrong my belief that we were under the building. "So, what did you think, Frank? Got your target yet?"

I knew what she meant but braced against the dashboard before answering. Ursula drove onto the street with terrifying confidence.

"Buckle up," Hildy advised from the back seat, where she was undoubtedly safer than I was from any head-on collisions.

I checked the seat belt. Tight.

"As far as targets go, Joanna's out, obviously," I said.

"Obviously. Good that she's on our side, though."

Hildy spoke over her sister. "She's got a really big brain."

"I gathered." The night before, Joanna had terrified me with the speed she'd worked things out. Just as Ursula was scaring me now with the speed at which she took us up FDR Drive. "And frankly, I don't think I stand much of a chance with your grandmother."

Ursula nodded, pulling around a slower-moving truck in a move that shocked the hell out of the cab driver she cut off, if the angry horn was any indication. How was poor Kennet the bodyguard ever going to keep up? "Tabby'd eat you alive. She liked you, though. I could tell."

Hildy was hanging over the seat to listen in. I wanted to tell her to brace for impact. "Suzanne told Delilah that Tabby said your name suited you. That's really good, Frank."

The cousins had an excellent communications network in place. "Yeah? You think?"

"Definitely. But I thought we agreed you had to get one of the guys. Fourth or Nicholas. What did you think of them?"

I discovered that the ride was more bearable if I just closed my eyes. If my fate was to go up in a fiery blaze in a Manhattan race to the death, then so be it. Instead, I concentrated on the two men.

"Handsome, both of them," I said. The noncommittal noises from Ursula and Hildy were translatable. *Duh*, they were saying. *Move on.* "Fourth is dark and Nicholas is blond, but they're both...um...stiff."

"And not in the good way!" Hildy cackled, and Ursula snorted but objected.

"Those are your cousins. Gross!"

"Aw, so what? They're not Frank's cousins. And technically, Fourth is my uncle, which is no less gross, I admit."

"Fourth is your uncle?"

Hildy began a singsong recitation. "Zaccharias Babcock III had a son, Henry, by his first wife. Henry married Millicent. They had a daughter, Melissa, and a son, Zaccharias Babcock IV, known as Fourth. Margaret and James had Ursula and Hildy. Fourth is the oldest member of the Portfolio and I'm the youngest. See? Got it?"

"Move on," Ursula said. "Back to Frank's assessment of her targets. Did either of them look...you know...susceptible?"

Hmm. I knew what she meant. "They both checked me out," I said honestly, "which was only fair. Since I was checking them out." Fourth had a commanding presence that made all the people around him tuck their heads in instinctively. I didn't get the sense that he was cruel—just that he expected a lot. And got it.

Nicholas wasn't the same. He was...what was he? "Nicholas acts like there's no one else in the room," I offered.

Hildy banged on the seat, which surprised me, and I opened my eyes—a mistake, as Ursula was using an exit lane with no intention of exiting. She'd apparently decided to pass a slow-moving Army convoy by whatever means necessary. Where were the police? Wasn't this glaringly reckless driving?

"That's exactly right," Hildy said. "Nicholas doesn't really notice anyone until he needs information. Then it's like he's using his tractor beams to pull you in. Reluctantly. Into the Death Star."

"Nerd," Ursula said fondly. "But she's right. Nicholas is

thinking of other things. Usually related to money. Do you stand a chance with either of them?"

"I have no idea. And I'm still not sure what I'm supposed to do with either of them once I get them," I confessed.

"Make them do something they wouldn't ordinarily do." Hildy seemed very sure of herself. "Make Fourth laugh, for example."

"Or cause Nicholas to add something up wrong." They both chuckled at Ursula's suggestion.

I clenched my eyes shut again. "I don't know how to do either of those things."

"Look, if either of them pays any attention to you at the gala, we'll call it a win. You've met them both. You saw them and they saw you. You looked totally hot tonight, and you'll be spectacular in that Cormac Heggerty."

"Which Timothy bought you! That's so fucking awesome!" Hildy crowed.

"Plus, you've got an undeniable air of mystery about you. Guys can't resist that shit. They're both going to be sniffing around for more at the gala."

"They won't have dates of their own?"

"Fourth will," Hildy responded. "Always a different stick-thin supermodel. They all love him because he's tall, so they can wear heels. They're like total glamazons."

"Nicholas, probably not. He doesn't really date much. Comes from graduating college so early. He was never with his peer group, you know? So he'll probably attend alone."

"Or bring one of his flunkies with him," Hildy added, "so he can make them look things up."

"Gee," I said. "He sounds like a lot of fun."

Ursula reversed her opinion. "He's actually okay. I sort of like Nicholas. At least you know what you're getting with him. There is no false front. That's kind of a relief."

"I guess." I wasn't so sure, and she must have heard it in my voice.

"Don't panic. Let's see what happens at the gala. You've got this."

Ursula's words were comforting, even if her driving wasn't. And the cost of losing was simply too high. "I've got this," I repeated, and then said it again a little louder so I'd believe it. "I've got this!"

"Yeah you do!" Hildy patted my shoulder. "And we've got it with you!"

Now all I had to do was, well, the impossible.

19

WESTWARD HO

TIMOTHY

I decided that the reason I was out of sorts was that I hadn't gotten the chance to treat Frank with as much contempt as she fed me every day we were on the trail.

I could have taken her to Michelin-starred restaurants and scoffed when she couldn't interpret the menu. I paced at the airport, waiting impatiently for Ursula to deliver her back to me. What would Frank have made of the dolharuebang at Jungsik, or the sea urchin from Le Bernardin?

I wouldn't know because Ursula kidnapped her. Dressed her up. Took all the fun out of bringing this country mouse to the big city.

Museums. Opera. There were after-hours clubs I could have walked her through that would have made those freakish eyes pop open in innocent shock.

By the time Ursula pulled up in her appallingly pink Rivian, I'd mentally scheduled about a month of opportunities into our brief weekend that Ursula had kept me from, and I glared at her through the glass.

She waved blithely. Ursula didn't smile often, but when something tickled her fancy, she was singularly focused. She hugged Frank from the front seat and my cowgirl climbed out, carrying a tan canvas duffel with excellent dark leather straps. She'd traded up from the ratty backpack.

On my credit card.

I didn't even get the entertainment of buying it for her.

I fisted my hands on my hips and sneered at Ursula. She laughed, silent across the distance, and drove away.

"Hi. Were you waiting long?" Frank breezed in like she belonged there. This sophisticated urban polish she'd acquired was deeply annoying.

"The plane is waiting," I said shortly, "if you're ready." Her answering smile was brilliant and perfectly neutral. She was treating me like a stranger she had to be polite to. I internalized my growl and took the bag off her shoulder. "I'll take this."

"I've got it," she protested, but I refused to listen to her. If she'd stuck with me, there would have been a redcap panting at her heels, begging to carry her bags.

Once on the plane, Max worked his usual magic to soothe my attitude. A large cup of Sumatran coffee with just a splash of cream. Fresh bagel, lightly toasted with cream cheese and lox, sliced by an artist. A fresh napkin, heavy and pristine, to catch any crumbs. My muscles slowly unwound, and I remembered that the villain here was Ursula, not Frank.

She sat across from me, absorbed by her phone. She picked at the croissant Max had served her but mostly ate the raspberry garnish instead. Her hair had been released from those controlling braids. As I watched, she slid her fingers through the dark locks to keep it out of her eyes. My fingers felt the ghost sensation of heavy silk against skin.

She must have felt my gaze. She looked up, questioning my attention.

"No glasses today?" I asked.

Her lips twitched in the beginning of a smile. "They're Ursula's. I left them with her."

"Of course they're Ursula's. She's exactly the kind of person who would have clear glasses just for the look."

Frank tipped her head in mild acknowledgment. "Yeah, but they do look good."

"They do," I allowed. "You should get some. They were sexy." She blinked. I did too. I'd suddenly veered into very new territory for us, and I backed out as quickly as I could. "What are you reading?"

She looked down to her phone as if surprised to see it in her hand. "Oh. Introductory Engineering Design. I'm going to be behind when I go back in the fall, so I'm trying to do some of the reading ahead of time."

Well, there could hardly be a less sexy topic. We were back on safe ground. "Smart idea. Don't let me interrupt you."

The next five hours were oddly awkward. This was our transition phase, between when she was the boss and when I was. Not that Ursula had given me that privilege. I checked my communications and was immediately distracted from Frank, her long legs curled under her as she studied.

Fucking Baldrick Starmer. The man was a black hole of need, and I was expected to fill that hole.

For the first time, I thought about chucking the legislative branch and taking up my father's role at Babcock. He sat at a desk. People reported to him. He told them what to do and they did it. No fucking members of Congress to give him ulcers. Boring. Hugely boring—but maybe boredom was not the horror I thought it would be.

I shoveled energy and resources into Starmer, cursing internally while I schmoozed him on the outside. The damned man just would not stay bought, and I suspected Fred Rose's greasy hand in the current defections.

Well, over my dead body. *I'm coming for you, Freddy.* You *can call that self-satisfied, swollen senator "Rick" instead of the "Baldrick" he definitely deserves.*

By the time we landed, I was sick of the whole mess and greeted a return to the Circle B with relief. My supplies had been delivered to the landing strip and were already stowed in the bed of the truck. Frank and I sped down the road to the land where I was the idiot...so how come I was looking forward to it?

"You sure you can go for the full nine nights?" Frank asked. "At the speed you were texting, they might not be able to do without you."

I rolled my head at the wheel, easing tension while still eyeing the road. "Remember that sat phone? They can still get hold of me. More's the pity."

"We could lose it." She grinned. "I know some deep, deep crevices."

She made me laugh. "I wish. No, they're going to survive without me until next Wednesday. Either that, or I'm going to commit some very justifiable homicide."

"That should be interesting," she mused.

Both Cal and Maria were waiting as we pulled up to the barn, as was Vaughn's first girlfriend, Chita, and two leathery men who were probably barn workers. They all watched hopefully as I passed a new box of chocolates to Maria and tossed a bottle of drinkable gold to Cal. "That's the best Scotch I've ever found," I said. "I'd like your opinion when I get back, if you're willing."

He eyed the Macallan with interest. "Never found without an opinion," he said. "I'll certainly let you know."

Then, because Maria clearly wasn't ready to share, I sacrificed three nights of Frank's pillow chocolates by giving boxes to the waiting crew. They were delighted, and suddenly, Frank and I didn't have to pack up Daisy and Clop, didn't have to saddle Swan or Whistler.

Proof that if you pay enough, you can get good service anywhere.

Everyone had to join the confab in the office about our planned route. "I'm thinking we head up Valley River," Frank explained, "and then do Markus Creek. I'm thinking a big counterclockwise route. Then up Deep Creek and finally up the Second Fork."

"Make sure you're going up and then back down those creeks," Cal said. "It's too early in the season to try for Red's secret paths. Don't get overconfident, Frank."

"They're not secret paths, Cal, but I hear you. We'll be careful. And Timothy has a sat phone. We'll call if we get in trouble."

"Now, that's clever! Mother, we need to look into that!" Cal looked at Maria, who shot him a significant look that made him shut up.

Huh. What was that about?

"We should make it to Daughtry Lake by Sunday. Timothy can fish on Monday, we'll start back on Tuesday, and we'll be home by Wednesday. Right on time."

Frank got Maria to write down the route, and then the whole tribe gathered to wave us onto the trail like a movie.

Chocolates and whiskey. Applied properly, they could change the world.

Whistler began singing his way up the first big slope and I joined in, feeling like Senator Starmer and all of his ilk were back at the barn and I was escaping them. *Watch me ride off into the sunset, Baldy. Never to fucking return.*

We got to the first overlook. Anticipating the beauty hadn't weakened the effect at all. There was a sense of vast, endless space all around me. Limitless oxygen. Massive distances, somehow defined and contained by the mountains that acted as faraway backdrops. This time, I knew that the water I was hearing was Frank's Main Street—the Wild River that formed the spine of our travels up its tributaries, and which splashed and dashed and roared and rushed as it flowed endlessly from high to low.

I couldn't quite grasp the entire view. Couldn't get my mental hands around it. Between every two mountains, a valley. A creek or stream that wound down and along the contours of the land. No gardeners to prune things, no landscapers to reshape the earth. No order—just the original order. Could anyone ever truly understand this wilderness? Know its nooks and crannies, its hidden coves and rivulets?

How amazing would it be to try?

I was sitting there, open-mouthed. Whistler stood patiently, and Clop bumped his nose against Whistler's rump. Frank, Swan, and Daisy waited ahead. We were in a moment of...real quiet. Not quite like on my plane, where the engines provided their endless drone. This was a kind of quiet where I could hear the air in my ears. Where I could almost identify the creak of deep roots stretching out into the earth below us.

And my fucking sat phone rang.

I knew it was Baldrick Starmer. I knew it.

I knew he was aware I was on vacation. And he was calling me anyway. Because some high-dollar donor wanted tickets to something. Or Starmer wanted me to get him laid again. Or he wanted to hint about Fred Rose and the models Fred knew who Starmer might be taking to dinner tonight.

I had a moment of complete insanity. I yanked the phone out of my coat's deep pocket and heaved it, still piercing me with its shrieking ring, as far as I could over the bare trees below me and down into the wild.

I couldn't hear the splash it made—the river was too noisy

here—but there was no doubt that I'd just heaved the phone into the river.

I stared, astonished, into the distance, paralyzed by my own impulse. Frank's howl of laughter brought me back to awareness.

"I was kidding, you know!" Her eyes danced in amusement. "You didn't really have to lose your phone. We could have left it somewhere and come back to pick it up later!"

"Uh," I said, and then had nothing at all to follow that up with.

"Nice arm," she said. Still laughing, she turned and nudged Swan into a walk.

Whistler and I followed while I tried to figure out my impulse. Should we go back? Should I get another phone? At the very least, I should have let my father know I was going AWOL. Or Fourth. He would have cared. Or Tabby. There were people who could cover for me.

If I went back.

Familia ante omnia, huh?

Fuck that. Not today, Tabby.

I inhaled deeply. We were under the trees again, and I got a strong dose of pine needles. They smelled good.

They smelled fucking awesome.

Better than the finest leather, the most mellow Scotch, the supple glory of a supermodel's thigh. I was riding through a nature-made cathedral of reaching trees and shafting sunlight, the warm and powerful horse under me making the transit all but effortless.

I was...free.

For eight days.

Awesome.

What now?

20

THE EPIPHANY

FRANK

Timothy was having some kind of religious experience. Or maybe a psychotic break. Hard to tell the difference sometimes.

After he threw away his umbilical cord, he was first dazed and then nervous and then angry. Finally, he got to the point where he was looking at everything around us as if he'd never had eyes before.

I kept an eye on him over my shoulder but left him to his mental gymnastics alone. Timothy unplugged—what a wild concept. How would he log in the coordinates of his samples?

This question occurred to him when we came to the split in the trail and I turned us to the west to follow Valley River. The trail went through a pretty narrow gap, and the rock walls rose quickly on either side. I checked on him in time to see him dreamily run his fingers along the stone, barely leaning out of the saddle to do it. His face cleared and he called out, asking me to stop.

Chisel and hammer. I knew the drill by this point, but I still enjoyed watching as he hacked out a splinter of rock and reached for his marker and...

And the phone. The one he didn't have.

He looked up, entertainingly confused.

"Write *start of Valley River*. That will be good enough, right?"

He blinked at me and then looked behind us, as if he was going to spot his phone lying on a tuft of dead grass. "Will that be enough?" he asked. He sounded sort of mournful.

"Sure it will. You tell me this is the mountain with your mystery substance and I can lead you right back here. Hell, you could probably do it by yourself."

He considered the land around us, and I knew he was scanning the trail in his mind. He nodded, wrote on the sample, and stowed his supplies in Clop's panniers. "You know this part of the world pretty well, don't you?"

He mounted and we continued up the riverside trail. "Some of it. My uncle was the one who really knew this place."

Timothy was quiet behind me through the twists and turns of the initial canyon. When the land opened up again, he rode beside me, Whistler ignoring the mud that was making Swan pick her way delicately. "It's hard to imagine that anyone could, you know..." He fanned a confusing hand in front of him.

"What's that mean?"

"Oh, you know. Know all this. Like, there could be anything at all behind that boulder. Or a way to climb that cliff and see what's up there. Or which of these pools is the best place to catch trout. You know?"

I smiled. "I do know. Red knew this land better than anyone, and he said he was constantly surprised by what he learned. There were at least four homesteads that were abandoned on this property, usually by hopeful gold mines that never paid out. One in the valley leading to Daughtry Lake.

Probably my ancestors. All of them empty by the time the Buckleys got the property in the 1850s."

"Wow. That's crazy."

"Doesn't even begin to consider the native peoples who lived here. Or passed through. There are pictographs at Kaia Lake, up Markus Creek, that are seven or eight centuries old." Timothy looked at me, astonished, and I nodded. "There was an archaeologist who stayed at the ranch four years ago. Red and I took him up to Kaia and he confirmed it." That was one of Red's last trips before his lungs betrayed him and I'd been consumed with worry the entire trek. I frowned at the painful memory.

"This place has such a history." He seemed sincerely interested.

"That's just the human history. There's a tree history, and the history of animals through here, and the geologic stuff is incredible. This whole region is…shit." I lost the word and then found it. "Geothermal. It's geothermally active. We're just down the road from Yellowstone. You know, Old Faithful and all that? There are hot springs and a lava pool up on Hartshorn. That's up Deep Creek. We can go up there if you want. We'll be there in a few days."

"I really never thought about this at all," Timothy said.

The canyon tipped inward again. We were about to enter a part of the trail where shadows lived permanently, save at high noon. "Let's eat some lunch. Good place to fish too. You catch a few trout, I can cook them for you."

At least three times, he reached for a phone that wasn't there and then looked startled, but his mood remained open and curious. We had a good afternoon and made it to the campsite in enough time to offer him a hike to the ridgeline overhead. We left Clop and Daisy on guard duty to watch Whistler and Swan, who stood placidly in Red's impromptu corral, and headed up.

After a day in the saddle, a hike felt pretty good. We'd just have time to get to the top, look around, and get back to camp before the sun went down. Timothy didn't hold me up, and I was impressed. He was a desk-and-office kind of guy, but his cardio conditioning was pretty good.

We crested the rise in plenty of time and stood to absorb the majesty.

"Holy mother of god," Timothy breathed. "It just goes on and on forever, doesn't it?"

"Well, not forever. But it's pretty nice."

"Yeah, it is." Then his attitude changed. I watched his face as he looked down the mountain, over the Albert River, and to the property on the other bank. "What...what is that?"

I knew what he was looking at. The scar on the mountains that ripped a wound into the wilderness. My heart broke anew. "That's not Circle B land on the other side of the river. That's now owned by a multinational corporation. They're logging it. See?"

There was no need to point out the obvious. Taking place away from highways or oversight, they'd stripped the mountainside bare. Dirt roads snaked around the steep terrain for truck access to the trees they'd felled. As winter's snows melted, they picked up the loose soil, which was melting into the creek and from there to the Albert River. Cal had already told me the Gallatin had fewer fish, and the lumber company had just begun their clear-cutting. It would only get worse.

"It's obscene," Timothy breathed.

"You should see what a mine looks like," I said cruelly.

He jerked back to me. "A mine? Just a...you know? Hole in the side of a mountain?"

I scoffed a bitter laugh. "You've been watching old Westerns. These days, people who are looking to mine some mysterious element? They take the top off a mountain. Literally."

"Wha-what? No. I mean—" His eyes went back to the clear-cutting, and I knew he was shook.

Unbidden, my hand took his. Palm to palm, his fingers gripped me.

He swallowed hard and turned back to me. "I swear I didn't know. This isn't what I want."

"Good." I sighed, pretending the warmth of his hand wasn't sending waves of tingles up my arm. "I hope you do buy the ranch. If you don't, that's what's going to happen here too."

Timothy's grip tightened and he tugged, so I faced him. "What? What are you saying?"

The thought was too bitter to deserve warmth or comfort. I dropped his hand and turned away. "Cal told me last week. He's been diagnosed with Parkinson's. He and Maria are moving to Florida after this summer. It's the Circle B's last season."

Timothy's silence had a bright alertness. He was thinking about this. Then he spoke. "What happens to the ranch?"

Nausea made my mouth water. "Either you buy it, or they sell to that lumber corporation. No one will buy it as a dude ranch. Over a hundred and fifty years in the Buckley family, and it's just going to come to...to an end."

My childhood. My future. My life with Red. Felled by bull-dozers and timber saws.

"That's—that's—"

I couldn't bear to hear this rich man sputter. "We need to get back to camp before the sun goes down. Come on."

One minute I was holding his hand, the next I was hating him with acidic bitterness. He wasn't the only one having a psychotic break.

21

CLOUD COVER

TIMOTHY

I must have followed Frank off that mountain blindly. We got back to camp and I couldn't remember a single step I took. I was thinking about photos I'd seen of industrial mining operations in West Virginia, where—Frank was right—they simply leveled mountains. Shredding the local ecology in the quest for coal, or whatever.

How did I think I was going to get the stone to crush? Was I going to hire fleets of workers to ride the trails to carve hunks of the living stone with chisel and hammer?

I'd assumed some sort of mine system. Tunnels. Havoc wrecked far below the surface. Men in hard hats with lamps on them. So why was I carving up stones along the trail?

And what about the land I was on? Whether I found a source of molybdenum or not, did I want to own a ranch? If I bought a twenty-seven-thousand–acre ranch with no concept of profit, what would Nicholas make of that?

Would Fourth want to trade his custom suits for wool trek pants and the dirt and horsehair of backcountry treks?

Would Joanna smugly inform me of the falling value of wildland?

I was a lousy conversationalist over dinner. That was a shame, since our first night on the trail meant my supplies were fresh and only needed to be heated. Jean-Pierre had packed up a Lebanese lamb fatteh. He'd even enclosed a twist of paper that revealed fresh pomegranate seeds, but Frank was indifferent. We ate in silence around the campfire she'd efficiently and automatically built, and when the evening chill forced us into our tents, she didn't even call out her thanks when she found her chocolates in her tent.

I had a hard time sleeping.

Even as awake as I was, I didn't hear the rain start. That was because it came down more as a cloying, irritating mist rather than the honest simplicity of raindrops. I emerged from my tent to find everything sodden and the air gray and cold and humid.

Clop was annoyed to find that I had put his panniers down outside the protection of the little bark roof over the corner of their enclosure. His blanket wasn't wet, but the dampness probably felt pretty nasty against the wet baskets. "Sorry, Clop," I said as I got him ready for the trail. "I'm still learning, and you're paying the price."

Daisy didn't look much happier, but at least her baskets started out dry. Like everything else, they were quickly soggy once we got on the trail.

"I got a cover for my hat," I called to Frank, looking for a bright comment.

"Proud of you," she said shortly. We'd only been moving for half an hour when she reined in and gestured me forward. "If you want to get to Valley Lake, it's about two hours ahead of us, but in this rain, the trail is going to be deep in mud. I think we'd do better if we left the valley."

I shook my head at her. "I have no idea where we're going. If you want to go up, we go up."

She cocked an eyebrow. The brim of her hat protected her eyes, but that was about all that wasn't covered in mist. "It will mean taking what Cal calls Red's hidden paths. Up there."

She nodded into the trees. I saw no trail at all. "You know the way?"

"Absolutely. Red and I took it all the time. We'll go up and over this mountain and get to Markus Creek a full day early. If you're willing. There's an exposed part that...might require a little nerve. But the horses can handle it."

"Then I can too," I said stoutly. No way I was going to be the wimp in this scenario.

So, up we went. I stopped once at an exposed hunk of rock to take a sample, marking it *Red's Hidden Path*. I showed it to Frank, who offered the first real laughter of the gray, drizzly morning.

Whistler's whistle was going full tilt, but I was too demoralized to sing along. A few hours later, his breathing was labored enough that he'd stopped whistling, which Frank noted had never happened before. I patted Whistler's neck in commiserating congratulations.

We never really ate lunch. We stopped periodically to rest the horses and gnaw on tough, leathery strips of jerky or energy bars. We drank our water bottles dry and refilled them from the rushing streams, treating them with purification pills that required we wait a full hour before drinking again. And we endured.

At the very least, the mud was at a minimum. The path Frank followed was largely free of the last snow. Pine needles showed through, offering a footing for the horses that was prone to a little slippage, but it wasn't bad.

And then we came out of the forest.

The mountain continued on above us, but we were on a

sharp shelf of land that wound along loose scree, down to the edge of the next hillside. It was a bare, ugly neck of land, splitting the gray, spitting sky like a bridge. The footing was terrible —all loose stone.

Might require a little nerve. Right you are, Frank.

She dismounted. "We need to lead the horses here, one by one. You stay with Daisy, Clop, and Whistler, and I'll take Swan over and come back."

"You're sure?" Seemed like I was getting the bitch job, but she nodded.

"That's the way we've got to do it. Be right back."

Whistler, Daisy, and I watched (Clop rested with his long nose against Whistler's rump) as Frank led Swan across the exposed ridgeline. My adrenaline got a workout when Frank lost her footing twice—it would be a long, painful slide down the rock field if she fell to either side—and Swan stumbled once. But Frank pulled her ahead and got her going. They made it to the far trees and I heaved a sigh of relief.

She looked back and waved and then started back up the hill to us...which was when I realized how hard the wind was blowing.

By the time she got back, she was bent almost double, offering the least resistance to the wind, and I had aged twenty years. "Shit, Frank," I said, unable to resist a hand on her elbow to pull her closer. "I'm doing the next ones."

"No, I can do it!"

She was tired. I could see it. She had to know it. "I weigh about twice what you weigh. The wind isn't going to push me around. Stay here. I'll take Whistler."

She opened her mouth to protest, but Whistler and I were already gone. I didn't have the balance to turn around and check on her, but the fact that I couldn't hear her feet setting up tiny rockslides behind me meant I'd won this one. For once.

I'd watched Frank carefully and knew what to do when

Whistler lost his footing. I ran ahead, Whistler broke into a trot, and we reached the other side with no harm. I rubbed Swan's soft nose in greeting and promised her I'd be right back.

My trip up the ridge reminded me of how much I'd relied on Whistler to anchor me, but the inconsistent, alarming tugs of wind didn't pose as much risk to me as they did to Frank. She apologized when I got back to her and the mules.

"I swear I didn't know the wind would be so bad," she said, but I waved her off.

"What's a little nerve among friends? Lighten up, Frank. We're having fun, right?" I gave her a grin, and she offered a confused laugh.

Daisy and I were off. The mule was smaller than Whistler, which meant less wind—but the heavy panniers meant she would be at greater risk for overbalancing. Still, there was a reason people went into the Grand Canyon riding on mules. Daisy was as sure-footed as a deer and made it to the other side without a single slip.

"Well done, girl," I told her. My water bottle was in Whistler's saddlebags and I took a breather. Last trip.

I met Frank halfway up the ridge. She and Clop were easing down the slope. The wind had pushed Frank's hat off and it dangled down her back on its strap. She didn't waste the energy to put it back on. So far, so good.

But the wind had picked up again. It felt like a hand pushing on my back and then on my shoulder sideways. Then no pushing at all. I was constantly off-balance and bent over, as Frank had been, to give the wind less to push on.

I met them halfway and turned carefully to join the descent. We'd almost made it when the rock under my boot shifted, sending me sliding down to the right. At the same moment, the same thing happened to Frank, but to the left. I flung out an arm, and she did too.

We formed the connection that, astonishingly, brought both

of us to a standstill. Clop uttered a bray that punctuated the big
kettledrums banging in my chest. Frank and I exchanged raised
eyebrows and we kept going, never letting go of our hand-to-
wrist grasp.

When we made it to the far side and roped Clop in next to
the others, I didn't think twice before pulling Frank into me.

I held her and she held me. Her face was pressed against
my chest, my head down to her damp hair. Two heartbeats
slowly synchronized as we settled.

She mumbled into my chest. "What?" I asked.

"That was really stupid." She looked up, and suddenly, I
was kissing distance from her face. "Please don't tell Cal?"

Her plea was so wistful that I lost track of the sudden
impulse to kiss those lips. I burst out laughing. "Not a word.
You're one hell of a risk-taker. Did I ever tell you about
skydiving in a wingsuit?"

She liked the question. Her adrenaline was fading,
unlocking her sense of humor. "One of those batwing things?
You didn't."

As we followed her invisible trail down the mountain, I
regaled her with my thrill-seeking adventures, which made her
laugh, swear, and proclaim me an absolute idiot.

"So, that scree-surfing party was nothing to me," I boasted.
She shot me a look of gratitude as Swan gracefully navigated a
path between boulders. "Why's she called Swan?" I thought
to ask.

Under the trees, we were a bit more protected from the
misty rain, and the wind stayed far overhead, looking for other
fools to try the transit. I could hear her answer easily—and the
smile in her voice.

"I was very fond of an adventure movie at the time. When
Cal said I could name the new foal, I chose Swan."

She glanced back with an arched eyebrow. Could I figure
out the connection?

It took me a good twenty minutes. My mistake was running through the kind of adventure movies I'd liked as a teen—*Alien vs. Predator* and the like. Once I remembered to think like a girl, I got it.

"Elizabeth Swann! You named your horse for *Pirates of the Caribbean*!"

Frank nodded, happy. "Tough and strong. Everyone thought she should be a pretty little girl, but really she was the hero."

I'd never thought of the movie that way (I'd mostly admired Jack Sparrow's dedication to rum), but now that she pointed it out, I could see it. "That's like you," I said thoughtlessly. She looked her question back, and I was forced to explain. "I mean, you're a hot babe. You could have...could have picked up any guy in that bar in Denver. Or taken Vaughn, for that matter. And instead, you're doing your own thing. You're the hero here."

"Sweet talker."

I thought about it and added to my thought. "You should have flamed out in D.C. And in Manhattan. But you found an ally and made those cities your bitch. Someone should give you your own pirate ship."

She laughed. I felt absurdly proud of making her happy.

When we came out of the forest and into another river-carved valley, I was relieved that our attempt to bushwhack across wilderness hadn't ended in disaster. But the mist had turned into actual rain, which—surprise!—did turn out to be more annoying than the mist.

The temperature was falling, the daylight was fading, and we were riding through clouds. The day was miserable.

"Less than an hour and I'll get us to a good spot to camp," she called to me over the thump of driving rain.

"Lead on, Macduff. I follow."

22

APRIL'S FOOLS

FRANK

I'd led plenty of treks with guests who assured me they were experienced in backcountry expeditions. One family insisted they'd hiked the entire Pacific Crest Trail, including their seven-year-old. I'd had a guy who was a retired Navy Seal. I'd had military veterans who wouldn't have pointed it out if their foot had been eaten off by a puma.

To my astonishment, Timothy the Arrogant Billionaire had proven himself as tough as any of them.

Free diving. Heli-skiing. The certifiable insanity of wingsuit flying. Sure. These were the kind of extreme sports that only absurdly wealthy people could pursue. I wouldn't have doubted that this privileged jerk had tried.

But now I believed he might have survived and even enjoyed them.

He came out of the near death of the scree field with his sense of humor intact. I had to admire that. And he should have made my life hell for my poor decision-making. He didn't. He held me when I was about to fall on the ground in desperate relief, and he made me laugh.

So, okay. Maybe I had a little crush on the guy.

Red's campground hadn't been disturbed in the four years since I'd been there. The tarps he'd left were dirty and wrapped in leaf litter and the dregs of old spiderwebs, but they worked just fine. I had a roof rigged over the corral in no time, and all four beasts huddled gratefully in its shelter, their combined warmth creating steam that rose from their newly brushed backs.

Timothy was getting to be a pretty good groom. The servants who managed his strings of polo ponies were going to be very surprised when they had less work to do.

The second tarp meant that rain didn't permanently hiss into the fire. Timothy and I could be reasonably dry as we sat side by side, waiting for our soup to heat up. He never did get fussy with me. Our conversation was easy, and we worked together companionably to get our dinner together.

I didn't know who Jean-Claude was, but the guy could put together a fantastic chicken tarragon salad. "No mayo," Timothy explained as he added spoonfuls to my camp plate, next to the far more typical stew we'd rehydrated, "so it'll keep for a day or two in this cool weather. Taste good?"

"Mm," I said, enjoying the delicacy of the flavors after a day of jerky.

"I have three small splits of wine with me," he said.

"You're making Clop carry wine? Is that quite kind?"

"Quite kind," he said with confidence. "We will drink them, thereby leaving room for rock samples. In this way, we don't force Clop to carry more and more as he gets more and more tired. Nice, right?"

I giggled. The man made me giggle.

"My concern"—he got back to his point—"is...shall we open one now? In celebration of reaching Marley's Creek in safety?"

"Markus Creek," I corrected, dreading whatever he was going to say next after acknowledging that I could have gotten him killed. Was this the lecture I deserved?

"Markus. Of course. I was thinking of Jacob Marley haunting Ebenezer Scrooge."

"Or Bob Marley."

"Bob Marley! I and I think that would be a better name for that river." Firelight flickered across his face as he aped a Jamaican accent.

"Agreed," I sniggered.

"The question at hand," he said sternly to me, "is...to champagne or not to champagne?"

"Jesus. You brought champagne with you."

"You can take the boy out of the city, but you can't take the city out of the boy. I'm getting one of them."

The introduction of alcohol made me distantly nervous. Despite my crush on the man, was he expecting more than I wanted to give? Then I saw the bottle he presented over his arm.

"It's tiny!" I grinned. "Where did you get that baby bottle of champagne?"

"Sweet, lovely Frank. This is a split. Enough for us to each have a glass and then maybe a swallow more. Rinse out your mug. I regret I did not pack the Baccarat. Crystal," he added, seeing my confusion. "The most beautiful tone when you clink glasses in a toast."

He got the cork out without making any noise. I wondered if that meant the champagne had gone flat.

"Not at all, my dear. You never want to pop a champagne cork but instead ease it out with the strength of the thumbs." He held up one of his thumbs and leered comedically at me, which had its intended effect. I laughed. "If you pop it, you'll lose all that lovely carbonation—not to mention quite a lot of wine. When you see someone pop a cork, you know they are unlettered in the oenophilic arts. Wine, Frank. That means wine."

He poured the golden liquid, and we clinked our mugs together. "Terrible tone," I offered, and that made him grin in appreciation.

"To us," he said, "and our refusal to expire."

"To us," I agreed, "for not dying."

"Well said."

The bubbles were crisp and bright, and the wine was dry and welcoming. It sent a wave of benevolent heat through me. "That's much better than any champagne I've ever had," I said, looking in admiration at my old tin mug.

"A nice year," Timothy agreed. "And now that the champagne has insulated you a little against life's annoyances, I want to make a confession to you, Frank."

I raised my eyebrows. "Wait," I said, holding up a hand. "Let me have another sip first. Okay—go."

"Good Frank, clever Frank, resourceful Frank, I am afraid I must tell you..."

"Yes?"

"...that I gave away rather a lot of your bedtime chocolates. Can you forgive me?"

I laughed, stretching my legs toward the blissful warmth of the fire. "I don't know. It's a pretty serious sin."

"I know." His face was drawn into comedic seriousness. Light glinted off the scruff of his red beard. "I do have that complimentary hand lotion we discussed, though, if that eases the sin."

I didn't want to grin. I wanted to match his serious mien. But I couldn't help it. "You don't really, do you?"

"Have some lovely lotion? Would you like it now? I'm not out of chocolates yet, but I could get it for you."

My hand on his arm pulled him down into his seat again.

"Calm down. I still have some of last night's chocolates left. Would you like one?"

"By no means. Those are for you. With my sincere compliments."

Our evening was silly and funny and warm. When I found I couldn't suppress my yawns any longer, I looked briefly at his handsome tent, glowing red from the lantern he'd left on inside. My old blue tent looked like a mule next to a quarter horse. Serviceable. Useful. Not at all pretty. If he invited me in tonight, would I go?

No. That would be stupid. Getting involved with men—all of whom were disturbingly possessive—was the fastest route to turning a pleasant trek into something much less fun.

So, I swallowed the last of my champagne and refused his offer to empty the last of the bottle into my mug. "I'm going to sleep. Thank you for a lovely evening."

"Oh, my pleasure, fabulous Frank. Sleep well."

How did he get the chocolates onto my pillow when I'd been sitting next to him just about every moment?

The next morning, for the first time, Timothy was up before I was. He'd brought life back to our campfire and had already put the coffee on.

"I've been sitting here trying to think of an April Fools' Day joke to play on you," he said, "but I'll be damned if I can come up with a single thing."

"Good," I said, scrubbing hair out of my face. "Can't deal with that first thing."

"Huh. You seem so put together by the time I get up. I had no idea you're not a morning person."

"Coffee," I said with grumpy desperation.

After that, he was blessedly silent, and I was able to pull myself together. One glass of champagne couldn't bring on a hangover, could it? I was grateful that he chose to chisel out his next fragment of rock from a little farther away so I didn't have to wince at the sound.

"What do I write on this one?" he asked. "You name it. You'll be able to find this place if you name this rock."

I thought about it. "Champagne?" I asked.

He shook his head. "Three splits. We could have two more with the same name."

"Just say Markus Creek."

"No." His eyes lit up with inspiration. "Marley Creek. No one will ever break this excellent code!"

At least he was amusing himself.

The rain held off, and we traveled up Markus Creek to get to the long finger lake at the top. Red had never given me a name for that lake. Timothy and I debated on naming it Bob, or maybe Ebenezer. We never did decide. On our way back down the creek, Timothy pointed at the mountain facing south.

"Look—the trees are coming up green. Spring in the mountains. Pretty, huh?"

It was pretty. It was lovely. That bright, fresh green was one of my favorite colors. On the other hand, I'd endured blizzards while the trees were green, so I felt a little less reassured about this than Timothy did.

We made a pit stop, and he carved yet another hunk of rock off a cliff face. He came back wide-eyed, feigning fear or astonishment. "Bear!" he hissed at me. "Big bear!"

"Oh, ha-ha. Very funny. April Fools."

He shook his head and pointed behind him and down through the trees.

Fine. I'd play along.

I was about to plunge down the hill when a strong arm wrapped around my waist and pulled me back. "Not April Fools. Look."

There was nothing on the riverbank. I was going to push

that arm from around me when bushes on the other side rustled.

And a mangy, skinny brown bear shambled into view.

"Fuck," I breathed. "Back up."

We tiptoed back to the horses and gathered ourselves. I didn't feel safe until we were mounted. A motivated bear could run as fast as a horse for a few hundred feet, but that bear didn't want us. It wanted fish. Or berries. Or something that wouldn't fight a bear just out of hibernation and weak from the winter. Still, one swipe from an angry bear's paw meant a mule, a horse, a human would have a hard time coming back.

"I guess it really is spring," I said as we followed the trail away from the bear.

"Are there lots of grizzlies around here?" Timothy asked. Not scared, exactly, but aware. Such a thrill seeker.

"They're launching a comeback. But they're not very thick on the ground. We probably won't see another one. I've only ever seen two, although I've seen signs before."

"So this was a big deal?"

"It was for me."

"Me too!" We shared a smile, pleased with our brush with the natural world. "I thought we were supposed to make a lot of noise to scare bears away."

"Well, not scare exactly. Not much scares a bear. But they don't like humans, so they usually get out of the way if they hear you coming. It's startling one that is dangerous. Especially if she's the mama. No bear babies with this one that I saw."

"Phew."

"Exactly."

We left the bear doing his bear thing on the river behind us and continued downstream to get to the Wild River. After a while, Timothy called out to me. "So, who else should we be on alert for? I mean, other than Bob Marley, the April Fools' Bear?"

I snorted, amused by the bear's name. The snort made me giggle, which made me snort again. I got slightly hysterical, riding along under growing spring sunlight with Timothy behind me, chuckling at my reaction. I actually had a nice little local-animals lesson all teed up. Guests always asked about wildlife, and I had my roster of beasties with which to entertain them. But every time I thought of Bob Marley, the April Fools' Bear, I lost my composure again and couldn't talk.

"Boy, you are just snorting up a storm over there," he said, which made me snort again.

Eventually, Swan came to a halt, her ears twitched back to the sound of my laughter. I just had to sit there, helpless, giggling. It wasn't even that funny—except that it was.

Timothy pulled up alongside and laughed at me. "You okay there, cowgirl?"

"The April Fools' Bear," I wheezed. "Bob Marley the Bear."

"You're insane. Come on, Whistler. This path looks pretty obvious. Let's you and me take the lead for a while."

Swan decided she could follow Whistler and Clop without my guidance, and I enjoyed the temporary surrender of responsibility while I took deep breaths and calmed down. Then I thought of the bear behind us looking up and saying *Ya, mon*, and then I was off again.

"The grizzly Rastafarian," I whispered to Swan. Her ears twitched at me. "Rasta-grizz. Imagine dreadlocks on the bear."

Hopeless. I was hopeless.

Timothy gathered rock fragments with every new cliff we came to (he took to calling them *April Fools' Bear 1, 2, 3*, trusting that I'd be able to retrace our steps), and he and Whistler offered their peculiar serenade every time we had to deviate from the Markus and trek uphill overland when waterfalls forced us from the streambed route. After a stretch of thoughtful silence, Timothy debuted a second verse to his "Whistler Whistling" song:

I'm climbing and climbing with Whistler.
We're going up and on and on,
Following my handsome horsey sister.
Lead us onward, Lady Swan.

The horse whistles, the man cries.
As for choosing songs, best be wise.
Sing loud to warn the bears away,
But don't forget: They dig reggae.

I applauded and wished I could sing, but I couldn't carry a tune in a bucket. Never mind. I could enjoy his deep voice just the same.

It was probably a reaction to nearly getting him killed the day before (not to mention Whistler, Swan, Daisy, and Clop) that made this trek downstream along the Markus so enjoyable. The clouds hadn't vanished, but at least they'd parted long enough for great, dramatic shafts of sunlight to illuminate the mountains. Tucked into the Markus Valley, the winds had faded to soft breezes. Tough grasses were poking their first bearded heads above the remains of the snow, and even the trail wasn't impossibly muddy.

There were no branches off this trail, so Timothy and Whistler remained in the lead, with sweet Clop plodding willingly along behind. Eventually, I told Timothy about the pumas and bobcats that hated humanity even more than bears, and about the possibility that one of the Yellowstone wolf packs might expand their hunting range over the border and into the wilds around Daughtry Lake, which I personally thought was great news. (The Circle B didn't do any ranching, though. We had no calves or lambs to worry about, so it was easy for us to welcome the wolves back.)

"Moose, now," I offered as I trailed along behind him. "That's what you want to worry about. A big bull moose stands its ground? Just give up. Turn around and go the other way. They can get grumpy."

"I bet," he answered. "Moose not smoking that sweet ganja, huh?"

"Definitely not. Moose are more like...Babcocks at a board meeting."

"What, power-mad? Determined to talk more than anyone else? Do moose measure their manhood by the size of their portfolios too?"

I chuckled but privately thought he'd shown more of his personality here than he might have intended to, given that I'd met all his sisters and girl cousins. Seven women and not one of them seemed to care about her net worth. The two remaining boys in the family, though—Fourth and Nicholas. I'd met them, too, and found them stern and formal. Proud. *I see you, Timothy. I know who you fear. And it's not a bear.*

Our easy mood lasted throughout the day. Once we made camp at the fork of the Markus and the Wild, we took care of the horses and mules and got our dinner together. Timothy apparently trusted me enough to doctor his various blisters in front of the fire, where I could see him do it, and that made me proud.

And then I offered the idiotic suggestion that eventually proved to be near lethal.

23

THE UNCERTAINTY PRINCIPLE

TIMOTHY

"You ought to pan for rocks in the streams, like the gold miners did. It would be a hell of a lot easier on your hands."

Frank's words were offered casually, but they ran through me like electricity. "Pan for rocks. That's a very interesting idea." Could I do it? How would I do it?

"I was kidding," she said. She gestured to the two rivers that met just past our campsite. "Anyway, you don't have the right equipment. Plus, you might have noticed. There's kind of a little bit of water flowing down from the mountains. See?"

The valley created over geologic ages by the Wild River was broad. It looked like a raggedy-edged meadow. But there was no doubt that we were sitting on a slope and water was definitely flowing downhill. These were mountain rivers, and they were moving fast. Wading in more than knee-deep would definitely challenge my balance.

Plus, these waters were glacier fed. A few degrees colder and they'd go back to being ice.

Still—it would be so much easier to scoop rocks from the riverbed.

"Stop thinking about this," Frank said. "I can hear the gears in your mind creaking. You can't do it. Besides, say you pulled a rock from the river that was just lousy with your Patton Oswald Mystery Element. How would you know which mountain it came from? You wouldn't. It's dumb. Give up the idea."

I spread my hands in an *I surrender* gesture, but the idea still nagged at me. I'd at least know which direction to go in to further my quest.

And all that loose stone was just sitting there, washed down from upstream and tumbling around under waterfalls. The bigger the falls, the more rocks I could pull out.

Using...what?

How about the cooking pot? That would do for a test run.

I watched the sky. Would the light hang on until after we finished whatever Frank was cooking? It had optimistically been labeled Orange Chicken, but based on the smell, they were referring to the color rather than the flavor.

If we bolted our food before the sun went down, I could volunteer to wash the pot in the river.

Right under that little waterfall over there.

Frank eyed me from across the campfire, and I smiled innocently at her. The clouds had drawn back, taking the rain with them. No need for the tarp that created a temporary shelter. We weren't sitting side by side this time, and I had a moment to regret that. Frank smelled good, even after a day on the trail.

She'd felt good when we hugged after crossing the scree field.

Her waist was trim and tempting when I'd pulled her back from Bob Marley, the April Fools' Bear.

And her laughter was infectious. I wanted more.

But not as much as I wanted to wash that pot.

"Jesus Christ!" she shouted when I came back from the

river, my jacket wet almost to the shoulder. "Are you insane? Do you understand how serious hypothermia is?"

"I got a whole potful," I said, putting the pot on the ground. I couldn't bear to lose any of my precious treasure while she was attempting to yank my jacket off me.

"Fucking idiot! Get out of this shirt!"

"It's wool. I'll be fine."

"You could lose a finger—and you'd deserve it! Get it off! How do you turn the heater on in your tent?"

My entire arm felt colder than the polar-bear swims at Vaughn's beach place in Rhode Island every New Year's. That water was near freezing too. Why was this so much harsher? My fingers weren't working right. I couldn't quite undo my buttons.

"Over your head if you have to. And the T-shirt."

"Well, now I really am cold. You just want me half naked."

"Get in the tent. Do you have dry clothes in there? I'm going to get you something hot to hold. Where's your damned mug? Hold this coffee. Damn it, Babcock! I told you not to do it!"

In all honesty, I hadn't realized just how far beneath the surface I'd have to reach. The water was so clear that I thought I'd barely have to go farther than the handle. And the current was so swift that I came close to losing the pot entirely. That would have pissed Frank off even more.

On the other hand, the stones I pulled up would be easy to package and filled with information. The assayer was sure to find something good.

And my arm was warming up just fine. I was pleased with the trade-off.

Frank fussed and cursed until long after sunset. She wouldn't let me come out of my tent, so I couldn't hide the next box of chocolates on her pillow, but she probably would have just yelled at me anyway. I went to sleep and woke the next day fully refreshed and happy.

I had a moment of shock when I thought she'd dumped my rocks back in the river, but then I saw the packet the orange chicken had come in. It was bulging with my stones and now bore a notation in marker that read *Idiot at Markus/Wild Junction*.

And oatmeal was cooking in the pot.

"Frank, you are a goddess among women," I told her.

"Well, you're a numbskull among men. With the emphasis on *numb*. Promise me now that you won't do that again, or we're going downriver and back to the ranch today."

Didn't she know I was completely amoral? "I swear it," I said solemnly.

She eyed me suspiciously. "All right. But I'm watching you. Eat your breakfast."

We cleaned the campsite to her rigid specifications. Before we mounted up, she stood at the edge of the river and looked up. "Not sure I like the looks of those clouds," she said.

"They look like the exact same clouds to me," I said. "What don't you like?"

She made a face but didn't explain. Instead, she looked down the river. "Two hours that way, we come to Deep Creek. That's the route I was planning. Up Deep Creek, eventually to Kaia Lake. There are smaller tributaries, and I'd like to check how the bridges are holding up. But we're going to get more rain. Maybe more than rain."

I cocked an eyebrow at her because she clearly wasn't done. "Yeah?"

"Yeah. Or we could do half a day's ride upriver and get back to Charla Lake, where there's a bunkhouse with a woodstove. It would be a better place to wait out a spring blizzard."

"We're getting a spring blizzard?"

She made the *maybe yes, maybe no* face. "Could be. Kind of feels like it."

I respected her trail sense, but we'd already been to Charla

Lake. I had samples from that trail. "Let's risk it," I said. "Head for Deep Creek. We'll be okay. We're tough."

She sneered as she eyed me, and I knew she was thinking about my wet jacket. But then she gave me the benefit of the doubt. "All right. Mount up. Let's do Deep Creek."

24

IT'S GOING WELL

FRANK

It took me the entire morning to get over my anger.

Except, tell the truth: My anger was based in fear.

Timothy obviously didn't understand the risk of hypothermia, but I did. Like the thrill seeker he was, Timothy was treating the whole thing like a joke. That was hard for me to forgive.

He read the lay of the land right, of course—he let me lead, and he never sang his Whistler song. He didn't try to make me laugh. He gave me space, which was smart.

Plus, the rain held off. I wasn't sure we'd made the right choice about skipping the Charla Lake bunkhouse, but so far, so good.

Before we got to the meadow where Deep Creek flowed into the wild, there was a broad, flat stretch of river that wouldn't get much past the horses' knees, although the mules were going to get their bellies wet. That was where we'd cross to the eastern shore of the Wild. I made Timothy carry Clop's lead in his hand in case Clop went down. That way, Timothy and Whistler could still survive. He grinned at what he clearly thought was overkill but obeyed me as I did the same with Daisy.

Since Timothy was still grinning when we made the opposite shore safely, I knew I had to set him straight. I built a fire so the horses would have some heat and then made us a hot lunch. Then I told him about the kid who had almost died.

"I was seventeen," I said. "Red was leading a group up the Albert River and I was his assistant. Nothing we hadn't done dozens of times. There's good trout fishing on the Albert, and that's what this group wanted. So we set them up for fly-fishing."

Maybe he caught the tension in my voice. Timothy listened quietly, holding Clop's cinch to the fire to help it dry.

"I was upriver with the mother. She'd gotten her line tangled in the bushes for the millionth time. That's typical for newbies. We really couldn't hear much over the water, but I glanced downriver and saw the next guy looking downriver. Then he was running. They were all running."

"Running downriver? In the water?"

"On the bank, through the rocks and fallen logs and big stones. Through those scrub bushes that grow up. It's not easy to make up any time, and everyone I could see was moving fast. I got the mom out of the water and went to see what was going on."

"What time of year was this?"

"June. Early in the season, but a lot warmer than it is right now. Anyway, the fifteen-year-old son had fallen and gotten swept up by the current. I still don't know how my uncle was able to get him to shore, but by the time I got there, this big, husky kid was barely conscious. He kept trying to pull off his clothes, saying he was hot."

"How long was he in?"

"Red said he was hanging on to a rock when Red got to him. Maybe seven minutes? Maybe ten? I don't know."

"What did you do?"

"We wrapped him in all the warm clothes we could find and Red told me to start a fire and heat stones in it, to wrap the stones in clothes and pack them around him. Then Red got on his horse and took off for the ranch."

"You guys needed a satellite phone."

I shrugged. The entire memory was tinged with that sense of helplessness. "The kid kept passing out. His muscles all got rigid. His parents were freaking out and his little sister was sobbing. We sat there, waiting for a seventy-year-old man to ride his horse to death."

"For how long?"

"We were a day's ride from the lodge, and Red made it in just over three hours. The sun was setting when we heard a helicopter. It was the rescue copter from Bozeman. They'd stopped to pick up Red, who guided them in. They couldn't take everyone, so there was this horrible moment where the mom and dad started screaming at each other about which one of them got to go. While their son was dying. Every minute counted. I couldn't get them to decide."

I felt the tears prickling behind my eyes and blinked them back. Timothy touched the sleeve of my coat, and I dashed my hands over my eyes. "Shit," he said softly.

"Finally, Red pointed at the mother and told her to get in the helicopter. They took off. God, it was so loud. So fucking loud."

"Then what?"

"The dad rounded on Red and started yelling. 'Take me back to the ranch, I have to get back to the ranch.' And Red almost dead from his ride. But he started to get on the mother's horse. That's when I started shouting. I made him get down. I told the dad I'd start back with him tomorrow, after the sun came up. If their daughter could keep up, she could come—otherwise, she'd have to come back more slowly with Red and everyone else."

"Did he freak?"

"Totally freaked. Another guest had to force him away and talked to him until he calmed down. We made camp right there on the river, even though it was miles from where we'd planned to stay. The next day, the dad and I tried to beat Red's record back, but he was a greenhorn. It took us most of the day. The whole time, he alternated between crying and screaming. That's my idea of what hell must be like."

"So...what did you find when you got back?"

I sighed. "The kid survived. He had brain damage, but he was alive. We heard later that the parents divorced. It was a mess." I ran out of story and sat there, drained. Timothy let me rest. "So that's why I gave you such a hard time yesterday," I finally said. "I was angry. I still am. But mostly I was scared."

He looked into the fire, nearly invisible in the morning light, and then made a point to ceremoniously hand me the cooking pot. "I didn't understand. I'm sorry. I really won't do it again."

I took the pot but studied him. "You already promised."

"Yeah, but I'm a known liar. This time, I mean it."

He was so casual, so easy in his admission, that I was left open-mouthed. He reached out with one finger and gently pushed up on my chin. "You're gonna catch flies, beautiful. I'll be good. Scout's honor."

"Were you ever a scout?"

He scoffed. "Acted as a scout to warn Vaughn someone was coming, sure. Boy Scout? Nah." He winked at me. "But I'm not an idiot either. I've learned my lesson." He nodded as if I could believe him. I was totally confused. "Shall we keep going?"

When we made the turn to follow the riverbank up the Deep Creek trail, I caught him looking at the water. Did it look like he was being a little more respectful?

We had a while before the valley closed in so far that we'd have to ride single file. I needed to get past the residual horror of the memory and hit on the first topic of conversation that came to mind.

"You know you mentioned the sat phone to Cal and Maria?"

"Yeah," he said. "And she shut him up about it. I'm thinking now that it would be a damned good idea to have all the trail guides equipped, don't you?"

"Yeah, but remember, Cal and Maria are selling up after this season and moving to Florida. He's got Parkinson's."

"Shit, that's right."

"I know." I shook my head. First Red left me, now Cal and Maria were planning an exit. Grim news. "And probably selling to a timber corporation." Timothy's jerk unwittingly tugged on the reins and Whistler huffed in annoyance. "No one else is going to buy this much land for a dude ranch that never made much money."

"I hate that idea. They'll destroy it!" His protest was heartfelt.

I laughed at the irony. "So will you. Right?" He looked at me and then away. Masking his guilt? "But if you buy it, maybe I can protect seven hundred acres. At least that's still a possibility."

"Pfft." He was dismissive—or at least pretending to be dismissive. "Let me know when you get Fourth to change his mind."

"Or Nicholas. Or Joanna. Or Tabby," I reminded him.

He laughed. "Oh, please try to get at Tabby. I'll pay extra to watch. We could sell tickets. Like pay-per-view."

Our ride had been fraught with too many high-emotion conversations. I had to consciously remind myself to avoid mentioning that Joanna and I had already discussed how I should avoid Tabby and focus on Fourth or Nicholas. "Your family is really intense," I said.

His laugh echoed from the stone walls that were drawing in closer. "That's an understatement. You know we all had to start taking finance classes in third grade?"

"Third grade?!" I goggled at him. Wasn't third grade for learning the more exotic colors and dusting off those critical spelling skills?

"Third grade," he confirmed. "We study in special Babcock-only after-school tutoring sessions, and we can't get any profit sharing or inheritances until we pass our final exams. And they are brutal. I passed them the first time I took them, of course." His tone was so pat that I knew he was lying. I shot him a scornful look, and he caved immediately. "Okay, it took me three tries, and my damned younger sister had to help."

I got the relationship wrong deliberately. "Your younger sister is...Suzanne? Or Quinn? I met them all at the meeting, but..."

"My younger sister is Joanna, world's most arrogant genius. And Delilah, too—Joanna's twin. Not that Delilah got that terrifying brain. She's more like me."

"She's the beautiful one, right?"

"Are you saying I'm not beautiful? I beg your pardon!"

"Excuse me for implying something so heinous." I grinned as I said it, even though Timothy was, in fact, beautiful. He had his ridiculously expensive hat pushed back on his head, and his face was spotlit by one of the day's last sunbeams. That cocky swagger, that strong neck, those hands—mm. He was beautiful, all right.

But yeah. Cocky. As hell. He began explaining how many hearts he'd broken over his lifetime as a Casanova, and once again I somehow knew he was making most of it up. So I sat back to enjoy the lies.

Or rather, I sat forward, as it was now necessary to go single file through the canyon, but his voice carried just fine over the rushing of Deep Creek. The path grew steep and we had to veer around, following the land up and over the shelves of rock, where the creek poured over in noisy waterfalls. I was on a switchback, climbing a steep incline, and so in perfect position to see Timothy below me. He was gazing longingly at the base of the waterfall. He no doubt believed those rocks held the key to whatever he was doing, but he didn't ask to stop.

I gave him credit for that.

In fact, he only requested breaks when he wanted to carve more hunks of stone out of the mountain with his chisel. We ate in the saddle and kept going up, accompanied by the amazing whistling horse. The tributaries we passed were all in full flow, but the low log bridges were still in good shape. We reached tree cover as the rain started.

"The best campsite is about an hour ahead. You okay to head for it?" I offered. "We could find flat places for the tents around here if you want to rest."

He was putting his rain cover on his hat and arranging his slicker so it covered as much of him and Whistler as possible. "I'm good to go."

So we kept going. Until I came to a rockslide and stopped.

He peered past me. "You can't make it over that?" Timothy asked.

"I can," I replied. "I'm looking at that boulder."

He looked where I was pointing, A large stone had fallen from above and was wedged into the streambed. The water had found a way, of course, carving a new path in the hillside. "Yeah?"

I grinned back at him, water sluicing off my brim as I turned. "There used to be a waterfall there. And now there isn't. Right there, see?" I gestured, and he was puzzled.

Then he grinned. "Really?"

"Really. If you want to pan for rocks, how about right there? Where there won't be any water to sweep you away?"

"You are a goddess!" he cried.

Which set an entirely new tone for what followed next.

25

CHEERFUL IN THE RAIN

TIMOTHY

I didn't usually form incorrect first impressions.

It was part of my job to see past false fronts, studied friend-liness, belligerent posturing. The ability to correctly read even people who wanted to be guarded was what made me a success on Capitol Hill. But there was no denying that I'd read Frank Robinson wrong.

The pretty, pushy woman who'd so irritated me in that Denver bar was nowhere in sight. Oh, she was still pretty, and god knows she could be pushy. It was the irritants that had vanished.

Her explanation for why she'd been so mad at me for wetting my arm? That was a pretty good tale she told. It really did make me think twice about the river we rode beside, or the streams and tributaries gushing down the mountain to feed the Deep Creek.

Yeah, maybe panning for molybdenum wasn't the greatest idea.

And then she looked at a hunk of riverbed—one that looked a great deal like all the other riverbeds we'd seen in our travels—and saw the waterfall that wasn't there anymore.

And she set me to pan for rocks in a dry pocket.

I climbed back on Whistler after stowing my catch in Clop's hamper and experienced the startling—could one say refreshing?—sensation of sitting on a rain-soaked saddle. Yikes.

But it just made me chuckle. Following Frank in wilderness was so much easier, so much more fun, than corralling some chief of staff or wrangling a representative. It was so much more direct, so much more concrete, than the endless veiled conversations where no one would say what they wanted, or what the cost would be to change their opinion.

Even the rain was pleasing. I'd sweated in the congressional sauna in the basement of the Capitol, run on a treadmill in the members-only gym, "stumbled" so casually into a conversation with a party leader—all surrounded by the rank sweat of stubborn old men.

The rain felt...fucking wonderful.

Frank checked on me a few times as we pushed higher and higher up the trail carved into the hillside, but each time I could smile and nod back to her. Yes, it was raining. Yes, the world was soggy and it was cold. Yes, I wanted to stop again and bang new blisters into my hands in search of more rock fragments. But I was doing just fine.

Strong. Easy in the saddle. Loosened up. No longer such a novice on the trail.

The campsite was a mostly flat piece of land created by some long-ago landslide. Deep Creek was thirty feet or so below us, far enough that we weren't deafened by the sound of the endless rivulets and waterfalls. A corner of rock formed a good pen for the animals. Frank pulled two convenient logs across the front, and we rigged the first tarp overhead so the horses would be protected.

Frank darted a look at me as I was checking Whistler's hooves, and I realized I was whistling the uphill song. Because I felt good. I grinned back at her.

"Don't forget to check Clop," she said.

"Have I ever forgotten to check Clop? I have not. Clop is my buddy, aren't you, Cloppy? My little headbutting donkey. My sweet-faced mule."

I continued to croon to Clop while Frank rolled her eyes and hid her grin.

We measured out their shares of grain and, satisfied with the horse-and-mule conditions, turned to our own dinner.

"If we rig the tarp between these trees, we can cover the firepit. There will be room for your tent here."

"Your tent won't be protected," I said.

"I'm fine."

"Not at all." Feeling very gallant, I swapped the bags with our tents. "I insist. I have the heater, after all."

She opened her mouth to say something and then shrugged. "Help me rig the tarp."

I was proud to have remembered the knot she taught me to use (which was brilliant—held like a locked door until you twitched the tail, at which point it unraveled neatly). I got my side tied up before she did and came to help her with her side.

She was straining to reach the branch she wanted. I reached out, and she sighed and handed me the line. I tied it, careful to get the knot just right as she was watching. Once I pulled it taut, we found ourselves under a roof at last, with rain beating on the tarp instead of on our hats. Success!

I grinned down at her and said the first thing that came into my mind. "I just want you to know, I'm having a really good time."

She blinked, surprised. Then her hand, cold as ice, landed on my cheek in a caress.

She was as astonished as I was, but I knew I couldn't stand

to let her fingers remain that chilled. I slid my far larger hand over hers, holding her to my face.

She looked up at me. I looked down at her. It would be the simplest movement to lower my face to hers. To duck under her hat's brim and taste those lips.

But this wasn't some supermodel. This was Frank, the woman I was counting on to lead me through the wilderness. I didn't dare make any assumptions. Instead, I studied those stunning eyes, the light inner circle almost lost in the black pupils, huge in the low light. She probably felt the muscles of my gentle smile in the palm of her hand.

She inhaled and said, "I don't know what to do."

I raised an eyebrow, my heart thudding at the potential of the moment. "Be brave," I advised.

She shook her head but did not look away. Did not withdraw her hand. "I'm scared of what you think it will mean if I *am* brave."

"Does it have to mean anything?"

Her brows were drawn together in concern. I let go of the tarp's rope and, with a damp finger, touched that little crease and then let my hand fall away. "I won't think anything," I said. And hoped it wasn't a lie. "If you want to kiss me, I'll be happy with just that."

I hadn't smoothed out her worry line with my touch. "Really?" she said, troubled.

"Try and see."

She was motionless for the space of several pounding heartbeats. Then she pulled her hand from under mine—but only to push the hat off the back of my head.

She came up on her toes, I leaned down, and it was as easy as that. Her lips, fresh from the rain, were soft and chilled against mine. A flash of heat went through me, so warm that I thought the sun had broken through the clouds. I looped a careful arm around her waist and pulled her closer. Her hand tangled in my hair. She exhaled, warm against my skin, and I didn't think before opening my lips.

For a brief, endless moment, the delicate tip of her tongue touched mine—and then she pulled away.

I let her go, already missing the feel of her against me.

"That didn't mean anything," she said. "Don't go expecting anything."

She turned away, head down, and got busily to work building the fire.

"Okay," I said, not sure how to play this. She was putting out waves of Keep Out energy, and I wasn't sure what that was about. "If you don't want to sleep with me, you don't have to worry. I'm capable of controlling myself."

"I'm not afraid of you," she said defensively.

I narrowed my eyes, trying to figure this out. On previous days, I'd helped her lay out a fire and get dinner ready, but she didn't look like she wanted me anywhere near her. Okay...I'd give her some space.

I started to set up my tent. When I was done, I set up hers. I could get the next box of chocolates onto her pillow without her seeing it, but maybe that joke would fall flat after the kiss.

What to do, what to do...

I sat as far from her as I could and decided to just ask the question. "Can I give you the next box of chocolates? Or will that be going too far?"

She sat back on her haunches. The night's meal (a revolting combination of dehydrated chili and mac 'n' cheese that smelled astonishingly good) was slowly congealing in the cooking pot. It needed nothing more than an occasional stir. Two baked potatoes wrapped in foil were tucked into the coals. Dinner was cooking, and she couldn't focus on that any longer.

So, she looked at me and sighed. "Sorry," she said grudgingly.

Still not seeing a path forward here, I was cautious. "Sorry for what?"

She stared off into the trees, where darkness was creeping closer. As if making up her mind, she looked back with determination. "I'm sorry because you're suffering for the sins of others."

Eyebrows up, I questioned that. "Wow. What does that mean?"

"It means that there have been a few guys who I've dated who decided that they owned me. And I have no fucking interest in being owned."

Okay. Now I knew what the problem was. "Well, I have no interest in owning you, Frank."

She shot her reply back like bullets. "Well, I have no interest in dating you, Timothy."

"Okay, then." Not being a fool, I dropped the conversation. She did too.

We ate our meal in near silence. There was the typical "Please pass the salt" and "Want more tea?" But no real conversation. I stood at the end to stumble down to Deep Creek to wash the pot, and she wouldn't let me.

"Put it in the food bag and we'll haul it up a tree. Wash it tomorrow. You'll break your ankle if you try to go down without any light."

I nodded, and we went on finishing up our camping evening.

"Good night," I said once we were stowed away and safe.

She paused before answering. "I actually would like a little chocolate," she admitted.

I snorted in appreciation and found her the box. "Please."

She opened the box and held it out to me. "Want some?"

It was a peace offering and an apology. I took one of the chocolates, careful not to touch her fingers. "Thanks."

"Good night, then."

"Good night," I said.

She was about to unzip the flap to her tent when she stopped. Staring at the ground, she said, "I'm not saying it wasn't a good kiss."

"It was a very good kiss," I agreed.

"Yeah. 'Night."

"'Night."

I laid in my tent and replayed her words. And the feel of her. The taste of her. Frank was willing—and reluctant. Delicious—and stubborn. Born to travel the backcountry—and sexy as hell in her pretend glasses and sophisticated suit.

Frank was a puzzle, one I didn't know how to solve. Yet.

Could I figure out a way to get her to lower her defenses?

26

KAIA LAKE

FRANK

I believed that every human was still an animal under our veneer of civilization. Every time someone said, "I dunno, I got a hinky feeling about that," or someone claimed their choice was based on intuition, I was absolutely sure that was the animal in us, reading things in a situation that the human brain couldn't perceive.

I trusted my intuition. I trusted a hinky feeling. Just because I didn't know why I believed something was no reason to discount it.

Almost one month ago exactly, I met a man in a Denver bar who I knew was a predator.

Timothy Babcock did whatever he had to to get what he wanted. More than that, he sincerely believed that he *deserved* everything he wanted.

This was a man who would do something illegal and risk prison because he thought he was entitled to whatever he could take.

And yet...I was lying in my raggedy old tent alone.

He was across the campfire from me in his air-mattress palace, leaving me alone. Even after a kiss that had made steam come out my pores.

I could still feel his warmth. Knew the strength in his arms. Felt the heat of his hands. Smelled him—smelled horse and clean sweat and the leather band of his hat and a scent that didn't come from some fancy cologne. Four days on the trail, he smelled like Timothy.

And it was good. So good.

I cursed Delbert Sharf again and threw in Casey Moffat and Walt Carlyle too. The men in my life who had taken something perfectly enjoyable and trashed it just so they could call me "the old ball and chain" or "the little woman" while expecting me to cater to every need.

If it weren't for not one, not two, but three possessive assholes, I could have been in Timothy's tent at that very moment, exploring every inch of that toned body. Satisfying my curiosity about a man with such big thumbs. Enjoying myself.

But no. I was alone and cold and free. Which was the way things needed to remain.

The trek up to Kaia Lake was hard. Timothy never complained—never even uttered a peep unless he wanted to dismount and hack up some more mountainside. But I could hear my Uncle Red in my brain, as clear as if he were riding his clever old Appaloosa beside me.

Frank, you must be some kind of bonehead to try for anything as high up as Kaia Lake on April third. Don't you know how many storms you're in for? I'm 'shamed of you, girl!

Red was never ashamed of me. Red was my entire family once my dad was sent to prison and my mother took up keeping company with Mr. Jim Beam. Red taught me how to work with horses and how to live lightly on the land. He bought me my first tampons and talked me through their use from the other side of the bathroom door. Red was the one who scared Casey Moffat so bad that my senior year in high school wasn't a constant nightmare.

But Red would have shaken his head at me for this trek.

By the afternoon, the temperature was falling, along with the rain. The wind was picking up. Timothy and I both had gloves on, and I was grateful for the warmth of Swan under me. When we finally made it to Kaia Lake, there was no view to be had—just more grainy, driving, wet snow, filling all of us with misery.

Red and I had built a real corral for the horses, but I had to use the first tarp for a roof and the second for a windbreak. The fire I managed to start fizzed and complained. It was an endless chore to keep it going. Finally, Timothy sat back and looked at me. We were both wet and cold and exhausted.

"Look," he said, "there is no question of not sleeping in the same tent. I need the body warmth and so do you. Come in with me. I won't kiss you, I won't touch you. There's still power left in my heater. We have to combine forces here."

The ghost of Uncle Red appeared behind Timothy, hands on hips and making faces at me. *See? I told you you were a fool.*

Warmth was our top priority. "All right," I said. "I agree."

"Finally. Come on."

I was determined to ignore any awkwardness—or any reminder of that kiss. He let me precede him into the tent, and I rolled my sleeping bag out on his plump, luxurious mattress. "How do you get this inflated each time?" I asked.

"Foot pump. It's easy. Zip the bags together?"

We'd be warmer that way. On the other hand, we'd definitely be in immediate body contact. I hesitated.

"Sharing body heat," he reminded me as wind rippled the tent walls. I could see my breath.

I nodded. We had to take off our gloves to zip the bags

together, and neither of us stripped down much. Hat, coat, boots—that's all I lost. He also shed a thick wool sweater that I secretly coveted and slid into the bag in heavy socks, wool pants, and a flannel shirt over a tee.

There wasn't a lot of room left, but without my coat, I was losing heat fast. Shaking my head at the awkwardness, I slid into whatever room was left in the bag.

I rapidly discovered that there was no way we were going to lie side by side on our backs. One of us—maybe both of us—was going to have to sleep on their side.

"You are very cold," he complained as he held out one arm.

"You are very warm," I countered. I turned onto my hip and held my head above his shoulder, all my muscles rigid to hold me off him.

"Oh, hang on. I forgot." I realized he was unzipping the sleeping bag, and I wrinkled my nose in dislike.

He fumbled on his far side and then presented me with...a box of chocolates.

It made me laugh. I couldn't help it. What an absurd thing to do as we were so desperately uncomfortable and awkward in one claustrophobic sleeping bag.

And when I laughed, I relaxed. The air mattress held me like a cloud. The arm around me pulled me closer to his chest, and I lay down my head, smiling at the russet box, still tied with its silk ribbon, lying on his chest. "How many more of these do you have?"

"This is the last one. As far as you know."

I didn't have to look up to know he was smiling. "I still have most of last night's box left. Better save that so we can survive if we get snowed in here for the rest of April."

"Smart thinking. I'll put it over here."

He shifted under me. His little portable lantern was turned off, and then the bag was zipped back up again. He turned to me and pulled me into him, both his arms around me. My face was buried in his neck, and there was suddenly just enough room.

For the first time in hours, warmth washed over my face, fell down my spine, felt like sunshine on the soles of my feet. Without any awkwardness, one of my legs was between his and the other was over the top. We were totally tangled together.

And warm.

And still half laughing.

"Thanks," I said.

"For the chocolate?"

"For not...expecting...anything."

"What I expect is that my trail guide does not turn into an ice cube in the night."

"That's wise."

"I've been known to have the occasional good idea."

"I'm sure. How are the blisters on your hands?"

"My hands feel extremely good right now."

His hands were on my rib cage, on my arm. He was flattering me...and I liked it. "And your aches and pains? Everything feeling good?"

"Are you flirting with me, Robinson? Because it's damned cold. I don't want to be judged when the temperature is this low." I snorted, pushing my nose against the hollow of his throat, and he uttered a yip. "Shit, you're cold. Don't do that!"

"Apologies." My smile probably wasn't as secret as I would have liked. He could probably feel it.

I felt warm. And comfortable.

I felt safe.

"Good night," I murmured.

"Good night back to you," he whispered. "Your hair smells like horse."

I snorted again. "Sorry."

"No, I like it. I might whistle to your hair, if you don't mind."

"Whistle quietly, Babcock. I'm going to sleep."

"You do you, honey."

Just how long would this snowfall last? How long would the chocolate hold out?

How long could I resist this guy?

27

THE LANDSCAPING OF HYDROLOGY

TIMOTHY

I blamed Frank for the massive boner.

Granted, she was sound asleep and not moving at all, but I could feel breasts against my chest. Her hair was under my cheek. Her long legs were mixed up with mine, and the deep mysteries of her crotch were riding sweetly on my thigh.

I was thirty-two. It had been years since I'd had such an adolescent reaction to finding a woman in my bed. Blame the dry spell I'd been enduring since Aleister Darling met me at the sea lion enclosure of the zoo. No time for honeys while I was cornering the market.

Except now.

With this honey.

Who was very clear that she had reservations.

I eased out of the sleeping bag without waking her—not easy to do. It helped that the air had warmed considerably since the sun came up. I found my boots and stuck my head out of the tent.

Kaia Lake was, as advertised, glorious. Ringed in tall mountains, the lake glowed blue against the fast-melting snow. It followed the contour of the land, ducking into coves that made me ache for a kayak. The place cried out for explanation.

Other things were crying out, though.

I went through the teenage experience of a quick yank while pretending to pee. At least I'd be able to look like a gentleman when Frank got up. I had the fire up and burning, coffee brewing, by the time Frank appeared.

Her hair was adorably mussed. She might have planned on being awkward, but I put a mug of coffee in her hand as soon as she appeared and she grunted her thanks. Awkwardness sidestepped.

She checked on the horses while I started to pack up. Could I keep the sleeping bags zipped together? Better not. It might feel like an attempt to own her.

"Kaia Lake as pretty as you hoped?" she asked.

I took a deep breath of the mountain air and nodded. "All these lakes—they each have totally different characters, don't they? This one looks like movies should be filmed here. You know? Pirates, maybe."

She shook her head. "Not pirates—elves and orcs and epic sword fights." She looked like a powerful elf maiden herself. I smiled at the idea, and she thought I was agreeing with her. "Who needs New Zealand when you've got Montana?"

"Right on!" I said. "You said it!"

Then she was happy. "It's going to be a muddy ride down. We should get started."

"Right behind you, boss."

I sort of missed Whistler's whistle when we were going downhill, but I couldn't blame him for focusing on his feet. The trail was slick with mud like gooey clay. It clung to his hooves and made it hard for me to advise on how to get down the hillside. But following Swan's path was working for us.

Until we got to the blowout.

"Huh," Frank said as she studied the gushing stream now flowing where the trail had been the day before. Her voice was all but lost in the crash of a new waterfall.

"Up and around?" I called, pointing up to the rocks above us.

She shook her head. "You and I might find a path to climb, but I wouldn't take the horses up anything so steep." Her eyes scanned the area and then focused over Deep Creek. She turned her horse and pointed back the way we came. "We'll go down the other side."

The trail was narrow, with a stone cliff on one side and the drop to the river on the other, but Whistler, Clop, and I did a careful turn, and Whistler's big feet remained steady. We headed back up to a primitive bridge over Deep Creek.

"Let's walk them over," Frank called to me. I let her go first, testing the bridge's soundness before she led Swan across. It didn't seem gallant to let the woman test the bridge first. Wasn't that the job for a mighty man? But Frank actively objected to the concept of ownership—which might include a little natural protectiveness—and she was the trail guide. So I shut the fuck up.

She and Swan made it across, and Daisy had no problems. I was bigger than Frank was, but the horses had me beat, weight-wise. Still, Whistler was no Skinny Minnie. We crossed carefully, the water frothed to whiteness below us. Before I could stop her, Frank ducked back over to get Clop, and we were safely on the other side.

"There's a trail here?" I called.

She nodded. "That's why there's a bridge. This goes down to Starvation—that's a creek that heads north into the mountains. There are petroglyphs up there and some guests want to see them. We'll go up Starvation for an hour or so and cross near the top. We should be able to get down that way."

"I'd kind of like to see some ancient petroglyphs myself," I said, which made her grin.

"Of course you do. Troublemaker!"

"That's me."

I'd thought the path on the far side of Deep Creek was rough. The one on this side looked like it hadn't been traveled in years. But Frank went on confidently, and Whistler, Clop, and I followed.

I guess there was no way to get to the point where Starvation met Deep Creek because the trail cut away from the river. We wound through trees still soggy with last night's snow, and the absence of river noise was evidence that I'd gotten used to the sound without realizing it. Now I wondered if I was going deaf before realizing I could now hear things. Whistler's breath. The cry of some bird of prey overhead. The sound of Frank ahead of us, humming Whistler's song.

"Hey!" I cried happily. "That's my song!"

"I don't know what you're talking about," she called back haughtily. She sent me a wicked grin over her shoulder. "I can't help it. It's very catchy."

"Yes," I said happily. "Yes, it is. The next time we go up, I'll sing you a new verse."

"Be still my heart," she said sarcastically.

"Oh, you love it," I muttered.

Since we were at such a delicate moment in what might prove to be a highly pleasing encounter, I was working on a verse that did not include how hard she'd made me by tucking into my body and breathing on my neck. The thought was getting in the way of my songwriting when we came around the corner and I could hear a stream again.

"That's Starvation," Frank said. "We're pretty far north of Deep Creek, but the trail will take us back again. There's a crossing down this way. Come on."

Whoever had made these rough bridges was a hell of a

builder. Several seasons of leaves had fallen on the one over Starvation and a large log had banged up against the bank below, but the wood was sound. We led our mounts over again in the same pattern, and I was just leading Clop over and complimenting myself on not possessively demanding that I go first instead of Frank when Clop, as usual, ran his nose into the rump of patient Whistler.

For the first time, Whistler was surprised by this. He threw up his head to neigh and backed into Clop.

Who bumped into me.

I skidded on some of the gooey clay left on the bridge.

And over I went into the water below.

28

ONE BAD STEP

FRANK

For a fraction of a second, I thought Timothy was teasing me.

Playing a little game.

Standing on a ledge below the bridge to grin up at me—dry, cocky, and perfectly happy.

I knew there was no ledge. I knew the creek had carved a good five feet into the earth at this point and was racing down the mountain with unrestrained fury. I leaped to the top of the bank, mere seconds of action that stretched like rubber into an infinity of time, and looked downhill, hoping to track where he'd been pushed. I'd leave the mules and Whistler and race down on Swan.

God, let me be able to find him.

And he was there, submerged and clinging to the log below the bridge. As I watched, his head went under the racing water, his feet pointing down the mountain and scrambling for purchase.

In that icy water, his muscle control wouldn't last long. I had bare seconds to get him.

I had a coil of rope at the bottom of Clop's panniers, but there was no time to dig it out. I ripped the short cord from the cover of Daisy's baskets—was it even ten feet long? Would that be enough?—and tied one end to Swan's saddle horn. Before I could lose my nerve, I played the cord over the side and started down.

"Look out," Timothy croaked and then gurgled. His head had gone under again. God, he must be so cold.

I got down almost to the water and he held up a hand, clinging to the log with just one arm. I should have been scared and trembling, but it was as if the ice had formed inside me too. Dispassionately, I watched my fingers fashion a loop knot and slip it around that reaching wrist. His fingers grabbed the rope once I had it on, but his knuckles were white.

"Back!" I called to Swan. "Back up!" I should have hooked to Whistler. He was bigger and stronger—but would he have known to back up on command? Was he trained? Why couldn't I remember?

The rope pulled taut and I heard Swan's saddle creak, but the tension held. I was cutting off the circulation to Timothy's hand, but if that was the worst that happened...

His head went under one more time and then he grunted, pushing against the log. As he slid agonizingly up the bank, the log crashed over and was swept downstream.

Timothy was now hanging by the cord—and by my desperate grip on his wrist.

But now he could push with his feet. Slowly, slick against the bank's muddy sides, he rose out of the water. First his chest was out, then his hips. I made it to the top of the bank and lay on my belly to haul him over the edge.

And then he was lying on the ground beside me, gasping.

Dripping wet. His skin was crimson, and his clothes were soaked.

His tent. I'd set it up somewhere and get him into the tent. With that weak little heater. Naked. Into the bag.

I knew it wouldn't work. He had no heat left in his body. The sleeping bag would just reflect back his own cold.

I knew the stages of hypothermia. His speech would start to slur. He'd become confused. As his body shut down all the capillaries to his skin, he'd decide he was overly warm and start peeling off clothes.

Next he'd fall unconscious.

Without help, he would...

He was looking at me, big eyes wide. "Shit," he said. "Tha... thas cold..."

The horror burst out of me in a giggle. "I don't know what to do," I said. Not that he could process my words.

I screwed my eyes shut and blocked out the appalling sight. *What do I do, Red?*

I didn't actually believe in ghosts, but if Red had been alive, I knew what he would have said.

The grotto. Get him to the grotto.

It was the last place I wanted Timothy to see—and the only place that would save his life.

Fifteen minutes on a fast horse.

I untied the cord around Timothy's wrist and used it to shift Clop from Whistler to Swan. I kissed my horse's nose and whispered to her, "I know you know the way. Follow us, sweet girl."

Then I slapped Timothy hard.

He groaned and his eyes flew open.

"You have to get on Whistler," I said. "I can't lift you. You have to get on! Timothy, now!"

I barked at him and his vision cleared. He was beginning to shiver—great convulsions that shook his whole body. But he fought his way to his knees, and then I was able to get a shoulder under his arm and help to lift him up. Whistler waited patiently as we staggered to him.

"I can tie you across the saddle if you can't mount," I said.

He shook that red head—where was that stupid hat?—and grunted. "I rye...I ride."

The heave to get him up was terrifying, and he nearly toppled over backward, but he still had some strength left and got his far leg over the saddle. I vaulted up, powered by raw adrenaline alone, and got behind him, yanking him up. For a few desperate moments, I knew I'd never reach Whistler's reins, and I didn't know if I could control the big horse just with my knees. Then Whistler turned his head to look back at us— and I had the reins.

Good damned horse.

Thank god.

"Get up, Whistler." I wasn't sure how well I could balance Timothy in front of me. He was so much larger than me that it was hard for me to see around him, but he gradually fell forward until he was all but lying on Whistler's neck. That good horse did not object.

The trail was tangled but still visible. The air was chilled on my front where Timothy's wet clothes had soaked me, but I wasn't going to die from it. Maybe it was Red's divine influence, but there weren't too many obstacles. The only downed trees could be stepped over, the only rockslides could be crossed. We wound along the Starvation trail, across the mountain pass, and up the winding path that led around the mountain.

Timothy was still shivering, but his muscles weren't working. When we finally got to the grotto, I walked Whistler past the corral and right up to the door.

"Stay on the horse," I begged Timothy as I dismounted.

The latch on the door still worked. I was inside in a rush of nostalgia. It smelled like woodsmoke and Red and the steamy heat from the hot springs. I gathered the old wooden wheelbarrow, relic of the mining days, praying it would hold Timothy's body.

He gasped when I dragged him off the horse and fell heavily into the wheelbarrow. It caught him across the thighs and I knew it must have hurt, but he made no protest. Possibly couldn't protest.

"Stay here, Whistler. Please god, stay here." I ground-tied him and hoped he wouldn't decide to go over the ledge.

I'd worked hard in my life. I had a good set of muscles. But I strained every single one of them wheeling Timothy through the cabin. Red's lantern was still there on the table, the kerosene still unevaporated. I lit the wick and replaced the chimney.

My hands were going to be full. There was no way I could carry it. Agonized by the delay, I ran halfway down the tunnel and put the lantern down. It would have to be enough light to wheel him in.

As I went, I thought about stripping him bare—but what more harm would it do if I just dumped him fully dressed into the hot springs? Nothing. All I really had to do was keep his head above water. Hiking boots would dry out. Wool clothes could steam in front of the fire.

I got to the edge at last, shaking with the effort. Failing anything better, I grabbed one of his hands and heaved up on the wheelbarrow, spilling him out, over, down, and into the water, head held up only by my grip on his arm.

He cried out when he went in and then moaned. I tugged until I dragged him around the edge to the underwater seat. I wasn't sure he wasn't still going to slide under the water, so I struggled to get my boots off with one hand.

My coat followed, and I regretted the time it took to peel off my pants and shirts. But if Clop and Daisy were still in the clearing and all my clothes were as fully soaked as Timothy's, I'd be at risk, too, when I went back to take care of them. So poor Timothy had to loll there in the water, slipping in and out of consciousness while I peeled my clothes off with agonizing one-handed slowness.

At last, I slid into the water in just my bra and panties, gasping at the bliss of the temperature. I could reach the diverter with my foot and half closed it, cutting off the cold water and raising the heat level. I pushed Timothy off the bench again and got behind him so I could float him out, getting his scalp and hair into the water. If people lost most of their heat through their heads, surely getting his skull into heated water would help?

And then I held him, not sure what else I could do.

How much time had elapsed? Why hadn't I forced my hat onto his head? What was I thinking, letting him cross the bridge when it was so muddy? When would I know if there was brain damage? His breathing was steady against my reaching arms, and the shivers had stopped. Was that good? Or had he entered a more dangerous stage where shivering stopped?

What if I'd killed him?

"Dunk my head."

I looked down, terrified and hopeful. His blue eyes looked back at me. "What?"

"Nose is cold. Dip me back?"

"You can hold your breath?"

"Yeah. Few seconds."

"Okay. Here we go."

I moved and he ducked his head back, water rushing over his skin. Too long?

He was turning his head back and forth under the water, pushing the warm water against his face. He lifted back up under his own power, and I was so grateful that I began to cry.

"Ah, baby," he murmured. "No cry. You okay? You get hurt?"

I hugged him back to me again. "No, I didn't get hurt. Can you tell me your name?"

He chuckled, but I shook him a little to make him take me seriously. "Timothy O'Toole Babcock. Director, legislative affairs, Babcock Holdings." His voice slowly got stronger. He told me the year and the president. He did simple math. He wiggled his toes and fingers.

And he said he should have grabbed some river rocks while he was down there.

With every right answer, my terror eased. "Thank god," I said. "Thank god, thank god. Thanks, Red."

"We're praying to Red now?"

"This is his place. He saved you."

"You saved me."

"After I almost killed you."

"Hush with that."

"Can you sit on your own? There's a bench here. Feel it?"

"Yeah. I feel strange, but nothing hurts anymore. I can sit."

"Will you mind if I go find Swan and the mules? Take care of Whistler? I won't go if you think you might be too weak."

"Go. I'm going to stay right here and bake out the chills. This place is a godsend. Where are we?"

"I'll tell you all about it. I'll be back as soon as I can."

"Don't worry about me."

Of course I was going to worry about him. I had a grim image of coming back to find him floating face down in the pool, but he was looking stronger and was thinking right. He wasn't going to drown in the time it would take me to gather the horses and our supplies. I eased the diverter open again, letting in more cold. Without the stream water, the hot springs became unbearable. He'd cook like a potato in stew without the strength to crawl out.

He probably watched me climb out of the pool in my underwear, but I gathered my clothes and went back up the tunnel. I found one of Red's old flannels in the trunk. It would serve as my towel.

Once I was dressed, I left the cabin area and nearly cried again to see Whistler standing so patiently right outside. "You're a damned good horse, Whistler. I'm sorry I ever laughed at how you go uphill."

He headbutted me affectionately, and I promised him extra grain if we found Swan and the mules.

When I turned him to take him back down the path, I found Swan and the mules waiting equally patiently at the door to the corral. Then I had to kiss her nose and the noses of the mules too. Gratitude and affection nearly overwhelmed me. Something had gone right.

Since I didn't have to go back down the path to Starvation, I took the time to comb all four beasts, check their hooves and pick them, and feed them an extra measure for being such good allies. The saddles and saddle pads would dry out in the tiny tack room, and if the mules and horses got cold, Red and I had built rough stables where they could shelter.

It took me four trips to get the supplies from the panniers back to the cabin, and I made all four trips with determination, resisting the impulse to tuck back down the tunnel to the grotto to make sure Timothy was still alive.

He rewarded my control with a surprise when I got back.

29

RECOVERY

TIMOTHY

I lost track of a lot of things once I fell off that bridge, but I definitely remembered two things: The blank astonishment when I left the world of sanity and fell into madness...and the sense that ten thousand thin acupuncture needles were being driven into every inch of me with vicious malice.

The water was so brutal that I didn't even register it as cold. It was beyond my power to understand. I remembered seeing Frank's face over me, I remembered the black nightmare of the log shifting loose, I remembered Frank threatening to tie me across the saddle.

I didn't remember anything else.

Until I had this otherworldly birthing experience, where I went from a drifting blackness to a very confusing warmth.

I knew now that it came from the hot springs Frank found, but all I remembered about those first moments was the slow realization that my skin was chilling the water it was in. I could only hold a single thought in my mind, and that thought was that if I moved a little, even just a hand—even a finger—then I could push the chilled water away and feel warmer water flow in to chill in its place.

My brain felt foggy, but I suppose the better analogy was that my brain was iced and slowly thawing in the heat. I became aware that arms were around me, holding me. I was safe.

Heat was pressing against my ears. That alone was the single most miraculous feeling I'd ever experienced.

Water lapped against my hairline. My scalp was giving up its chill. Heat was pouring into me through the thousands of capillaries just under the skin. My nose was still desperately cold, my cheekbones almost certainly covered in ice.

But everywhere else...

I wanted my boots off. My toes were still surrounded by ice.

Clothes folded around me in the water, clinging to me. But they clung with warmth, not with the pain of the creek.

And Frank was here. I knew it was her even before I opened my eyes.

When I did, I was floating on my back. I could roll my eyes up to see her behind me. She was staring into the darkness around us, seeing nothing. Her forehead was wrinkled. Girl was thinking hard.

She was so beautiful.

I told her I wanted to dip my face back, thaw the icicles still clinging to my skin. Tears leaked down her cheeks, and I was afraid she was in pain, but she wasn't. She was grateful that I was okay, which was far more than I could have hoped for, given how mad she'd been when I just went in up to my shoulder.

She tested my mental acuity, and apparently I got the answers right because she let me sit up. All my muscles felt like the day after a punishing workout, but everything was working.

Frank wanted to see to the horses, which made sense to me.

I didn't even know how she'd gotten me here to Aladdin's magic cave, but I felt sure horses were involved. When she got out, her nearly nude body was long and pale and delicious. I'd been thinking I would check after she left to make sure none of my bits had frozen off, but I didn't need to after that.

Dick working just fine, thank you.

After she left, I took an extremely long time to unlace one boot. Now I knew what it would feel like to be a hundred years old. Everything had to be done as fast as possible, which was agonizingly slow. When I pulled my foot from the soaking leather, I groaned in pleasure as the hot water wrapped around my bones. God, what bliss. So good I had to do the other boot.

I managed to get both boots out of the pool and onto the ledge and then sat for a while, trying to decide if I could get my coat off.

As it happened, sliding out of it was pretty easy. It was fighting to get it out of the water and onto the ledge that wore me out.

That left me in a few layers on top and bottom, but I could take my time. With each layer shed, I felt better, if fatigued by the effort. And I knew Frank would be back eventually, so I thought I'd better turn from physical to mental effort and compose the third verse of Whistler's song.

I sang it for her when she came back, proud that my voice sounded strong.

> If you take a dip, then you're a drip.
> You won't even need to strip.
> Your temp will fall straight down to zero.
> Fear not 'cause Frank's a fucking hero.

She offered me a full-throated laugh, which was all the appreciation I could ever want. "How are you feeling, Shakespeare?"

I sighed. "I'm better. A lot better. I don't think I want to get out, though."

"I don't think you should. I want you to eat something, though." She dragged my soggy coat away and sat beside me.

With a smile, she handed me...one of her chocolates.

"No way!" I protested. "Those are for you."

"Quick energy," she insisted. "The sugar will get to you very quickly. And you're also going to eat the last of the apples, and I'm cooking a stew that you're going to have to eat. Plus, drink all this water."

"I don't think I can do all that."

"Not all at once, no. But nibble the chocolate while I cut up the apple."

She fed me like a mama bird tends to its babies and I let her do it. I wasn't strong enough to object. I did have a good idea, though.

"Can you help me get this sweater off?"

She got wet in the process, but my chest felt so good, so free, without that sodden wool against me that I dared to ask her to help me take off more.

With clinical detachment, she did. When I was sitting in nothing but my boxer briefs, she gathered up my entire soggy wardrobe and told me she had a fire going in the cabin. She'd put my clothes in front of it to dry.

The whole time she was gone, I worked on deciding if the concept of a cabin in a cave was entirely normal and I just wasn't as thawed as I thought I was.

She was holding my inflated air mattress when she came back with my sleeping bag over one arm. "There's a fire in the cabin, but it's actually warmer back here because of the hot springs. I think you should sleep here when you're ready."

"What do you mean, there's a cabin? Is it in this cave?"

"How about I show you everything tomorrow? I'm hoping you feel strong enough to get out. You should sleep."

I had to agree. I was exhausted but not sure I could even get out of the water.

"Before you try, drift over to that corner," she said. "See how the water is flowing out there? That's our toilet. As long as you aim over the edge, you can pee or even poop into the water and nature will carry it far, far away."

"Dreamy." I smiled. "I was sort of wondering."

"I'll give you some privacy."

"Thanks. Don't go far. I'm not sure I can get out."

But in the end, I was able to boost myself out, and Frank gave me a rough old shirt as a towel. She turned her back when I peeled off my shorts, and I collapsed, naked, onto the mattress and pulled the unzipped sleeping bag over me.

And heaved a massive sigh of pleasure. I'd been cast out of solid, ancient lead. Astonishing I didn't pop the mattress under my weight and sink a bit into the floor.

"I'm really sorry," I said when Frank checked to make sure I was safe and dry. "I didn't mean to scare you."

"It wasn't your fault," she insisted. "I think it was more my fault. I wanted to tell you *I* was sorry."

"No, not at all. It was...my error." My words were slurring again, but this time it was from the rushing wave of fatigue. My eyelids were closing despite my intentions.

"No—" She was determined, but I never heard the end of it because sleep ambushed me.

I think it must have been much later when I felt her weight settle onto the mattress beside me. There. Now *that* was better.

And then I knew nothing at all until daylight was creeping down the tunnel, and Frank was gone.

A stack of clothes waited beside the mattress. I eyed them. Yes, they were my clothes. It was a silent reminder that I wasn't supposed to wander around Eden naked.

I sat up slowly and tested my strength. That worked out okay, so I carefully rose to my feet. Not bad. My muscles ached and my jaw was sore. There was a crimson ligature mark around my left wrist—she'd hauled me out on a rope, right? And I had an impressive bruise blooming in a stripe across both thighs. Wonder where that came from.

I took my time. Used the hot springs potty. Dressed and even attempted to rake my fingers through my hair in some primitive attempt at grooming.

Then I went slowly and gingerly up the tunnel to see if I could find Frank.

30

THE REVEAL

FRANK

I was tired.

I lay back on the stone and felt like I'd been very efficiently drained.

The morning was worth looking at. The air was cool and the clouds were fat and angry, but sunlight was shafting down like the finger of god. Daughtry Lake was a vivid blue, except for the black shadow cast by the storm clouds.

The panorama from the shelf outside the cabin was jaw-dropping. No matter how many times I gazed over the rough meadows, the thick forests, the towering mountains, I still couldn't get used to it. Millennia ago, the river had carved a wide basin among the steep cliffs. Elk grazed on the tough high-altitude grasses, and foxes hunted for the wily snowshoe rabbits. There had been a golden eagle aerie above the mine opening for as long as Red had been alive, and I saw the female soaring over the valley. Glad to see she was alive and not tormented by the bald eagles.

My favorite view.

My home.

And now Timothy was here.

Red had kept this place secret, even from his best friend Cal. I was the only one he'd ever brought here, and I knew why.

This place was untouched. I wanted to keep it that way.

But...Timothy was sleeping in the grotto.

Cal and Maria were going to sell the land.

I couldn't afford to buy even this parcel.

Clear-cutting for timber would reach this hidden valley eventually. Or Timothy would discover his mystery element and cut the mountain down.

And once he woke up, the secret would be told.

So, yeah. I was tired.

The wind picked up, but in the niche carved into the rock, I was protected. My coat and my coffee were enough to keep me warm. Warm enough. I closed my eyes and waited.

Timothy was quiet. Of course, there wasn't much to make noise when you were walking in socks on solid stone. So he was standing on the ledge before I knew he was awake.

I smiled to see that his jaw had literally dropped. He stared at the view, open-mouthed. That was a reaction I respected, so I left him in peace.

Eventually, he sat on the rocks next to me and sighed. "Where are we?" he asked.

I nodded to the valley stretched out below us. "That's Daughtry Lake, and there's Second Ford, which flows down to the Wild River. We're about a two-day ride back to the ranch."

His eyes were still moving. Still trying to come to grips with the view. I handed him the ancient binoculars that lived in the cabin. "Look up there on that cliff. See the mountain goats? No, not on the grassy part—look on the stone. Wait, look where I'm pointing. See the grass? Now look down. Keep going. Farther. Okay, see the—"

"Holy shit! What the hell are they holding on to?" I grinned. Mountain goats were fun to watch. "Jesus! There's a baby!"

"Yeah. It's that season."

He took the binoculars down and peered to see if he could see them without the optics. "We need to get you a better pair," he said carelessly.

He didn't see my wince. There was a lot about this place that could be upgraded with his kind of money, but even if I won the lottery, I wouldn't replace Red's binoculars. "Want some coffee? No, don't get up. I have your mug here."

He noticed that hot water was bubbling in the small basin beside my seat, the coffeepot sitting in the middle and staying warm.

"That's a hot spring too?"

I handed him the coffee. "Nah, this water is from a boiler set behind the fireplace. It would be cool if it was from a geyser, huh?"

He blew on the steam from his coffee and sipped cautiously, following the path of the water with his clever eyes. "That pipe goes right through the stone. Who put that together?" he asked.

I bumped up my eyebrows. "I'm a stonemason. Remember?"

He looked back at me, his eyes focusing on me. "I'm... what?"

I nodded. "I'm going to make pancakes. You ready for breakfast?"

He shifted on the rock to face me more directly and ignored my question. "Tell me about this place. Please tell me where the hell we are."

And thus would my secret come to an abrupt end.

"Red was going through old records one winter," I said, resigned. "This was back in the 1970s, and he was bored out of his mind. Big snow. This was back when Cal's father ran the Circle B, and Red was the hand left on the property to take care of the horses in winter. Anyway, he found a cracked old ledger that said when my forebears first arrived here, an old guy in the town told them there was a mine by what was then called Second Fork Lake, but it was played out. No gold, no nothing."

I eyed Timothy, hoping he'd make the connection and tell me what the hell mineral *he* was looking for. He nodded at me to continue.

"So that spring, Red went looking for the mine. He'd been up here plenty of times, looking for the old Daughtry homestead. It wasn't our land anymore, but he still wanted to find the spot. Back then, the trees here were smaller, and he spotted a hole in the cliff from that end of the lake. There are lots of natural caves around here and he investigated every one he came across, but this was the one that turned out to be the mine."

"Did he hike up this cliff?" Timothy looked over the edge to the drop. "Was he part mountain goat?"

I smiled. "Happens he *was* part mountain goat. But he found that the original miners had hacked out a path. That end of the terrace goes around the mountain to the back side, which eventually gets you to Starvation Creek."

"No thank you. Seen enough of that."

I huffed my agreement. "And when he finally got here, he found the dregs of a mine. You saw the woodstove inside?" Timothy nodded. "Cast iron. Weighs a damned ton. How they got that out here, I have no idea. They were tough, though."

"I guess."

"Of course, Red noticed that the mine had a surprise inside."

"A hot tub."

I smiled at the description. "A hot tub. Right. Red was young back then. He decided he wanted to make the cave into his home away from home. So he started building. This wooden wall across the opening"—I knocked on the logs behind me—

"was his first project. He told me there were lots of animals that liked the heat, and he had to discourage them."

"Animals?"

"He said it took a few years to persuade the rattlers to nest somewhere else."

"Shit!" Timothy looked at the terrace with new eyes, wondering if he had missed something.

"Still a little cold for them. Snakes love to bask out here, though. We get along fine. They don't bother us, we don't bother them." I heard the *us* with a pang. The last time I was out here, that meant me and Red. Now it seemed to mean me and Timothy, and that was...sad.

"If you say so. Snakes are cool." He still looked a little concerned, and I respected that response too.

"So, he built the wall over the entrance, alerted the former occupants that there was a new sheriff in town, and started moving a few things in every time he came out here."

"He did an amazing job. That cabin...it's so snug. I'm very impressed."

"Thanks." I smiled.

He cocked his head. "Wait. Was Red a stonemason too?"

"He was more of a carpenter."

"So who built that beautiful fireplace in there?" I smiled modestly. "And this rock we're sitting on...did it start out shaped into a perfect lounging spot?"

Modestly, I allowed that I'd done a fair amount of chiseling in my day. He wasn't the only one to hack up stone.

"And you let me wreck my hands when you could have gotten those fragments for me?"

I shrugged. "You knew I was a stonemason. You could have asked."

He made a noise that expressed contempt and admiration. "Go on. What did he do next?"

"I'll skip over a bunch of slow trips over the years and get to

Red's sister. Or rather, Red's niece, who married a drunk. Nice guy, but you know. Liked his beer."

"Yeah?"

"Oh yeah. So one night, the niece's husband came home from the bar by way of driving into a little old lady who'd gotten it into her mind that she had to get an ice cream from town. Word was she had a tiny bit of Alzheimer's, but that didn't stop anyone from realizing that my father was a menace. He was convicted of vehicular homicide and sent up to the big house. I was six at the time."

"God." He was listening carefully, all his attention trained on me.

"Yeah. His sentence keeps getting extended because he gets involved in shit-bad decisions. Like failed jailbreaks. And my mother sort of fell apart. She didn't object to beer much herself. It soon became clear that she wasn't able to care for herself, much less a snotty little kid, so Red brought me to the ranch. I followed him around like a shadow."

His mouth was curved into a thoughtful smile. "I'll bet you were cute."

"Adorable. Always angry, never let an argument die, full of grudges. Wouldn't follow an order from anyone...except Red. Who let me take out my rage on hay bales. And then taught me that I couldn't be angry with horses. And started letting me ride drogue on his backcountry treks."

"He became your father."

I scratched at my neck. "Yeah. He really did. And I think about it now, and I can't believe he was so kind. You know, he wanted to live out here during the winter, but he had to keep his place in town because I had to go to school. He never asked to be a father, but he sacrificed everything for me."

Timothy pursed his lips in thought. "Not sure it was entirely one-sided. Who came up with this system to keep the coffeepot warm?"

The thought lightened my mood. "Yeah, that was pretty much me. We worked on it together, and it tickled Red. And after I graduated and went to tech school, I carved us these rocks to sit on."

Timothy looked down. "So these *were* carved? I thought this was natural."

"Thanks. That's the goal. If anyone ever spots the grotto from down there, this place has to look like no human has ever been up here. So that's why we're sitting on rocks and not on some folding lounge chairs."

He laughed, delighted. "That's brilliant!"

"Thanks." I patted the stone fondly. "Red did a spell in the mines in his youth, so he did the big work and I did the fine stuff. We carved out those sleeping shelves together, and I built the fireplace behind the woodstove. And I figured out how to make the bathing pool—the hot tub."

"What do you mean, make the hot tub?"

I waved a hand, trying to encompass the issue. "The hot spring is actually too hot to sit in. The miners left an old tin bathtub in a wooden frame. They used a pail to fill the tub and let it cool down enough to sit in, and Red liked that—except the tin had rusted, and he said it was hard on his ass."

Timothy chuckled. "I'll bet."

"So I suggested two changes. First, I got Red to carve out a big hole in that cave, and then I used my masonry to tile it in smooth stones. I made the bench, too, so we could soak in peace."

"I thought it was a natural ledge!"

"Good. I like it that way. Then I rerouted a stream. It used to create a waterfall over the entry path, but we hacked a new watercourse, and now it flows through the grotto and down the natural channel the hot springs carved over the ages. We think it goes underground for a mile or more and then ends up down there at Daughtry. Maybe. I added a diverter so we could adjust the temperature, and then we broke down the wall between the hot spring and the hole. Hot tub created."

He looked at me wide-eyed. "You're a fucking genius!"

"That's true," I agreed.

"No, really. I think that's inspired. Your cave has both hot and cold running water. Literally running. And it certainly saved my life yesterday."

I inhaled at the reminder. "Yeah. I guess it did."

"Shit. This is amazing."

"I know." We sat in silence. The wind shifted, blowing into the niche. "You have no coat on."

"It's still wet. Thanks for hanging it up for me."

I grabbed the coffeepot. "Let's go inside. I think it's going to snow again."

"So we're staying for the day?"

I looked at the clouds. "Yeah. We're not taking any more risks."

"Fine with me. Spa day."

31

A GOOD NUTRITIOUS BREAKFAST

TIMOTHY

Frank made pancakes on the woodstove. It shouldn't have felt any different than every other meal we'd had on these treks. She was the trail guide, she took care of cooking. That's the way it was.

But now we were inside. There were walls around us and a door that didn't entirely keep out the cold, white light of a snowy day. We weren't hunkered around a campfire. No, she was busy at the stove, and I sat waiting on the rock ledge that made what she called the sleeping shelf, a long, skinny table in front of me.

It felt peculiarly domestic. Like I was the 1950s husband come home from work, waiting for the wife to serve up my dinner.

This would, I knew, infuriate Frank. I cast around for a conversation topic that would distract us both. There was plenty left to still discuss, but when I saw her move the kerosene lamp to get rid of a shadow on the frying pan, I spoke without thinking. "This is why you want a mechanical engineering degree."

For me, it was light dawning. For her, it was a shrug. "Yeah. Obviously."

"And why you liked the idea of hydroelectric power."

She flipped a pancake with a practiced flick of her wrist. "I wouldn't mind a freezer in here. Red used to take a few deer during the hunting season, but most of it we had to pack out in time to get it to the ranch before it rotted. Or attracted predators."

There was a set of shelves tucked into a niche behind her. I saw canned foods as well as ancient, faded canisters with tight lids marked SALT and SUGAR, but it wasn't much of a pantry. A few books tilted at crazy angles. Which novels or how-tos would Red (or Frank) have kept on hand? I made a note to explore later. "With a battery system, you could run some lights too."

She nodded. "There's a lot I could do if I could just figure out how to engineer things. I'd love to install a water purifier so we didn't have to treat every single sip. I'd also like to calculate how much stone I can remove so I can carve a tunnel to the corral."

"There's a corral?"

She slid a short stack of pancakes in front of me. "Where did you think Swan and Whistler were? Do you have no loyalty to Clop or Daisy?"

"I dunno." She had little packets of maple syrup, and I poured one on the flapjacks. "Clop was the one who backed me into the stream, so..."

"Forgive him. He and Daisy followed Swan all the way to the corral yesterday by themselves."

"They did? That's pretty amazing."

"Well, Swan has been here, like, a million times, so I guess it's not that surprising."

I shook my head, my mouth full of deliciousness. "That's a good horse," I mumbled. "Whistler too."

"Good horse," she agreed. "Anyway, I want to be able to get to them without going outside if the path is icy. It's a long way down. And that's another thing. Can I engineer a safer route up here that still keeps the secret?" She came to a halt and stared into the middle distance. "I suppose it doesn't matter now. Cal and Maria are selling. This won't be my home for long."

"Oh, come on now. I could buy the ranch."

"Yeah, but you'll only do it if you find your mystery element, and then you're going to be worse than the clear-cutters."

"No, I won't! I'd take care of this place!"

Her expression said *I'll humor you now, but I don't believe it.* "Okay," she said. "That's good." She sounded way too depressed.

I patted the bench next to me. "Leave those. Eat these with me. Come sit down. It'll be okay."

She ignored me but slid her pancakes onto a cracked plate and took her place at the table. She picked at her food, uninterested in eating.

"You know how I forgot you were a stonemason?" I asked.

"Yeah?"

"Well, you forget what I do."

"I know what you do. You bully people on Capitol Hill."

"Yes, I do—and I'm good at it. But why do I bully them?" She looked at me blankly, so I finished the thought. "Because my family corporation is in real estate. We buy land. That's what we do." I cocked an eyebrow significantly, and she frowned.

"You...you buy land?"

"We buy land," I confirmed. "We also sell it, but we all have our personal portfolios."

She shifted to face me. "What are you talking about? What are you saying?"

The depression had faded under her growing attention. "How many acres did you say the Circle B was?"

"Twenty-seven thousand."

"Okay. Ranch land...say that's an average of two thousand dollars an acre. Timber lands go for more. We'll say twenty-five hundred. So, the entire ranch is worth...what is that? 67.5?"

"Million?"

I grinned. "Yeah, million."

"Shit." Her face fell again, and I put my hand on hers to regain her attention.

"You know I'm a billionaire, right?" She frowned. "Don't think badly of me—it's not my fault. As soon as I passed our company finance exams, I received my legacy of three hundred and fifty million. That's just part of being a Babcock." I certainly had her attention now. "Even if I didn't increase that amount over the years—which I certainly have—the price of the Circle B is about a fifth of that."

She drew back, her brow furled. "That's a lot of very big numbers," she said weakly.

"I know. And it's not polite to talk about money. But I'm telling you that if Cal and Maria want to sell, they should come to me first. I love this land—and that view." I gestured to the closed door that was blocking the panorama.

Despite my reassurances, Frank looked more alarmed than ever. "And what if you find your element?"

I shook my head. "Let's deal with that when it happens."

"And what if you don't find the element? Then you'll go somewhere else..."

"Would you quit making trouble? I told you, I increased my fortune. You don't hang around Washington, D.C. without picking up some useful tips. I can buy the Circle B and also get wherever has a repository of mol—um."

Her anxiety broke and she laughed at me. "You might as

well tell me. You now know every secret I've ever had. Tell me. What are you looking for? Because I know it begins with *mol*."

It occurred to me in a flash that I didn't *want* to have any secrets from Frank. "Molybdenum," I said. "There's a guy at the U.S. Patent Office who says they're in discovery for a battery that runs on molybdenum."

"What the hell is molybdenum?"

"You mean besides a really funny word? Molybdenum is a mildly worthless mineral extracted from solid stone. Right now, it costs twenty-two dollars a pound. In six months?"

"How much?"

"Well, iridium is going for about seven thousand five hundred per pound. Molybdenum is going to be bigger than that."

"Holy...I mean...shit!"

"Yep." I leaned back in satisfaction. "So, the idea of spending a few million on a ranch? I'm just not that worried about it, Frank."

She watched me, her oddly beautiful eyes serious. "Really? Will you buy the ranch? And protect the grotto?"

I grinned. "I thought you were going to protect the grotto. If you win the bet, I mean."

A smile began and slowly bloomed on her face. "I am fucking going to win that bet! Oh, this is so great!"

She launched herself at me, throwing her arms around my neck. Laughing, I caught her, relishing the feeling of her breasts against me as she laughed. *Oh, you do feel good, Frank.*

She pulled away and I let go, but she didn't sit back. She paused, her face so close I could feel the heat of her blush.

"How do you feel?" she breathed. She was watching my mouth.

A bolt of adrenaline shot through me.

"I feel good. How do you feel, Frank?"

I realized I was watching her lips, too, when she smiled at my question. "I feel really good. Really, really good."

My lust and my dick were rising, but I didn't dare anger her now by making an incorrect assumption. "Is this because I said I'd buy the ranch?"

She sat back on her heels but didn't slide her arms down from my neck. Her grin got cocky. "You mean, am I interested in you because you're so stinking rich?"

"Well, yeah."

"I'm interested in you, Timothy, because you make me happy. The money isn't the point."

"Oh." I felt stupidly glad. "That's good."

She slid a hand forward but only to trace a finger around my ear. It sent shivers through me. "Timothy," she said, leaning forward and putting her lips up close to my other ear.

"What?" I said thickly.

"Tell me you have condoms."

My hands on her ribs slid without my conscious command to draw her up and into me. "Honey, I always have condoms with me."

"That's really good news." I felt her lips close over the lobe of my ear. There must have been a direct nerve roadway to my cock because it felt like she was sucking on something else. I groaned and tilted to pull my ear away—but only so I could find her mouth with mine.

The kiss taught me the difference between Frank uncertain and Frank sure of herself. She inhaled me. I felt drawn into her, felt that I needed her closer still. The taste of her tongue, the lure of her lips, the tease of her teeth all lit up my nerve endings. I had to pull her to me, my hands on her beautiful ass, to see if I could stop my heart from exploding out of my chest.

It wasn't until I felt the cold stone against my back that I realized we'd fallen backward. Had she pushed me down? Was there anything more exciting than that?

Yes—there was. There was Frank swinging a long leg over to straddle me. God, she was going to make me come like a kid, miles too soon. Who needed a condom when you erupted in your boxers?

I fought to calm down, to exert some self-control while Frank writhed against my groin, applying a fraction of the pressure my cock needed. She lifted from the kiss, and we both gasped for more air. "God," she said. "You feel so good."

Her eyes were closed, lost in the sensations, and I was capable only of echoing her words. "So good." I just had to trust that she knew I meant *she* felt good.

She inhaled sharply when I slid my hands from her ass, and we both waited, breathless, to see which way I'd head next. I could slip my hands down, riding over her thighs until my thumbs met at the seam of her trousers, where I knew I'd feel damp, hot cloth.

Or I could be a grown-up. Take my time. Slide my hands up those lean ribs until I filled my hands with the curve of her...

...Oh, heaven. Her breasts fit into my hands, custom-made for curve to fit curve. She leaned forward, pushing into my hands, and I grunted at her responsiveness.

Her nipples hardened against my palms. She moaned and threw her head back. I groaned and wondered if the top of my head was going to lift off my skull entirely.

She leaned back, easing the pressure of my hands, and I felt a bolt of panic. Was she having second thoughts?

She wasn't. She was reaching for her hem, crossing both hands over her belly to grab hoodie and T-shirt in one and stripping both over her head. "I need to feel your hands on my skin," she said and reached behind her for the clasp.

My movement came straight from balls that were tender and radiating need. I sat up and caught her ribs, carrying her over in one move so I could lie over her. "Wait," I groaned. "Wait. Just a minute. Let me just—"

Her hands were still behind her, arching her breasts up to my touch. I shifted until I could caress one peaked tip with my mouth. Frank was a plain-cotton kind of girl, and I couldn't have been happier about it. With just one finger, I tugged down on the cup until the nipple, pink as a rose, popped free to the air.

I had to suck on it—to flick that tight little bud with my tongue.

Frank moaned and shifted. The tension of the fabric eased and the bra slid down. Her arms came around me, and she held my head to her. "Do it again," she said. "Again. With your tongue. Oh yes..." With the bra unfastened, I could divide my attention between both crests, licking and sampling and nibbling as inspiration took me. "Too many clothes," she breathed. Her hands rucked up my shirt and sweater, and I stopped caressing her long enough to fight out of both. The air on my back suddenly cool, the sensitivity on my chest suddenly hot.

The bra disappeared. Her hands on my face, she guided me to one breast and then the other. I went willingly. We fell into this madness so quickly—like falling into a creek—that there was no time for logic or wise reflection. There was only skin and kiss and move and feel. Only heat and tingles and the growing drumbeat of need that might just have been my own thundering heart.

Frank pushed on my shoulders. I lifted to find out what she wanted, and she easily rolled me over so I was on my back. The cold made me gasp.

"You didn't have mattresses on your sleeping shelf?" I asked.

"We filled them each summer"—she was kissing my chest —"with fresh hay. Sorry."

As she seemed to be kissing a path downward, I felt no need to express regrets. I'd already forgotten the faint, distant chill. She reached my stomach, and I placed my hands lightly on her luxurious hair. Not to push her head down—never that—but to ride in bliss if she headed south of her own accord.

Which she did.

My toes curled in my socks when she kissed my belly button, fingers fumbling with the fly of my trousers. "Want help?" I croaked when the thick wool fabric defeated her fingers.

"Let me do it. Please." She rose to bring both hands to the situation, and I imagined all the polite, proper responses I would have made if I hadn't suddenly lost the ability to speak.

The tab surrendered. She slid the zip down slowly, teasing me with the sensation over my cock.

"Timothy," she said, not suffering from my inability to speak. "Mm. You really are a billionaire, aren't you?"

She surprised a laugh out of me. I wanted to tell her that my cock was no bigger than anyone else's but that she'd inspired me to new degrees of girth and hardness, but I was struck dumb by the anticipation and excitement that was crushing me. I managed a grunt. "Uh," I said.

She liked that. I could feel the smile in her mouth when she slid her lips over the head.

Fireworks. Electrocution. Wetness.

My fingers were fists in her hair. I was probably pulling, but she didn't seem to mind. She slid wetly, hotly, along my length once. Twice. Three times.

That was the point of absolute no return. I jerked myself up and pulled from her mouth. "You're going to make me come. Come so hard. What do...what do we want here?"

Her eyes were shining, and her lips...oh god, they were red. From sucking me. "I think we want the condom, then," she said, and I had a panicked moment when I knew where my stash was in my D.C. townhouse and in my Manhattan apartment, but where were the rubbers when I was in Frank's secret sex grotto?

Unable to speak coherently, I unwrapped from her and nearly tripped over my trousers when I lunged for Clop's panniers. One hand holding up my pants, I fumbled until I found my shaving kit and fought out the slippery little foil packet. I bumped the hell out of my hip when I whipped back to Frank and hit the breakfast table, but who was counting one more incomprehensible bruise?

She'd taken the opportunity to heartlessly, ruthlessly skin out of her clothes and lie on that cold stone without a stitch on. The sight stopped me cold in admiration.

And concern.

"Let me get the air mattress," I said, now able to verbalize. "I don't want you getting cold on that stone."

She rose on an elbow. "Then get that on," she said, nodding to my hand, "and let me ride."

Oh yes.

God, yes.

Yes, please.

32

EXCELLENT RIDING WEATHER

FRANK

I swung a leg over Timothy's hips to line myself up with that impressive cock when he insisted on stopping long enough to grab discarded clothes to slip under my knees.

"I don't want you to scrape yourself on this stone," he said, his concern melting the last resistance in my heart. Yes, he was cocky and arrogant and had no idea the power that even a little money could hold over most people.

But he was also the man who'd brushed French fries off a seat. Who cared about my knees. It would have killed him if I'd said it out loud, but Timothy Babcock was a nice guy.

The realization left me smiling from a mouth suddenly dry with the need to impale myself—to fill myself—with the strength of him. Still, experience was a hard teacher.

I had a hand wrapped around his cock, seconds away from seating him properly, when I paused until he opened his eyes and saw me.

"This doesn't mean...doesn't mean you own me," I insisted.

He nodded. "I don't own you. You don't own me."

"That's right." I was satisfied, save for the slight objection I felt at the thought that he wasn't owned either.

But that was easily dismissed. I centered him and eased down, pushing myself open on his thick cock.

He gritted his teeth and screwed his eyes shut in concentration, which was good because it took me a moment to get all the way down on him. Twice I had to stop and pull out just enough to inspire a new rush of wetness within me, but I finally sat down on him.

The heat of him. The penetration of him. The fullness.

I sat straighter, thrilled at the slight change in angle, and threw back my head. My hair tickled my ass. Was it teasing his balls too?

The thought of teasing him was motivational. I put my hands down to his ribs and lifted my hips to slide his cock outward. That was good.

Then I sat again. And that was also good.

I knew enough about sex to know that a slow build brought a better orgasm. I, like most women, needed a little time to get into the pattern.

Except...

Except...

I was riding faster. Pacing along. Then loping along. And then I was running away with my mount, finding the speed and impact that centered every nerve ending at my core. The rest of the world faded away. There was only Timothy. His cock. His hands, hard on me but not hard enough.

"I swear," he gasped, "I can do better. I swear. But I'm afraid —I think I'm—God, Frank—"

I nodded. "Me too. Hang on. Just another...just a minute. Hang on."

He shouted, and his thumb came down hard on my clit. Then I was shouting, too, cresting waves of heat and energy like a waterfall slamming into the receiving ground.

Once the wave crested, I could only exhale, my breath forming around the words *oh* and *my* and *god*. I collapsed on his chest, limp.

Blissed.

Stoned on the relaxation.

I drifted until I realized his arms were around me. "Hey. Take a breath."

"Huh?"

"You stopped breathing."

"No I didn't."

"If you say so. Nice to have you breathing now." He was smiling. I could hear it in his voice.

"Shh," I said. "I'm wrung out."

"Lift your ass just long enough for me to get this condom."

That, I could do. I didn't know what he did with it—I kept my eyes closed and he never moved out from under me—but I suspected his T-shirt was used to hide something sort of nasty.

But that was fine. I lowered my hips again to rest against his now-calm cock. "I might fall asleep," I admitted. "If only I wasn't kind of cold."

He shifted under me, and I snapped out of my doze with a start. He sat and then stood easily, cradling me in his arms.

"Hey! Put me down! You'll hurt yourself!"

"Hurt myself," he scoffed. "Right. Don't insult me, cowgirl."

The lamp was still over by the stove and didn't shed much light down the tunnel, but the walk was short and he was unlikely to trip, so I relaxed and enjoyed the journey. I put my arms around his neck and spent the brief time kissing his neck. That made his fingers tighten on me.

I gave him credit for the graceful way he managed to sit on

his ass with his feet in the water and then ease down, never letting go of me. We settled into the hot water, and I sighed at the wonder of it.

"Damn, that feels good," I murmured, my head on his chest.

"Damn, it does," he agreed, sitting on the underwater bench. "Did you say there was a way to make the water hotter?"

I tried to reach the diverter with my foot but couldn't without leaving his arms. "Over there. See it? Push it this way."

He shifted, slinging down a little to reach the freshwater door and ease it shut.

"Leave a little trickling in. We could get stuck."

"We'd die happy. I'll open it again when we're ready."

I sighed. He leaned his head back against the ledge, and we melted into the heat. Ahh.

Eventually, the arm under my knees relaxed and I shifted, floating my legs out behind him and turning so I was ass-up in the water, linked to him by my looped arms. I rested my chin on his shoulder to keep from going under entirely. It was almost too hot to bear. I loved it.

An idea occurred to me, and I opened my mouth and it slipped out like a colt. "If I had power," I said drowsily.

"Could be hydroelectric or geothermal," he offered sleepily.

"Right. Solar too. If I had power, I could run a winch on the ceiling."

"That ceiling?"

He was looking up, but I was looking at his ear. "That ceiling," I agreed.

"For what?"

"We could attach a bench to it," I said, "on long chains."

"Okay." He meant *I'm following you—go on* but didn't have the energy to say the words. I heard him anyway.

"Submerge the bench. Sit on the bench. Bake like this until the meat is about to fall off the bone."

"I'm getting close to that now."

"Want to get out?" My foot was now brushing against the diverter. I could cool us off quickly.

"No."

"Me either. So we sit on the bench and roast. And when we're just about to expire from the heat, I push the button and engage the winch and it lifts us from the water into the cooler air."

He was silent in the faint light, the hot spring's current stirring the water gently. "And on a track. So it would slide us over the water to the air mattress. We could fall into it and recover."

"Nice." Almost time for cold water. Almost, but not quite. "Not a bench," I said.

"No bench? I like the bench."

"Slats of wood linked together. Like a bench but flat."

"A bed in the water?"

"No. A...a shape..." I was too relaxed to come up with the right words. "The winch makes the shape of a bench. Each slat can be raised or lowered independently. So bench shape when bench needed."

"Flat shape on air mattress." He got it. I loved that he got it.

"Lower us to mattress. Sleep on bench."

"So good. Make that."

"Yes. I will make that."

"My brain is cooking."

"Me too." I flicked my foot out and the cool water slipped into the pool's current, curling around reddened flesh and flaccid muscles.

"That feels good."

"So good."

"Lie here more."

"Yes. More."

I nudged the diverter a little wider and our bathwater became more refreshing. I was able to push back from Timothy and find the bottom with my feet. I'd made the pool deep. It came up to my ribs when I was standing, and Timothy had recovered enough to eye the view with interest.

"Come on, billionaire. Let's go nap on the air mattress."

"Oh. You think we're going to nap, do you?"

"How many condoms did you bring?"

"Enough for now. Help me out."

33

ALL GOOD THINGS

TIMOTHY

When I packed the luxurious hand cream, I'd done it as a joke to go along with chocolates on the trail guide's pillow. I certainly hadn't considered how enjoyable it would be to stroke that lotion onto every curve of my trail guide's supple body.

We nibbled on the last of the chocolates and drank the two splits of champagne, cooled in the mountain stream Frank had cleverly diverted into her grotto. We filled the pool with the kind of bodily fluids that would have been disgusting if the endless current didn't continually wash us and the pool clean.

We talked. We slept. We kissed. A lot. And we wore no clothes at all for forty-eight hours. I'd thought the entire valley was beautiful before. Now I knew it was my own personal garden of Eden.

But duty called, as it always did. All good things had to come to an end. Not only did I have a gala to attend, but Frank said Cal and Maria would send out search parties if we didn't appear on time.

Reluctantly, I yanked that ill-fitting door open that morning to a surprising burst of sunshine and soft air. The blizzard had given up while we were otherwise occupied, and the spectacular valley had gone back to April.

"I want to stay," I admitted. "I've barely gotten to know Daughtry Lake."

Frank smiled at me from Swan's back. "I understand that. This is an incredible place. Buy it from Cal and Maria and you'll have all the time you want."

I smiled back at her, flush with a deep affection that overwhelmed me.

We started down a trail that was little more than a deer path, but Swan and Whistler picked their way down with relative ease, our mules following docilely. We passed a rock outcropping and I made Frank stop.

"Show me, stonemason. Give me a demonstration. Here's a good place for a sample."

Smirking, she took my chisel and shovel in practiced hands and fractured out the perfect size with about three quick taps.

"That was so fast that I'm actually impressed. And mad that you haven't been doing that all along." I took the sample, but she held on to it until I bent and ducked under her hat to kiss her.

She held on and pulled me to her, and then the horses had to wait. We pushed our trousers down to our knees, and I grabbed one of the last of my condoms so we could fuck up against that rock wall. I was learning what turned her on the most by this time, and I drew out her pleasure until she clung to me, shrieking, when she came.

"Oh god," she said once she was rational again. "You're going to scare the horses!"

The horses were placid. Clop and Daisy were lipping some spring leaves, and Swan and Whistler were resting with one back foot up on the edge of the hoof. They were all but asleep.

I marked the sample *Scared Horses* and showed her to make her laugh. Then, although she didn't need my help, I boosted her into her saddle for the pleasure of feeling her ass.

She winced as she seated herself. "I have been ridden hard today." She grinned at me.

I, on the other hand, felt great. All my joints had been oiled. My spine was newly supple. My head was clear. I admit that I missed the excellent hat that had gone overboard when I fell into Starvation Creek, but the view had gotten a lot better since then anyway. I wouldn't want anything to block the sight of Frank, riding in front of me with the grace of a lady centaur.

We camped on the Wild River and made one last attempt to pop my air mattress. "After this," I said, holding up the final condom, "I'm eating you and you're eating me until we get to a drugstore."

"What a shame," Frank said sarcastically. "Let's do that first. You know, to practice."

It was the best backcountry trek on record.

But all good things must come to an end. Real life was waiting when we got back to the ranch, and it was annoyed I'd been ignoring it.

Maria Buckley was waiting at the barn when we rode in, Cal lingering behind her.

"Timothy Babcock!" she yelled as soon as we got close. "I am not your secretary!"

As a greeting, this was one I wasn't familiar with, but I tried to keep up. "And I'm not your auto mechanic, Maria. How are you doing?"

She was grumpy. The chocolate had only bought me so much goodwill, then. "My ear is about to fall off from taking phone calls. You get into this office right now and handle this. Before some senator calls out the National Guard. Good lord, who could possibly need anyone so badly?"

She followed me into the office, berating me until Cal

hooked an elbow through her arm and pulled her into a do-si-do. "Good whiskey," he said to me with a nod.

I nodded back as he led her out to the horses and Frank. Lesson learned: Eighty-four–year–old Macallan was a longer-lasting bribe than Italian chocolates.

The list of messages Maria had taken started with my assistant Johnston trying to find me. I could see the exact moment, noted in Maria's careful handwriting, when Johnston caved and told Baldrick Starmer where I was, because he'd begun calling with irritating regularity. I could imagine those calls. *Is he back yet? Not until Wednesday, sir. How about now? Nope, still not Wednesday. What if he's dead? We'll know on Wednesday.*

The most irritating part was that I knew exactly what he wanted. No matter his excuses, in the end he wanted to party out of the public eye. His wife was delighted when he didn't head home during congressional recesses, but the man had been identified as a drunk at a D.C. nightspot, so now he was on a Puritanical streak, publicly lecturing on purity and restraint. Which, of course, meant he wanted me to host him at my town-house. With some friends. And a lot of booze.

The entire situation suddenly wearied me.

My father had called, as had Tabby's assistant. Jean-Claude left a long message about taking the train from D.C. and setting up my Manhattan kitchen. His rant about the aubergines that had been delivered entirely defeated Maria's ability to spell.

I called my assistant Johnston first. He was an officious little shit who kept his ear to the ground in Washington. His gossip was invaluable. Good enough that I kept approving the bar tabs he submitted for reimbursement. He was nearly in tears when I finally got him on the phone, and I was treated to a ten-minute monologue about all the things any normal idiot could have handled in my absence.

Outside the open office door, Frank laughed at something

Cal said. They were unpacking the mules. Most of the supplies went into the barn. My things had already been stowed in the bed of my truck. Frank was caught in a sunbeam like the star had just entered the production.

God, she was beautiful.

"So, do I tell Kelly you'll make the donation? Mr. Babcock? Are you there?"

I'd missed something. "I'll be back in D.C. on Monday, after the gala. Handle it for now."

"Yes, but you'll call Starmer? And Westhouse. And Miller, and Thompson—and Henry says he's got a line on a cave-diving expedition in North Korea if you're willing to risk their Navy."

The idea of that trip had jazzed me a few weeks ago. Scuba-diving off the coast of the dangerously reclusive Hermit Nation seemed like a thrill. Now it sounded...stupid.

"I'll call him when I get home to New York. Anything else?"

"Everything else!"

"Anything that won't wait until I answer some more of these calls?"

"Call Starmer! He's going to blow a blood vessel!"

In fact, I left Starmer with his high blood pressure while I called my father, who was unamused when I told him I'd accidentally lost the phone in a raging river.

"You should have gone in after it," he said. "Those things are indestructible. Can you get it back?"

Go into a river swollen with glacial snowmelt? I'd learned so much in eight days. "I'll get another one. I'm heading to the airport. Home in six or seven hours."

"Good. It's about time. I'm tired of doing your job for you when you're supposed to be doing my job!"

I scrubbed my hand over my face. What would happen if I just dragged Frank back to the grotto?

"I've got to go, Dad. I've got a list of senators to call."

"Better you than me! Some of those guys are very determined!"

Didn't I know it.

In fact, I was unable to pick that burden up again. I opted to text Starmer when I got back to my laptop in the plane. But there was one more call I had to face.

Vaughn answered with a grin in his voice. "Shit, I'm glad you're back in cell phone range, Baby-cock!"

"I hear you've been plagued by my fans."

"It's like a great big Where's Waldo, brother. The whole world is searching for you. Glad you didn't get swept down the Wild River. Have a good time? The place is pretty amazing, right?"

"Vaughn."

All it took was me saying his name to get his attention. "What? What is it? What happened? Oh, shit. It's Frank, right? Goddamn it."

Vaughn was scary smart sometimes. "I'm sorry. I sure didn't mean for it to happen."

"Oh, fuck. I never should have set you two up." I had nothing to say to that. I definitely understood his reaction. "Well, shit. I'm never going to stand a chance, am I? How serious is it?"

My eyes went back out the door to where Frank was laughing as she carried my samples box to my truck, her arms drawn straight by the box. She was canted backward to balance against the weight, and Cal scuttled alongside her, attempting to take the box from her. *Girl doesn't want your help*, I thought.

"I'm not sure how serious. But I like her. A lot."

"And does she like you a lot?"

I sighed. "I hope so. I think so."

Vaughn cursed some more and then gave up. "Mazel tov, man. Invite me to the wedding."

I laughed. "You'll be at the gala on Saturday?"

"The department store thing? Yeah, I've got my tuxedo all ready. You going?"

"With Frank."

"God. I'm going to have to look at her hanging on you, huh? Fine. I'll up my dosage of depression meds."

If Vaughn suffered from depression, it was news to me. "Thanks for being cool, man."

He blew a raspberry into the phone, making me wince at the noise. "That's me. Always a bridesmaid, never a bride."

"There are any number of women in Manhattan who would love to make you a bride, man."

"Introduce me to some at the gala. Someone like Frank."

"She's one of a kind."

"I *know*. I was the one who found her!"

"I'll set you up with someone great."

"Taking scraps from Baby-cock. This is what my life has come to. Call that blowhard senator, will you? I've talked to his chief of staff so often that I think we're besties now."

"On it now. See you Saturday."

"You're an asshole, Baby-cock."

"I am. But you're still Coxless."

I hung up feeling lighter. Vaughn was a good guy. I'd set him up with someone if he wasn't such a slut.

I found Maria brushing Clop and wrapped an arm around her. "Maria, don't answer your phone for half an hour. I haven't called the senators yet, but..." She turned to rail at me in objection. I held up a hand. "I'll get in touch with them as soon as we get to the plane, and after that they'll leave you alone. But if I start calling them now, we'll never get home." I planted a kiss on her gray, curling hair. "In thanks for being my secretary this week, I'm going to send you the best chocolate you've ever eaten. And more whiskey for Cal."

She grumbled and darted a look at me. "And me. Whiskey for me. He won't share."

"Is that because you didn't share your chocolates with him?"

"He doesn't even like chocolate!"

"I do too!" Cal was grooming Whistler and stuck his head around the horse's large rump. "You're just too greedy to share!"

"Oh, pshaw." Maria scoffed in the way of a long-married couple. "As if you wouldn't be just as happy with a regular old candy bar!"

Their squabbling made me smile and raised a slight envy in me. What would it be to know someone that well? To argue and bitch and know that they didn't take it seriously?

It wasn't until Frank and I were driving down the road that I realized I hadn't brought up the question of buying the ranch. But Frank had forgotten about it too. I'd deal with it back in Manhattan.

Once onboard the jet, Frank wouldn't sit next to me. "This is where I sit," she said from her place across from me.

I patted the chair next to me. "Come over here. These seats recline to bed levels. Bet I can make you come so hard you scream at thirty-thousand feet."

She looked over her shoulder nervously. "That guy will hear you."

"Max? He'll stay away. Come over."

She shook her head at me. "I'm telling you right now that there is not even a hint of the exhibitionist in me. If that's your kink, then you should know that now."

"So, no joining the mile-high club?" She rolled her eyes, and I was disappointed. Still, a long trip with Frank was better than a long trip without her. I unbuckled and switched seats to sit next to her. "Fine. I'll be good. Want to watch me email a bunch of senators?"

34

A DIFFERENT HIGH VIEW

FRANK

I spent the ride across the nation wrestling with a question I couldn't actually ask:

When Timothy wanted me to sit next to him, when he wanted to have sex with the steward about ten feet away...was that billionaire stuff?

Or was it possessive stuff?

I'd broken up with Delbert Sharf because he thought he owned me, and at that time he was the most successful man I knew. He was part-owner of a construction company in Denver that I'd worked for, and Delbert had a truck *and* a nice Toyota sedan. I'd thought at the time that he was a great match, and I should get over the fact that he would only go out with his friends and not mine, that he insisted on holding my hand until every man in the room had identified me as "taken."

Was that so bad? Was I crazy to imagine he thought of me as another possession?

Timothy was obviously used to getting whatever he wanted. Wasn't that part of his appeal?

What was the matter with me that I cared where I sat?

Just how independent did I need to be?

Timothy alternated his attentions—half the time facing texts and emails on his computer and half the time telling me scandalous and very funny stories about people I'd only heard of on the national news. We ran in very, very different circles.

Gilbert picked us up at the airport, grinning happily and uttering a whole string of singsong syllables that clearly meant something.

Timothy turned to me. "That is a good question," he said, which surprised me, since I'd understood nothing Gilbert said. "Would you like to be taken to Ursula's? Or I can put you up at a hotel, if you prefer?"

Sunshine bloomed in my chest. If he was offering me alternatives, he wasn't trying to own me. "Can I stay with you?"

He grinned and took my hand. "Home, Gilbert." He nudged Gilbert aside and held the door for me himself. "After you."

So polite. It was nice. I tried to hide my grin as I slid into the back of the big Mercedes. Timothy tucked in next to me, and Gilbert rounded the car and sat in the front seat.

I whispered to Timothy, who leaned down to hear me. "Do you think Gilbert listens to Bob Marley?"

He snorted with laughter. "Do you think he's the April Fools' Bear?" Then we were both snorting.

The humor died, and I wondered why we weren't moving. "Is there a problem?" I asked. "Are we not going?"

"Waiting on Max."

"The steward?"

"Max runs my houses." *Houses*, plural. Of course he did. "He's dealing with the luggage. It won't be but a moment."

Ah. Of course. I sat, feeling awkward, since Timothy was now studying me.

"You have the most unusual eyes," he said. "They're spectacular."

"Um, thank you."

"I can't decide. Sapphires? Or diamonds? Which do you prefer?"

I laughed out loud and then realized he was serious. "Um, Levi's? Columbia hiking boots?"

He grinned and brushed hair from my cheek. "You're going to be fun to spoil."

Weight settled into the car from the trunk, and then Max was in the front passenger seat by Gilbert. Timothy closed the partition, shutting us away from the other two in the car, and I breathed deeply in order to suppress the uneasiness.

Did men spoil women if they didn't think they owned them?

The elevator ride from the parking garage to Timothy's apartment was blindingly fast, given that we rose to the forty-eighth floor even before my stomach settled back where it was supposed to be.

The apartment was astonishing. I'd felt more at home in Ursula's Connecticut mansion. Everything at Timothy's was ultramodern and alarmingly white. The vast living room was walled in windows. The view of the sky and the city was floor-to-ceiling, and it overwhelmed me.

"It's not as good a view as from the grotto." Timothy came up behind me, putting his hands on my hips and pulling me back into his chest. "But it's not terrible. Right?"

I stared, open-mouthed. "You could look down at this city for a year and never see everything. It's so confusing!"

He chuckled. "If I found some binoculars, we wouldn't find any mountain goats, but I bet I could find a fat guy watering his plants in his underwear. Interested?" I laughed and turned in his arms. He felt warm and strong and reassuring. He kissed me. It was a gentle kiss that made no assumptions, and I was grateful. "Come on. Let me show you around." He led me across the acres of white rug, past a dining table with twelve chairs. "This is the kitchen, and that's Jean-Claude. Jean-Claude will prepare whatever you like, won't you, Jean-Claude?"

A man who was not wearing chef whites, like I would have expected, nodded at me. "Ma'am," he said.

I nodded back, and they waited to see if I was going to announce some food I couldn't live without. I looked to Timothy. "I live on dehydrated mac 'n' cheese. What do you think I'm going to ask for?"

Jean-Claude shuddered and Timothy laughed. "Anything will be fine, Jean-Claude. Thank you. C'mon." He walked me through the servants' area, where Max and Jean-Claude each had their own rooms. (Each, I noticed, with its own private bathroom. Fancy.) We came to a large, lovely bedroom with a separate seating area, which Timothy offered me. "Would you like to stay here?"

I was confused. "In your room?"

"This isn't my room. This is the guest suite. Down here is my bedroom."

I had to duck back into the doorway to get over the sensation that we were at risk of plunging over the edge. His room was the corner of the apartment, and this time, two walls were nothing but windows. It was like an eyeball without a lid. Like an eagle's aerie. "Jesus," I muttered.

"You don't like it? A decorator did it for me." Timothy looked at the room suspiciously.

I accepted the view and considered the room itself. It was all dark brown and manly but still extremely modern. All the fixtures were sleek and lacked any kind of handle or detail. The massive bed had overhead spots, as well as what looked like huge silver bullets for reading-light sconces. It looked like a magazine ad.

It was totally impersonal.

"You really live here?" I asked.

"Why? It's no good?"

"It's good, it's just...where are you in this room?"

"Where am I?" He was honestly confused. "I'm right here, honey."

"No, I mean...where's your shit? Like, the crap that builds up. I don't know. The book you're reading. A note reminding you to pick up milk. Something—anything—that makes it look like a human lives here?"

His brows were almost touching, and I felt bad for making him look so confused. "Huh," he said.

"I'm sorry," I said quickly. "I'm crazy. Don't listen to me. I'm just sort of overwhelmed."

He was turning in slow circles, considering his space. "You're looking for Red's binoculars."

"No!" I was horrified. "Obviously not!"

He turned back to me and explained, "Not that specific thing, of course. I mean, there isn't anything here that's attached to me. I guess this looks pretty...antiseptic, doesn't it?"

The word did sort of fit.

He went through a door that turned out to be his closet. I peeked in and goggled. It was an entire separate room filled with a men's clothing store. It had an island full of glass-fronted drawers with perfectly rolled socks in it. And Max. Max was there too.

We had a conversation with him that made me very uneasy.

35

WHAT THE VALET SAW

TIMOTHY

All Max was doing was going through my luggage. I had no idea why Frank seemed so confused by this.

Granted, Max was pulling out garments that reeked of horse. Trousers thick with mud. Wool shirts that probably just should have been thrown away. He cast each one into one of several laundry baskets with pinched fingers, clearly wishing for some nice long tongs.

"I'll be done soon, sir," he said. "When I finish with yours, I'll tend to the lady's bags. But I wasn't sure which room she would be staying in?"

I looked to Frank to answer and found her wide-eyed. "I'll unpack my stuff," she said defensively.

"Very good, ma'am. I will, however, attend to your laundry."

"Oh, the hell you will!"

I put a hand on the small of Frank's back. "Max won't mind. He does all the laundry. He likes laundry, don't you, Max?"

Max sneered at the single sock he pulled from my pack.

Once white, it was now red from the grime. "I live for laundry," he said dryly.

Frank crossed her arms over her chest. "I can do my laundry." She turned to me and whispered, as if Max couldn't hear her, "I don't want him washing my underwear."

I tried not to laugh because she was clearly serious. "He doesn't care, honey. Promise. It's nothing to him."

Her nose wrinkled in distaste, and she frowned.

Max spoke up. "I'm happy to show the lady our laundry facilities and help her with any questions she might have."

She looked relieved and nodded at him. "Thanks. I can pay."

I smothered my laugh, but Max didn't. "Very kind, ma'am. There will be no charge."

Frank looked from me to Max and back. "You guys have never been in a coin-op laundry, huh?"

"Yes, I have," I answered quickly.

"As have I, ma'am."

Her eyes narrowed. "Were either of you actually doing laundry?"

I shut up, and Max acknowledged her question. "Well, no, actually."

"I didn't think so. Anyway, I bought a bunch of new underwear when I was with Ursula that I haven't worn yet. He might think they should be washed."

"New underwear?" I said hopefully.

"From that woman Ursula knows, who makes, um, underwear."

If I knew Ursula, we weren't dealing with anything as prosaic as *underwear*. "Right. You said you bought new lingerie." I asked, "From whom?"

Frank ducked her head. "Magda."

Jackpot. I'd bought gifts for various girlfriends from Magda, and Frank was going to look good in them.

"If they are brand new, ma'am," Max said, "let's wash them first. To make them more comfortable on your skin."

Frank inhaled and then braced her arms on the island. "I'm not comfortable talking about underwear with you, Max."

"I understand, ma'am."

"I can wash my own drawers."

"Indeed. I have lingerie racks for drying. I'll show you where."

"You really think I have to wash them first? They're brand new."

"Well, I would. But they are yours, not mine."

She thought about it. "And how would you wash them? Like, the delicate setting?"

"Oh, no, ma'am. Lingerie requires special care. I would hand-wash them. Several times."

She studied him, brows drawn. Then she dropped her hands and wheeled back. "Okay," she said. "Max can do my laundry. If that's really what you guys expect."

"Oh, very good, ma'am! I shall tend to that right away. And shall I put your cleaned clothes in the guest suite?"

Max was doing me a favor, pressing her on which bed she was going to sleep in. She looked at me uncertainly, so I rocked my head toward my bedroom. "Stay with me?" I asked.

She paused and then nodded. I couldn't hide my grin. Max said, "Very good, ma'am. I'll get started on the laundry right away."

He gathered up his laundry baskets and backed out the service door, which Frank apparently hadn't noticed. "Where does that go?"

"Into Max's kingdom. We don't go in there." She wanted to question that, but I put a hand to her waist and backed her out of the room again. "Let me show you where you'll be sleeping."

It took a few tweaks to talk her out of her boots. She wanted reassurance that Max wouldn't come back in the room unex-

pectedly, and she couldn't relax until I used the voice command
to lower the shades over the windows. "You really have no exhibitionist in you, do you?" I kissed her neck, and she turned in
my arms, surveying the room. Closed doors, covered windows.

I felt her relax. Her arms came around me. "Told you. I'm
sorry if that disappoints you."

"Nothing about you disappoints me."

"Not even that I don't fit in here? That I still smell like I've
been in the backcountry for eight days?"

"You smell like some very special hand lotion to me. But if it
worries you, let me introduce you to the bathroom."

I made love to her under the paired rainfall showerheads,
tracing rivulets over her breasts, down her flat belly, to the soft
curls at the fork of her legs. She sighed and leaned back against
the tiles when I knelt and lifted one of her long thighs over my
shoulder.

I licked her slowly, adding my heat to hers as steam rose
around us. I didn't increase my pace or pressure until her
fingers tugged at my hair and she was trembling against my
mouth. And when she came, I lowered her gently so she sat,
her legs splayed around mine while she recovered.

When she opened her eyes, she was my Frank again.
Amused, tough, capable. Funny. Her hand snaked out and
found my cock, still rock hard. "Tell me you have another stash
of condoms in this palace."

I smiled and then groaned when her fingers wrapped
around me. The drive to feel her pressure—to bury myself deep
inside her—was only slightly appeased by the grip she took. I
covered her hand with mine, encouraging an even tighter hold.
My thoughtful, witty reply evaporated. "I have condoms," I said,
and wondered how long it would be before she let me make
medical appointments for both of us. Once we were both clean,
we could discuss birth control that would allow me to go bare-
back with her. No more condoms.

But I wasn't such an idiot that I said it out loud. Not when she was as suspicious as she was.

Maybe tomorrow.

Once sheathed, I pulled her to her feet and turned her to the wall. I bent her forward with a hand against her back, and she responded. She lay her face against the tiles and arched, spreading her legs. I fit into her like we were formed to be together, barely bending my knees to center my cock at her entrance.

I fucked into her slowly and she groaned, her eyes closing.

No. Watch us.

I wrapped a hand around her waist and pulled her from the wall, still seated deep inside her. We shuffled together until I could put her hands on the glass of the enclosure. I wiped the condensation away with my hand until we could see ourselves in the mirror.

She exhaled a surprised *Ohhh* and I rocked into her. Her breasts came up against the glass, which must have felt cold. But she couldn't look away, pressing her forehead to the glass.

"So you do have a little bit of the exhibitionist in you," I panted. "You like to watch us, huh?"

"God," she said. Her fingers were splayed against the glass, and the heat inside her was volcanic. "Look at us."

"Yes. Yes. Look at us. Watch me take you."

"Timothy—oh. Help me."

"Help you..."

"Make me come. Please. Make me come. I need it."

What she needed, I would get for her. I settled into a steady pace, rocking into her heat, her tightness. When she rocked back to meet me, I slid my hand down her belly, landing on her clit.

She jumped and moaned. "Watch," I gasped. "Don't look away. Ride my finger." Her breathing was irregular, her spine writhing. I increased the pressure from both sides. "You're so beautiful. Frank. Frank."

She came, and I was deeply grateful. I let go of my control and pounded into her while she was still spasming. We came together.

Then I dried her carefully and took her to my bed. We lay there, naked and drying, half asleep and happy.

When her beautiful eyes opened to me, I knew I couldn't tell her I wanted her to move into my life forever, so I rolled to my back and gathered her in. "Want to see something outstanding about my place?" Not waiting for her answer, I opened the shades, which rolled back to reveal Manhattan at night, thousands of lights illuminating the darkness.

"Jesus," she said. "That's...that's amazing."

"It never really gets dark here."

"Terrible stargazing, huh?"

"Well, unless the stars you're looking for are celebrities. Then it's the best place in the world."

I felt her grin, and she poked at my ribs. I propped my head on my arm and held her while we considered the city.

"Your place is amazing," she said.

I shrugged, reminded of all the things I didn't have. "I guess."

She rose on an elbow to look at me. "You guess? This place is—it's unbelievable."

"Thanks." I guess she didn't hear real gratitude in my voice because she kept looking at me. "There are some things I'd like to change," I said.

"What could you possibly want to change? I mean, seriously."

I slid out from under her and sat on the edge of the bed. When that wasn't enough, I paced naked in the room. "I need a terrace. A big terrace. For entertaining."

"A terrace? Like, a balcony?"

"Like, a balcony the size of the apartment. No one can throw a respectable party without a terrace." Like Fourth had. In his penthouse duplex.

"You couldn't throw a party in your living room? It's the size of a football field."

She wasn't going to understand. I sat on the bed to focus on her. To make her see. "I shouldn't have to share this floor with three other apartments. I need a library"—like Joanna—"and a home office." Nicholas did half his work from home. "And there should be a separate entrance for the staff." Tabby insisted her guests should never see a staff member unless they were serving something.

Frank's eyes were wide. Then she burst out laughing. "Seriously? No one has all that!"

"Everyone has that!" My cry was too childish. Too loud. She would think I was being petulant, and I supposed I was. "The members of my family who have managed their money the best? They have all that."

"Ursula doesn't."

I dismissed the comment. "Because Ursula doesn't care. She lives in Darien, not Manhattan."

"That's bad?"

"Well, it's not Manhattan." I reached out and took her hand. "I'm going to show you around New York City tomorrow. Or rather, I'm going to show New York City you. They should be honored."

I touched the smile she wore with my fingers and then my mouth. So recently sated, I didn't let the kiss escalate. It was peaceful. Tender. Touching.

"I have my final dress fitting on Saturday," she said, "and Ursula says I need a spa day, so she's got some stuff set up."

The idea of a spa day reminded me of her secret mountain hot tub. Sated mere minutes ago, my dick twitched. "Spa day?" I grinned.

"Not like that! She says there's some hair treatment I need to have."

"What could your hair possibly need?" I stroked her head, and she grinned.

"I have no idea. Apparently I'm okay for Montana but not so much for Manhattan."

"She's crazy. You're perfect. Tell me about your dress. I'm going to buy you some jewels."

"No, Timothy, really. I don't need jewels."

Sure she didn't. What woman didn't like a gift box from Tiffany or Cartier? "Just tell me what color your dress is."

She waggled her eyebrows at me. "I won't. It's going to be a surprise. And I'm getting ready with Ursula at her house on Saturday, so you'll have to meet me at the gala."

"I'll pick you both up."

She shook her head. "You want to negotiate with Ursula, fine by me."

I got a text on my watch. "Jean-Claude wants to know what time we want dinner."

She looked alarmed. "Jean-Claude is still here? While you and I were rolling around in the bedroom?"

I kissed her nose. "He lives here. He and Max are always here. Unless we're in D.C. Then they're always there. Are you hungry? Shall I tell him eight?"

"I need some clothes."

"I'll loan you a robe." And buy her one of her own tomorrow.

"I can't go to dinner with Jean-Claude in a robe! What did Max do with my pack?"

It took a very long time to get her to agree. I had to promise her that Jean-Claude and Max would both wear blindfolds to serve us, which she correctly assumed was a joke. Eventually, I persuaded her into a robe and out to the dining room, where every course she ate was a revelation.

Watching her experience things that seemed so simple made the meal special for me.

Tomorrow I was going to take her to every place that was important to me. I was going to watch those eyes go wide. Hear her surprised laughter. Cherish each time she grabbed my hand.

And I knew just where to start.

36

URSULA'S TAKE ON THE SITUATION

FRANK

"Wait, say that again. He had all of Manhattan to show you, and he took you...where?"

I grinned, remaining still under Cormac's final tweaks to the dress. "To meet his polo ponies."

"Jesus. What an idiot."

"No, it was awesome! He's got a beautiful gray named Baron Rothschild of the Wind—"

"Pretentious."

"—who's called Puppy. As soon as Timothy walks into the stables, he opens Puppy's door and the horse follows him everywhere. Like a dog."

From her seat on the bench, Ursula eyed me. "And you loved that."

I couldn't understand her skepticism. "Of course I loved that! Who wouldn't? He's got nine horses and one of them thinks he's the mama. It's so stinking cute!"

"That *is* pretty cute," Cormac agreed. She was sitting on the floor, her mouth full of pins, working on the hem.

"I suppose." Ursula's tone said she didn't suppose at all.

I scoffed. "You're only saying that because he's your cousin. If it was anyone else, you'd know it was adorable."

She shifted and finally agreed. "I suppose. I'm still getting used to the idea of you sleeping with him. He was the most annoying teenager. Perpetually in trouble with his pal Vaughn."

"I know Vaughn," I said. "He's why Timothy and I met. And don't you think Timothy might have changed a little since he was a teen?"

"All men are perpetually teenagers. They all have a chronic case of arrested development." She looked up as Hildy bustled in. "What did you find out?"

Her younger sister plopped onto the bench beside Ursula as Cormac touched my leg to get me to rotate again. "The manager at Riverside says the event is completely sold out and people are begging to get more people in. Your secret PR campaign must have worked. The paparazzi are already staking out places for the red carpet. It's perfect."

Ursula smiled in satisfaction. She looked to me. "You're going to be online tomorrow, Frank," she said. "Maybe even in print. *Mysterious Beauty Attends Beckford Gala.* Thanks, Hildy. Nice networking."

Hildy preened. "It helps that the Riverside venue is a Babcock property and that I'm the special events manager."

Ursula nudged her sister. "And that I'm a PR genius. Not that anyone at Babcock gives a damn."

"This is a little confusing," I admitted.

"Confusing? Okay, I can see that," Ursula said. "But you have to pity poor Timothy. In my opinion, he always ends up with women who are desperate for his approval. It's because he has such low self-esteem."

I jerked at her words, annoying Cormac in her hemming. "Low self-esteem? Are we talking about the same guy?"

"Oh, I know he comes off as Joe Cool, but he's always felt like a lesser Babcock. He and Nicholas used to be as close as brothers, did you know that? And now they seem to hate each other. I don't know what happened, but I think it has something to do with why Timothy always wants these pretty little babes who look up to him and worship him and ultimately annoy him. You're a big step up for him. Like, a major improvement. So, if you feel confused, just think of what it's taking for Timothy to hold it together."

Her point of view pushed me off-balance. Was she right?

Had I misjudged Timothy? Like, a lot?

"All right," Cormac said with sudden authority. "I'm done here. By the time you finish at the spa, I'll have this ready. You will be stunning tonight, Ms. Frank. Make sure you tell them who made your dress."

I stepped off the platform and slipped out of the heels. Not the cruel stilettos Ursula mourned for, but still, they were higher than I was used to. "I promise. I know my lessons. I stay mysterious, except that my stunning dress was made by the amazing Cormac Heggerty."

"Right," Ursula confirmed. "But gown, not dress."

"I'm sorry?"

"Your gown was made by Cormac Heggerty, not your dress. That's a gown you're currently rocking. And may I say, you were born to wear that."

"I agree," Cormac said. "Perhaps you'd be willing to be in a photo shoot, Ms. Frank?"

Hildy clapped and Ursula nodded emphatically. I wasn't quite so sure.

"She'll get back to you," Ursula said, nudging me to the curtained-off changing area. "We'll need to discuss rates, of course. She's an unknown, but she will already have excellent press coverage, so we'll need to negotiate a fee."

Cormac grinned at Ursula. "Of course. Do I assume you're her agent?"

"For now. We'll talk. Go on, Frank. Get back into those dungarees. We've got lots of stops to make before we make you famous."

"But I don't want to—"

"Of course you don't. No one does. Go on. I'll call the spa to tell them we'll be a few minutes early. Cormac, you're a miracle worker."

"I know."

Timothy had called the grotto a spa, so I was expecting something a little more, well, natural. The place Ursula swanned into was...not that.

In fact, the entire place was like being tucked into a peach-colored satin jewelry box. Everything that wasn't tufted silk was supple cream leather. The air smelled very faintly of summer-fresh peaches, and hidden speakers were playing some audible narcotic. It was a soundtrack of distant chords and ever-changing melodies that never resolved into anything. Every room featured something that splashed water gently into a basin.

All the voices were hushed. All the rules implied. We didn't raise our voices, we didn't question the plan, we didn't refuse the heavy robes worn over bare-naked bodies or the quilted slippers. No one in that place had any muscles. They barely had spines. And yet their determination was epic.

As soon as we got there, we all started drifting. We drifted into treatment rooms, where soft-voiced, beautiful women somehow abraded every inch of my skin without me wincing even once. They positioned a huge arm over me, covered my eyes with a towel, and turned on a waterfall that rained down on me. "We'll be back in twenty minutes," the handmaidens said soothingly. "Try to take a little nap."

At first, there was no chance of napping. I was lying on a bed stark naked, save for the towels across my eyes, breasts, and coming up between my legs to cover my crotch. The entire place, which was not a shower stall, was getting soaking wet. The towels were sodden. This was...decidedly odd.

But nothing happened except the warm water sluicing down and the strange, hypnotic music playing. Without me realizing it, my muscles lost their will to work. My body puddled as all this water undoubtedly puddled on the floor. When the air shifted and a cooler breeze reached me, I woke up. The handmaidens were back.

I *had* fallen asleep. It was the damnedest thing.

After they sponged me completely dry without ever interrupting my modesty (they used an ungodly number of towels; their laundry bills must have been staggering), I was rubbed down with things that smelled of wildness. They told me the name of the lotion, but I didn't recognize it. Ting-Ting or something.

I was poured into my robe and taken to another room, where a man with quite astonishing hands massaged me. He was flattering, telling me I was in wonderful shape. I felt that was pretty much par for the course here in the peach jewel box, but then he mentioned that he could tell I didn't eat a lot of sugar, and that seemed more like knowledge and not just schmoozing.

I was grateful that his massage wasn't trying to get me to sleep. He actually woke me up, which was a relief, and we talked about muscle fatigue and glute strength and the valuable role played by tiny little muscles in the back that he called millipedes.

Or something like that.

I met Hildy and Ursula in a waiting area that was all ivory

lounging couches, each with a rolled towel at the foot and a neck pillow waiting on the side table. "Are you dreamy?" Hildy asked me happily. "I'm totally dreamy."

I grinned to see her so peaceful. Her usual abundant energy had been toned down. And her skin looked great. "I'm dreamy," I said so I wouldn't interrupt her sense of tranquility.

Ursula still looked like she could win a debate on any subject, but her skin was glowing too. "Dreamy," she agreed, even though her massage clearly hadn't taken any of the stiffness out her spine either. "Facials next, and then hair. Last will be mani-pedis. How are you enduring all this, cowgirl?"

I appreciated her checking on me. "Well, it's an experience, all right."

She chuckled. "It is that."

"The number of towels that shower thing used up—doesn't that seem like...a lot?"

"Oh yeah." She stretched out on her lounger and wiggled her toes. "Tell me, does it make you happier to remember that Timothy is buying all those wet towels for all three of us?"

I thought about it and stretched my toes out too. "Yes. Yes, it does."

37

THE GALA

TIMOTHY

My afternoon had been very productive. Once Frank finished with all the primping and prepping for the gala, I'd be able to tell her that Cal and Maria had agreed to my price and the Babcock acquisitions team was already handling the paperwork for me—a definite advantage to being a part of Tabby's Portfolio. The purchase would be complete in days.

I eyed my reflection in the plateglass window of the Babcock Riverfront Events Center. My bow tie was perfect, my shirt snowy. I looked good in a tuxedo, and I had the discreet touch of style in the onyx-and-gold shirt studs and cuff links. This outfit was like a second skin to me. I'd spent a large portion of my life in one or the other of my several tuxes. So why was I missing the hiking boots, the wool pants, the unflattering lines of a puffed-up down jacket?

Must have been the excellent hat that I missed. Pure cowboy. Max had already ordered me a new one to replace the one I lost in Starvation.

Cal had been touched when I told him I wasn't going to change the name of the ranch. Circle B would do as well as a brand and a name for a Babcock as it would for a Buckley. The continuity pleased him. And me too.

Johnston sidled up to me. My D.C. assistant looked, I thought, like a weasel had fallen into someone else's dinner jacket. "Preston is here," he said, "with his chief of staff. Not his wife." Everyone knew that Senator Preston had made his mistress his chief of staff so he had an excuse to be seen with her in public. His deputy was doing double the work and his power on Capitol Hill had halved because of it, but what else was new?

Johnston went on filling my ear with the petty, daily scandals that passed for news in legislative circles. He was scanning his phone at the same time, watching for mentions of the gala. I glanced down as he scrolled along a site that was posting red-carpet fashion in near-real time from the press scrum outside the main doors.

"Hold on. Show me that." I stopped his scrolling finger and slid back.

Frank. From right outside, moments ago.

Poured into a gown. Or rather, the gown had been poured onto her. If she'd been nude, she couldn't have shown off her body more effectively.

My god, she was sensational.

What color was that? I'd have to see it in person to decide. There was blue—that would mean sapphires. But there was a lot of gray too. And black. As the fabric stroked over her skin, it shifted color and gleamed wetly. The only thing that would do her justice would be diamonds.

Her hair was up but loose. I didn't know how that was possible, but it was. She had post-sex hair. Not a man alive wouldn't want to find the pins, or whatever held it up, and pull that hair free.

Her eyes were huge and glowing. I was too experienced not to appreciate the touch of a master makeup artist.

And all that beauty was mine.

I looked up, thrusting the phone back into Johnston's hand. Ignoring him, I moved through the crowd to the main entrance. Where was she?

How soon could I get to her?

I needed to be at her side. Not just to drink in her sexy, mysterious beauty but also to protect her from the wolves that were going to descend. Sniffing around her. Annoying her and touching her.

Christ, they might try to dance with her.

I'd have to kill them.

Cooler heads would have warned me to chill out a little before I got to her, but there were no cooler heads around. Vaughn hadn't arrived yet, and he was hardly the kind of guy to counsel caution.

Not about Frank.

So, by the time I found her, I'd sort of lost my mind. She hadn't gotten far from the entrance. She was with Ursula and Hildy, talking to some greasy asshole who thought he had the right to put a hand on her elbow. I saw red.

I shoved between them, putting my arm around her slippery, silky waist, and leaned down to claim her with a kiss. Her mouth opened in surprise when I got to her, and I slipped my tongue in. Not brutally. Not gross or anything. Just a hello touch.

She pushed away, bumping into Hildy, who reached out to steady her. "Timothy!" Frank said.

"You're gorgeous, baby. I've been watching you."

She looked down at her dress reflexively, and I took the occasion to shoot a glare at the guy. "Timothy Babcock," I said aggressively, shoving a hand at him. "Frank's with me."

He gaped and shook automatically. He fled the moment I let go of his hand. *That's right. Move along.*

Ursula barked a laugh, and Hildy had her hand over her ridiculous rosebud mouth. "Testosterone much, Timothy?" Ursula asked me.

"What? I was nice. I introduced myself."

That was my first clue that I'd played this evening all wrong. Frank backed up until Hildy and Ursula flanked her. Her energy did not match mine. "That was rude," she said pointedly.

Far too late, I remembered that she didn't ever want to feel owned. And I'd just claimed her in public.

Like an idiot.

I held my hands up in surrender. "My apologies."

"Not to me," she said. "To that guy."

"Oh, go on. He just wanted to drool on you."

Frank glared at me and turned to Ursula. "Shall we get a drink?"

"By all means."

"I'll get drinks for you," I volunteered, but Frank froze me out.

"Thank you, no. I'll see you later."

I'd been dismissed. By the most beautiful woman in the room. In the world.

"Damn," said a voice beside me. It was Vaughn. Late to the party, but right on time to see Frank slap me down. "That's got to sting."

"Oh, fuck off."

"Baby-cock, now you know how I feel."

"I *said* fuck off."

"Yep. You had her and you lost her. I can relate."

"What are you doing here anyway? I haven't lost her."

"Yes, you have. And I'm here to support the Beckford

Department Stores program to fund clubs for high school kids in poor areas who want to get into fashion design."

I paused. "Is that really what we're doing here?"

Vaughn laughed and slapped my back. "No. We're trolling for beautiful women in shapewear that lies about what they really look like once those gowns come off. We're drinking midshelf liquor and wondering which of these people we can use for our own nefarious ends. Just like every other gala."

"Good to see you, Coxless."

"You too, Baby-cock." And I knew he really had forgiven me for taking his girl.

Assuming I still had her.

The venue was huge. A great place for galas like this one. A band played from the stage, and a runway had been built halfway down the room for the inevitable student fashion show after dinner. The far end was right on the river, with million-dollar views of Manhattan across the water. An industrial catwalk had been turned into a promenade above the crowd, and already partygoers were strolling up there, where the rubbernecking for celebrities was at its peak.

I had to decide: Should I track Frank from above? She'd be much easier to spot up there. On the other hand, I'd have a hard time bodychecking any more lechers who wanted to brush up against her. But if I stayed on the floor, I could lose sight of her in the crowd.

Vaughn continued to tease me throughout the evening, coasting along in my wake and commenting helpfully on things he saw. My frustration grew until we got to the stage, and I realized how much better I could see over the crowd if I was up there.

Which was when the idea occurred to me.

"Watch this." I elbowed Vaughn and then gestured to the band leader. A quick whisper, a hundred slipped from hand to hand, and the next song they played was Bob Marley's "One Love."

They'd been playing regular potted palm music up until then, so the band looked quite pleased at the change. The drummer in particular got into it. People looked around at the sound, but I was watching Frank, who was talking to some gray-hair old enough to be her great-uncle Red.

She heard the music and turned around, surprised. I caught her eye and pointed at her from across the room. *Bob Marley*, I mouthed.

She laughed in astonishment, and then she and I together mouthed, *The April Fools' Bear*.

And that was all it took. "We're back together," I said in satisfaction to Vaughn.

"One song? A hundred bucks? There's no way."

"Watch and learn, little man."

I made sure we sat together at the overblown dinner, and I murmured in her ear as the various vice presidents and angel investors of the school talent-show program droned on. The lights went down for the fashion show, which I supposed was surprisingly good, based on the applause and murmurs, but the low lights gave me the chance to grope my girl—in the most genteel way, of course.

That silky fabric felt amazing when my hand was sand-wiched between satin and supple breast.

Frank nudged my hand away, which made me chuckle. Too exhibitionistic for her? That's fine. Instead, I could fondle as much of that luscious ass as was available on the chair.

Across the table, Vaughn stuck his tongue out at me in the darkness. He was seated between know-it-all Joanna and bubbly, babbling Hildy. *Too bad, brother. I've got the better seat.*

That was what I thought, anyway.

Once the lights came up, I learned pretty quickly who the April Fools' Bear really was.

"Can you stop pawing at me, please?" Frank's hiss startled me. Weren't we both having fun? Her nipple had pebbled against my hand. She was enjoying it.

Wasn't she?

"Baby," I said, confused.

"Don't call me that. You're behaving like...like an ogre. Can you stay away from me for a while, please?"

She rose and moved off quickly, losing herself in the crowd of people who'd stood after the fashion show ended. Some headed to the bathrooms for a pee or a bump of cocaine to make the evening go faster. Some to the dance floor to grind against someone whose skin felt as silky as the gown.

Like Frank.

I stood in time to see her intercepted by a tall, blond man. She cast a fierce glance at me over her shoulder and took his arm.

Nicholas.

He smiled down at her and led her toward the dance floor. I started after them but then came to a halt. My desire to go caveman on my cousin was pure and right and good...but Frank would not see it that way.

Vaughn had made it around the table. He was by my side once more. "Back together again, are you?"

I glared at him.

Nicholas thought he'd won? Snuck off with my woman?

Oh, we'd see about that.

38
THE FRANK ASSESSMENT

FRANK

I should have known better.

I was cursing myself for falling for it again. Guys with two cars—or their own plane and multiple home addresses and valets who knew more about washing women's underwear than I did—saw women as possessions. I knew it. I just hadn't listened to my own common sense.

And here I was, staying in this man's apartment. Using his credit card to buy things I would never, ever use again. Sleeping in his bed and, like a fool, shattering in his arms. I never should have come. I needed to get out. I needed to go home.

Why hadn't I brought my rifle?

I was edging around black jackets and murmuring "Excuse me" to various beaded evening sheaths when a tall figure blocked my path.

"Slow down," the low voice said. "He's still watching. You don't want to look like you're running away."

I looked up and into eyes the color of Timothy's. But that

was where the similarities ended. His cousin Nicholas was all angles and sharpness. His face had a model's cheekbones, and his eyes had the focus of a sniper. And I was now the subject of his interest.

"Nicholas," I said. "Um, hello."

"Hello. I gather you're fleeing in disgust from my cousin. And who can blame you?" The ice in the eyes thawed as he offered me the dawning surprise of a slow smile.

"Blame me?" I said stupidly.

"Come with me," he said, turning and presenting me with his elbow. "You'll punish him if you dance with me now."

I cast a look over my shoulder at Timothy, whose pale skin had gone dark pink with anger. *You do not own me.* I sent the thought as clearly as I could in a single glare and took Nicholas's arm.

"Rumor has it," he said as he led me through the crowd, "that you're now sharing his bed." I looked up at him, startled and angry. "Oh, don't be mad at *me*. Trust me, what Hildy knows, most of the Portfolio will know eventually. She adores you, by the way. She's just a little indiscreet."

We reached the dance floor, and he drew me into his arms with so much assurance that I didn't have even a moment to explain that I'd never done this kind of dancing before. It turned out that my protests weren't needed. With Nicholas leading, I apparently *could* do this kind of dancing.

"I guess I just don't like everyone knowing my business."

"Used to a more isolated lifestyle." He nodded down at me. His arm was light around me, but I still somehow knew where to put my feet, how to turn. "I've read the report. Oh, think nothing of it."

He had to say that, since I'd accidentally scraped the edge of my beautiful shoe along his ankle, stepping wrong when he mentioned a report. "I'm sorry," I said, flustered. "You've read what, now?"

I got that slow smile again and found that I was unable to turn my face away from his. Nicholas was exuding some kind of magnetism, and I was made of iron. "You didn't know. And why should you? My grandmother—the chair of our board?"

"Tabby?" He nodded. "She's scary."

"She is indeed. She keeps a fleet of investigators on retainer. I imagine they were working on your file before she gave her closing speech at the board meeting." I came to a halt, beyond shocked. He stopped, too, kindly sheltering me from the other dancers around us. "Yes. I'm sorry to be the one to tell you. She does it to anyone who catches the interest of someone in her Portfolio. On the positive side, your report ends on some excellent notes, and Tabby says she likes you. So, that's a very big hurdle crossed, I must say."

I realized my mouth was hanging open, and my eyes flew to the last place I'd seen Tabby. She was still there, on the promenade overhead. Instead of being dressed decently in pale gray, like any old lady should be, she was wearing head-to-toe gold sequins with huge shoulder pads. She looked awesome. Like she could power a city.

Tabby wasn't watching me with those clever eyes. Instead, she was talking to the large, florid man I'd last seen in the Senate hearing room. The one who'd made Timothy abandon me to shore up his senator.

"Fred Rose," Nicholas said, following my gaze. "Head of Rose Realty, archenemy of Babcock Holdings. Oh, they're tiny compared to us, but a nuisance just the same. I must say, his color doesn't look at all good."

He didn't sound alarmed. Quite pleased, in fact. I restored my focus to him. "What report? What did it say?"

"Verbatim? All right, give me a moment. Let's see. Francesca Annette Robinson of Ennis, Montana. Thirty-one years old. High school GPA of 3.3. Completed required coursework for a certificate in stonemasonry from the Finishing Trades Institute.

One semester of mechanical engineering at the University of Colorado, withdrawn for lack of funds. Two credit cards, both maxed out. I didn't know a credit limit *could* be as low as nine hundred dollars."

"All right, that's enough."

"You don't want the good part? About how you're helping Timothy in one of his schemes? Possibly...no, probably only quasilegal. The Denver bar waitress bribed by the investigator didn't hear much. But she did know Timothy was fighting with his partner in crime for a while."

"Jesus. You people are terrifying." When had he started me dancing again?

"Yes." He smiled down at me with evident warmth. "Hildy and my sister Suzanne have both informed me that you're now sleeping with Timothy, which I understand can be a satisfying event. Still, the man isn't known for his subtlety, so when I saw you fleeing, I thought you might like an assist."

There was no part of this conversation that I was in charge of. "An assist," I repeated woodenly.

"Well, Timothy often finds himself in competition with me. I'm not entirely sure why. We have very different sets of skills, so he knows he can't compete with me financially, while I cannot compete with him socially."

"I'd say you're doing okay," I said darkly.

"So kind. Thank you. My point is that Timothy often growls at me. A puppy learning to bark, for all that he's bigger than I am. Still, if you want to make him jealous, you could do worse than dance with me. While he glares."

I darted a look around. "Where is he?"

"Above us. Trying to hear what we're saying, which is ridiculous in all this noise. If you could throw back your lovely head and laugh at something particularly witty that I said, I imagine that would be most effective."

"I'll be sure to do that as soon as you say something particularly witty."

I'd caught him by surprise. He threw back his magnificent head and barked his laughter to the ceiling.

Or to Timothy.

"You are charming," he said. "I can see why he's so besotted."

"He's not besotted."

"Beg your pardon, lovely lady, but he definitely is. I've seen Timothy ignore women who were chasing him, as well as women who wanted him to chase them. He has shockingly poor focus on the subject. But he can't look away from you for a moment."

"That's because I'm a possession to him."

His eyebrows went up. "How uncharacteristically intelligent of him to value something so rare." I looked at him in shock, and he went on. "I really think you deserve to have a choice in your next steps, don't you? By which I mean to say, is Timothy the only Babcock worth your attention?"

Ursula danced past, grinning at me over Nicholas's shoulder. She was reminding me that I wasn't here to make Timothy jealous. I was here to win the bet.

So, I smiled up at Nicholas. "What do you mean?"

He flicked up an imperious eyebrow and appeared to be laughing at me. "I mean that I should like to take you out. To date you. To see you socially. To treat you properly. And to prove that Timothy's style is not my style. Are you interested, my dear?"

He was shockingly handsome. Cut on a much finer scale than Timothy, who could endure an early April dunking into a glacier-fed stream without complaint. That event would have carried long, lean Nicholas over the edge. But was that such an important quality in a potential date? "Tell me what you're proposing. Keeping in mind that I live in Montana."

He chuckled, those blue eyes glinting. "Well, I should like to take you somewhere public. Somewhere various Babcocks could take note of the event. My grandmother is holding a prewedding ball for my cousin Quinn at the beginning of May in anticipation of her June wedding to Andy, her fiancé. I think that would be a charming time to begin our relationship."

Suddenly, I understood him. "Oh. Timothy isn't the only one competing. You sounded like you were above all that juvenile stuff, but you just want to take me to that party because Timothy will be there. You want to rub his face in it."

"Rub his nose in it," Nicholas corrected. "Like a puppy who piddles on the rug. He needs to accept, once and for all, who the better man is."

I pulled away from his arms. "Thank you for the invitation. I'm sure you'll be able to find another way to rub that puppy's nose. Be careful that the puppy doesn't bite back."

He watched me coolly as I walked away. I was sure Timothy did too. With no place else to go, I headed for the only sanctuary I could think of: the women's room.

Where I was found by the COO Babcock. Queen, her name was. No, it was Quinn.

"Frank," she said, surprised to find me sitting on the plush little sofa. "Are you okay? Is everything all right?" I opened my mouth to answer, but nothing came out. She dropped beside me and rested a hand on my forearm. "Was it Timothy? I saw you dancing with Nicholas. Ursula said it was going well. What happened?"

I answered honestly. "Nicholas asked me out."

"Oh, that's awesome! So, you win the bet, right?"

"I do." That was good. Why was I fighting back tears?

"Oh, dear. Let me see what we can do..."

She pulled out her phone. Pretty soon, that bathroom was flooded with fascinated Babcock women who all wanted the details. Since various other women kept coming in, regarding our knot with undisguised interest, I didn't want to explain.

But Quinn had a strong streak of the mother in her. She gathered me up and told the others she was taking me to her townhouse for the night. She summoned her fiancé (a guy I instinctively liked, named Andy), tucked me into her limo with them, and drove me to her home.

Texts from Timothy began pinging into my phone. I ignored them.

In solidarity, Quinn did the same.

Once at her huge townhouse, she led me into a spectacular guest suite. It even had its own living room. The suite had all the warmth and charm that was lacking in Timothy's decorator showcase. Quinn gave me a pair of soft flannel pajamas and a robe and slippers. "There's ice water on your bedside and snacks in the fridge there. Feel free to raid the kitchen. And if you're up before ten, don't be surprised if no one else is. I intend to sleep in."

I supposed dimly that I was in Babcock overload. Paralyzed by the speed with which my life had changed. "Thank you."

She put a warm arm around me and hugged me. "Whatever else you're thinking, know that you're safe here, and warm, and we'll talk it all out tomorrow. Try to sleep, and let me know if you need anything."

I sat on the bed after she left and looked at my phone's dark screen. Timothy's texts had pinged in until I shut off the phone. If I took it off airplane mode, any messages on it would flood in.

Of course, those messages didn't have to be from Timothy.

Could be something important from Cal and Maria...which I had no resources to help with.

Could be a message from my mother...who had never remembered the number of my cell phone since the first one I got in junior high.

No, if there were going to be any messages, they would be

from Babcocks. And did I want to talk to...any Babcocks? Nicholas?

Timothy?

No.

No, I did not.

I left the phone on airplane mode and peeled out of the dress like a snake shedding a skin that had become unendurably tight. It was flannel for me from now on. And tomorrow, Timothy and I were going to have it out. I had a few things I wanted to say.

Including something that would blister his damned ears.

39

ONE THREAD PULLS…

TIMOTHY

I didn't usually demand privilege. People who did were almost always asses. But the bartender at the gala was just being obstinate.

"I know there's a bottle of Macallan 25 back there," I told him, "because this facility is owned by Babcock Holdings. And I am Timothy Babcock."

The bartender, clearly hired more for his frat-boy good looks than his brains or skill, nodded to me while shaking a martini for some pompous banker. "Yes, sir," he said. His agreement meant nothing. He still wouldn't get me my drink.

There were too many people between me and the ladies' room, where Frank had disappeared. I needed my drink now so I could get back to her. I fished out my wallet and reached out to shake the bartender's hand, the hundred in my palm.

He looked down, startled. "Oh no, sir. We can't—"

"Go into the storeroom and get the bottle of Macallan that's back there. I know it's there. I've seen it. Excuse me," I said to the guy who'd pushed up. Just by looking at him, I knew he worked in short-term bonds and did way too much cocaine.

"I just need two tequilas," he said, shooting a look of apology at me. "Like, now."

"Yes, sir."

I glared at the bartender. "*After* you go to the storeroom."

"I don't have keys to the storeroom, sir. I can't get that for you. Which tequila, sir?"

I noticed that my hundred had disappeared into his pocket and was just about to demand a chat with his boss when some serious energy appeared at my side.

"Ha-ha," my sister Joanna said distinctly. "You lose."

Mr. Two Tequilas was shifting urgently, so I eased away from the bar long enough to focus on her. "I lose? Why do you say so?"

She grinned. "Guess who just asked out your girl?"

All my frustrations fused into one grim presentiment that swept down my spine and kicked me in the balls. "You're shitting me."

"Absolutely not shitting you. Nicholas just asked Frank to go to Quinn's pre-wedding ball with him."

I strangled my scream deep in my throat but couldn't restrain the scowl and the hand I sent tugging at my own hair. I scanned the room. For Frank. For Nicholas. For someone I could punch or persuade or carry off. "How do you know this?"

Joanna was still at my elbow, grinning through her strange one green, one blue eyes.

"Frank told me. I was in the ladies' with her and she spilled the entire deal. Said you lost an important bet. That sound right to you?"

"Goddamn it." What were the chances that Frank would make this up?

Poor.

What were the chances that Joanna would make this up?

Better...but still poor.

I'd be damned if I'd check with Nicholas for verification. I needed Frank.

If you couldn't ask a sister, who could you ask? "Can you get her out of there for me?"

"Can't." Joanna was scary smart, but she was also a brat. She'd been a brat since our childhood. "She's gone."

"Gone?" I turned back to her, restraining the urge to shake her. Just a little.

"Gone. Quinn just took her home."

"What? Quinn? How did *she* get into this?"

"Oh, she was in the ladies' too. You know how motherly Queen Bee gets. She saw that Frank looked sort of shell-shocked and just swept her up."

My heart sank. "What do you mean, Frank looked shell-shocked?" Had Nicholas upset her? I'd rip him to shreds. I had a good forty pounds on him. It had been decades since he and I had wrestled, and I was pretty sure I could take him now.

"You know," Joanna said with maddening happiness. "Too much Babcockness, I'm guessing. I think we kind of broke her. Well, you, mostly."

"Me! What did I do? I was out here the whole time!"

She laughed at me. "That's not the story Frank told us. You were groping her, huh?"

"Jesus. She said that? To you *and* Quinn?"

"Oh, hell no." I was relieved until she went on. "She told *all* of us. The seven female members of the Portfolio."

"You were *all* in there?"

"Shit, brother. You were lucky Tabby didn't show. She usually knows when things like this are going on."

"Well, how the hell did I miss this? How'd you know to go into the ladies room?"

"We texted each other, of course. You, Fourth, and Nicholas aren't on the all-girl chat."

It was a conspiracy. I was doomed. "How long ago did they leave?"

"Oh, I'd guess it's been a good twenty minutes now. Quinn grabbed Andy, and off they went on either side of Frank, like bodyguards. Even if you'd been right there, you wouldn't have gotten within three feet." Her grin was insulting. She was enjoying this.

What was I supposed to do now? My brain was tires spinning in the mud, and Joanna was enjoying every minute of it. Fuck me.

"And you're sure she didn't leave with Nicholas?"

"Ha." Joanna found that funny. "Nicholas is no longer your problem, Timmy. Your girl is pissed at you all by yourself. My advice? Let her cool off at Quinn's for the night and try her tomorrow."

I'd already pulled out my phone and sent a text to Frank.

TIMOTHY BABCOCK
Where are you?

No dots answered me. Joanna was still watching me, grinning. She, at least, was having a good time. I switched conversations and texted Gilbert to pick me up. "Thanks, sis," I said absently and left her at the bar. Waiting for Gilbert at the door, I went back to texting Frank.

Can I come get you?

I'll come to you

Are you with Quinn

Still no answer. The tension in me mounted higher. By the time Gilbert got to me, I was snapping at him and anyone else around me. Next, I tried Quinn.

TIMOTHY BABCOCK

You've got Frank?

Is she okay?

Tell her I need to talk to her

God curse the fucking solidarity of women. No response at all. What if this really had been an emergency? It was just irresponsible to leave me hanging like this.

TIMOTHY BABCOCK

Andy

Be a man

Tell me if Frank is with you guys

ANDY RIGGINS

She's fine

We're almost to Quinn's

She can sleep here tonight

Is she okay

Better you give her some time to cool off, man

Try again tomorrow

Gilbert had pulled over to the side of some industrial Brooklyn road, waiting for directions. I used the intercom. "We're going home, Gilbert."

His reply was incomprehensible, but it included the word *Frank* and went up at the end like a question, so I made the deduction. "She's staying at Quinn's tonight. Just take me home."

Does she hate me

You know

She does now but wait until tomorrow

Female capacity for forgiveness keeps the world going round right?

Hoɔe you're right man

Don't suppose you can tell me what I did that was so loathsome

Sleep

Things will be clearer tomorrow

Thanks a lot for that, you so-called brother. Where was the Man Code when I needed it? Andy didn't know about bros before hos? Of course not. Andy probably hated that kind of thought.

I kind of hated it myself. But any port in a fucking storm.

I lay my head back against the seat and worked through how I was going to sweet-talk Frank when she finally answered me.

Starting with telling her about the ranch.

40

...AND THE SWEATER UNRAVELS

FRANK

Quinn's guest suite featured blackout curtains and silky, soft sheets under an equally soft down comforter. I had no sense of time when I woke up. I had to get out of bed and peer out the window at the only part of Manhattan that wasn't permanently soaked with sodium-vapor lights. It was still dark out.

So I went back to sleep.

The next time, I could see that I was looking into a garden, and the sun was up. It was past nine, which meant I'd slept later than any other time in my life, excepting sick days.

I showered and found some kind of cream in the massive bathroom that would scrape all the makeup off my face. I stared unhappily at my only footwear—those cruel, beautiful evening sandals—and thought that I'd go barefoot until I could beg Quinn to borrow some sneakers.

But she'd out-thought me. I went into my sitting room in the robe and found she'd left me a pair of drawstring sweatpants, a soft cotton T-shirt, and a hoodie made of kittens or something. The tag said cashmere.

Oh. So that's what all the buzz was about.

She'd left me some kind of slip-on shoes that fit me well enough. They were a little big on my feet (Quinn was taller than me), but the heavy socks helped.

I could have put on last night's lingerie, but the entire evening was tainted for me. I went commando.

I padded down the thick carpeting on Quinn's staircase and followed her voice to a massive, sun-filled kitchen, where she was sitting at a kitchen table, phone to her ear and exasperation on her face. Behind her at the stove, Andy waved a spatula at me happily.

Quinn looked up and saw me. "All right, Timothy. I'll tell her. She's up now. No, you have to wait. Well, I won't let you in. Just wait. Let the girl have some breakfast. She's fine. I'm looking at her. She's fine. No, you can't talk to her yet. Let her have a single cup of coffee. I'm hanging up on you. Stop calling!" She clicked off the call and regarded me, laughing. "Well, if you wanted to make him miserable, I'd say you're doing a pretty good job of it."

Andy handed me a cup of coffee and pointed me to the chair by Quinn. "Cream, milk, sugar? What do you take in your coffee?"

"Just a little sugar. Thanks. I don't mean to make Timothy miserable, and I'm sorry if he's annoying you."

Quinn grinned. "Timothy has been needing someone to make him miserable for a long time now. You go ahead and do what you're going to do."

The Babcocks confused me. Why was I getting more support from them than they were giving to one of their own?

"I'm making Quinn a scramble," Andy said. "Caramelized onions and spinach. Would you rather have mushrooms?"

They fed me. Were kind to me. Told me to relax and take

my time. I wanted them to adopt me. The third time Timothy called Quinn, she picked up.

"Yes. She's had breakfast. No, you can't come pick her up. No, not Gilbert either. I'll ask her." She turned to me. "Do you want to meet with him?"

I nodded. "I'm ready. Thank you."

"Timothy? I'll send her back to you with Ahmed. No, we will get her to you. No..."

I interrupted. "It's a thirty-four–block walk, if I understand the grid. I'll walk it. I'd like to stretch my legs anyway."

Both Quinn and Andy protested, and I had to remind them that I was not a Babcock. No one was going to snatch me off the street or hold me for ransom. Apparently all the Babcocks knew my credit cards were maxed out anyway. I was no kind of target, and the April morning looked nice out the window.

So, I hugged Quinn like a sister and kissed Andy's cheek and took myself for my first solo journey through the Big Apple.

My pace got slower and slower the closer I got to Timothy's building. The street scenes were fascinating, and window-shopping in the various stores and shops was dazzling. Everything in New York was colorful and bright and brash and rude and fun.

But internally, my landscape wasn't so bright.

And I was a long, *long* way from Montana.

When the security guard buzzed me up to Timothy's apartment, he was waiting in the elevator lobby. He wanted to hug me, but I held him off. "Please wait. I want to talk to you first."

"Yes. Yes, of course. There's some things I want to tell you too."

We sat in his ultramodern living room, facing each other on a sofa that was obviously chosen more for its looks than its comfort.

"Can I go first?" Timothy asked.

I held up a hand. "I know how charming you are. You're going to apologize and make me feel better, but I really need to make two points. Please let me go first."

He sat back, ducking his head as if chastised. "Please," he said.

I squared my shoulders and sat straight. "Thanks. Okay, the first thing I need you to hear is that I really, really dislike it when someone feels like they own me."

"I know. And I'm sorry."

"Last night, you were like a dog pissing around his territory."

"I just didn't want anyone bothering you."

"That's for me to decide."

"But we're together. Aren't we? You and I?"

My frustration built. "We aren't together. There has been no commitment."

"I'm ready to commit to you, Frank."

My scorn erupted in a huff. The idea of him taking such a thing so lightly! "You've known me for a month. A month! You can't make a commitment to someone you've known for such a short time!"

"Sure I can. And it's been more than a month, hasn't it?" I shook my head. He tried to take my hand. "We've been through so much together."

I pulled my hand back, anxiety crawling through me. "Not enough for that. Besides, not only have you not committed to me, but I haven't committed to you. So, you don't own me. Tell me you understand that." My voice had risen as I spoke, surging with the need to make him understand.

"I understand," he said, but I knew with perfect assurance that he was telling me what I wanted to hear.

I studied the skyline out those vast windows without actually seeing it. Finally, I nodded. *Okay*, I thought. *We can continue to work on this.*

"You had two things, right? Before my turn?"

That's what he was doing—letting me babble on before he got to the groveling. I wasn't getting through to him at all. "Exhibitionism!" I all but shouted. "Don't grope me in public! Ever!"

He looked wounded. "I thought you liked it."

I glared at him and hissed. "I have a hard time sleeping with you with your guys in the apartment!" I cast a thumb toward the kitchen as being representative of both Max and Jean-Claude.

"You can call them servants, you know. It's not a bad word."

"That's not the point!"

"All right. I get it. No more touching. It was dark last night, though."

"It wasn't dark enough. And there were people all around us. Your own family, for god's sake."

"They don't care."

"*I* care!"

"I get it. Calm down. No being possessive, no public touching. See? I'm listening. Now can I go?"

The man who handled the U.S. government was going to plead his case. I was ready. "I feel like I've been heard. Thank you. You go ahead."

I thought his apology would be flowery. He'd use pretty metaphors and wave his arms about. Make his point with passion and concern. He didn't.

He said four words, attempting to suppress a grin.

"I bought the ranch."

This was so unexpected that it took me a few seconds to make sense of the sounds. "You...you what?"

"I bought it. The Circle B. The lawyers finished it up this morning. Cal and Maria were delighted to sell it to me. They're renting back to get through their final summer. So...no timber company. No logging on the land. No clear-cutting."

My heart leaped as he spoke. My eyebrows went up. My mouth formed the "Oh!" of my shriek of joy as I launch myself at his neck.

Laughing, he caught me as I hugged him. "I *thought* that might make you happy."

My arms seized in paralysis as I wrapped around him. "I can't believe it! Oh, Timothy, that's so awesome!" He chuckled happily, and I finally regained control of my own muscles. I pulled back far enough to see his face. "That's so great— because I won the bet!"

His face locked up like my arm muscles had moments before. His smile seemed frozen. "What, now?"

"The bet!" I was too excited and rose to my feet to pace the room. "I won the bet. Last night, your cousin Nicholas asked me out. So I win! Oh, Timothy!" I faced him, hands clasped under my chin in overwhelmed gratitude and relief. "The grotto— Daughtry Lake! It's all safe now, and I have access for my entire life. I can't believe it!"

The pressure brought tears to my eyes, but I wasn't blinded enough to miss that he was now avoiding my attention. He shifted on the sofa and picked up the decoration on the glass coffee table—a small brass bull—to fiddle with it. "Well, we need to modify the bet just a little."

Like the sun going behind a cloud, a chill tried to lace down my nerves. "Um, what?"

"Just a little. Nothing, really. I'm going to make you a new grotto. A better one. With electricity. And a bigger hot tub."

"The grotto isn't a hot tub," I said, growing still in my rapid fear. "Why would I need a new one?"

"Not just a new one. A *better* one."

I strode to the sofa and took the bull out of his hands. "What are you talking about?" He still wouldn't look at me. "Tell me."

He stood but shifted until he stepped around the coffee

table on the other side. Not by me. He paced to the window. "It's nothing. Really." It was clearly something. I felt the same way I had when I realized the puma was hunting me. "I just got the assayer's report back, that's all."

"The report," I said woodenly, fear like a physical spike, ripping my organs around. "What did it say?"

He wheeled back and tried to take me in his arms. "That we're going to be very, very wealthy."

I shrugged him off. "Tell me," I said again.

He exhaled heavily and then pasted on a big, fake smile. "The only place on the ranch with molybdenum is the Daughtry Lake region. So, I'm going to make you the most amazing grotto anywhere else you want. Charla Lake, or up by Markus Creek. Anywhere you want."

My bones were heavy. My muscles slack. "You're going to mine at the grotto?"

"I'm going to make a fortune at the grotto," he corrected me. "Billions."

"You already have billions." My voice seemed to be coming from very far away.

"One," he said. "One billion. It's not enough."

I lifted my eyes to him. "How can that not be enough?"

"Come on, Frank." He tried again to slide an arm around my shoulders, but I pushed off, my muscles working again. "It's one little setback. This is good news, honey."

Oddly, I was grateful for the endearment because it broke my paralysis. "You know I loathe being called honey," I said. I walked to his bedroom and found my wallet. Coming back, I pulled out his credit card and laid it on the coffee table, along with the bronze bull that I was somehow still holding. "You can have this back."

"Frank," he said as I crossed to the kitchen. "Come on. Don't be so upset."

I pushed through the swinging door and hit someone on

the other side. No surprise. Max and Jean-Claude were both pretending they didn't just have their ears to the door. "Max, can I have my luggage, please? Where did you put it?"

"Your luggage, ma'am?"

"My backpack. My duffel. Can I have them, please."

Timothy had followed me. "Where are you going?"

I ignored him. "The pack, please, Max."

"Yes, ma'am. I'll get it. And your laundry."

"Just the stuff I came with," I called after him. "I don't want any of the new stuff. Thank you, Jean-Claude. You're an amazing cook. Excuse me." I pushed past Timothy and headed for the bedroom.

"Frank," he called after me. "Calm down."

I turned and fixed him with my stare. "Do I not appear calm?"

He had no answer. In his bedroom, I found my clothes where Max had folded them neatly into drawers.

Max appeared with my pack, holding a zip-top plastic bag. "I brought this for your shampoos, ma'am."

I studied it. Would I accept a plastic baggie? Yes. Yes, I would. "Thank you, Max."

Timothy leaned in the doorway, watching with his hands crossed over his chest. "You're leaving?"

"As you see."

He scoffed. "And how are you going to get home? If you're turning in my credit card, how are you supposed to get back to Montana?" I refused to answer. I had no answer. "Come on, Frank. If you're determined to go, I'll fly you back. Don't be crazy, baby."

Baby. He dared to call me *baby.* "I don't want anything from you. Nothing. Leave that underwear here, please, Max. I bought that with his credit card."

"Shit, Frank. Take the damned underwear. What do you think I'm going to do with it?" I shook my head at Max, who put the pile of Magda's comfortable bra and panties back in the drawer. "I know your credit cards are maxed out, Frank. There's no way you can buy a ticket on your own."

"I'll hitchhike home," I said, determined that he would not see the tears that threatened to fall. Going home had always meant Daughtry Lake and the grotto. It meant Uncle Red. Now Timothy owned all that.

I felt a gentle hand on my shoulder and wheeled. Max watched me with concern. "I'll get you a ticket, ma'am. You can pay me back."

"Max! I forbid it!" Timothy was furious.

"With my own money, ma'am. Of course." Max pointedly ignored Timothy.

Impulsively, I kissed him in thanks and hoped he wouldn't be fired. "The construction jobs will have opened up by now. I'm a stonemason. I make a good living. I'll pay you back, Max."

"I have no doubt. Take your time, ma'am."

"Oh, for god's sake." Timothy wheeled from the door and stalked away. We heard the door slam.

He was gone. That was my cue to sit bonelessly on the bed and melt into tears.

Max and then Jean-Claude wiped my tears and told me I'd be okay. Max bought me a coach seat on a red-eye flight to Big Sky and tried to persuade me to let Gilbert take me to the airport. I called Ursula instead. She was about to get on a call with some architectural preservation society, but she sent Kennet, her driver.

"He's yours for the day," she said. "And you'll tell me all about it later?"

I said I would, even though I wasn't sure I'd ever want to talk to a Babcock again.

41

THE SLAP-DOWN

TIMOTHY

Summoned for dinner at Fourth's apartment.

Sometimes a good thing, more often a bad thing. It could mean he had some new scheme he wanted to talk over in a less formal setting than his almost-at-the-top office at Babcock Tower. That would be a good thing. I loved being flattered.

On the other hand, Fourth was known to do his dressings-down in private. If I'd done anything wrong, this would be it.

I defied anyone to say I'd done anything wrong, damn it. Let them try.

Of course, I hadn't actually done any work in the week since Frank stormed out.

Maybe I'd even been ignoring a thing or two.

Maybe.

But if Fourth wanted to lecture me, then bring it on, Mr. Tough Guy. Maybe he'd find I wasn't the cheerful guy everyone got to kick like he expected.

Fourth actually had a butler. Like, a guy with a British

accent who always wore this tuxedolike suit and spoke in hushed tones as if someone had just died. "Mr. Babcock," he said when he opened the front door. Fourth's apartment took up the entire ninety-second floor (he also owned the ninety-first and ninety-third floors, too, but ninety-two had the front door), so the butler could have greeted me at the elevator. But god forbid guests didn't have to bang on the door. Like security hadn't already verified that I was an invited guest. "Please come in. Mr. Babcock will see you in his office."

We began the mile-long walk through the massive apartment, every long hallway reaching into the distance to the walls of windows that showed (from this elevation) Central Park. Fourth's balcony terrace was annoyingly huge.

One day very soon, I'd have a place bigger than this one. Then *I* would summon Fourth to visit *me*.

We turned right at the vast living room and traveled past the small salon, the formal dining room, and the informal dining room. The butler opened both doors to the office and announced me like I was a stranger. "Mr. Timothy Babcock, sir."

My butler was going to wear Armani suits exclusively. And only speak in French.

Fourth was at his desk. He beckoned me in like I was a suitor or a vendor. "Timothy. Come in."

I was about to make a crack—calling him Your Majesty would set a nicely insolent tone—when I realized that Nicholas was in the other chair.

What the hell.

And on the sofa...Andy. And Regina's boyfriend, Emmett, who was a street thug with a very useful knack with dogs.

And Vaughn. What the hell was Vaughn doing here?

Plus, smiling from an armchair was Suzanne's guy. "The nanny?" I burst out. "You brought the nanny into this?"

In truth, I'd always liked Benjamin, but this was looking like an ambush, and I was pretty sure everyone here was on Fourth's side.

Except me, of course.

"Sit, please, Timothy." Fourth was, as usual, implacable. Fourth wouldn't utter a yip if he found himself on fire.

Not that marble would burn.

"What the hell is going on?" I asked. "What is this, an intervention?" I put as much scorn into my voice as I could. "You going to persuade me to stop drinking that demon alcohol?"

Fourth looked faintly interested. "Why? Are you drinking too much?"

I rolled my eyes, and he told me to sit again. I thought about standing, but everyone else was seated.

I sat.

"Thank you," Fourth said with his usual attitude of expecting to be obeyed. "You're here tonight, Timothy, because I know some things I don't want to know."

I kept a poker face as I considered. Was it the molybdenum? Had he figured out my plan? "Like what?" I asked belligerently.

"Like as the Babcock Holdings chief executive officer, I should be above dealing with petty matters of personnel. And apparently, I am not."

"Personnel?" He'd confounded me. "What about personnel?"

Fourth turned to the sofa. "Can we hear from the office of the chief operating officer?"

Andy opened his mouth to speak, but I interrupted. "Hang on. Why aren't I hearing this from Quinn? If the COO has a problem, let her tell me directly."

Fourth held a finger up to Andy to put him on pause. "It has come to my attention," Fourth said, "that the women of the Portfolio have a chat group of their own. I have found it expedient to put together the male version. Thus, this group."

"Those guys aren't even Babcocks!" I glared at the sofa grouping.

"Andy will be a Babcock in June when he marries Quinn. I have reason to believe that Emmett and Benjamin will also be changing their names after news of their respective engagements will not divert attention from Quinn as the bride." Emmett held up a palm, and Benjamin leaned forward to slap it briskly. "And Vaughn might as well be a Babcock, as often as he's been in our houses and lives. With him, we are a seven-member group, which gives us parity with the women. Therefore, I am inducting them now into the all-male version of the Portfolio. As CEO, this is my right."

"Right, because you decided it was your right," I grumbled, but Fourth ignored me.

"Andy, you were saying?"

Quinn's chronically cheerful fiancé was also her assistant, so he *did* have a handle on what was going on in the COO's office. "Herbert Smith, head of personnel, came to Quinn on Thursday to report that one of Babcock's employees has registered an official complaint." Andy looked at me hopefully, but I shook my head. I had no idea what he was talking about. "The employee, a Johnston Scott, said that Timothy was being irrational and vicious. He threatened Johnston and attempted to make him cry."

"Attempted," I said in disgust. "He *was* crying. Like a baby. Attempted, my ass."

Fourth leaned forward. "You don't deny these charges?"

"Come on." I was irked by this line of questioning. "Johnston is a weasel. Everyone knows it. He needs to be made to cry regularly or he devolves into a subhuman."

Nicholas made a *tsk, tsk* noise. "Timothy, Timothy, Timothy."

"You shut up. What are you even doing here? Why don't you crawl back into your calculator?"

Andy spoke over whatever Nicholas wanted to say in reply. "Johnston also reports that you haven't been working this week."

It was a total attack. I ducked my head and jutted my jaw defensively. "Congress is in recess anyway. There's nothing happening in Washington, D.C. right now."

"Nothing happening?" Fourth repeated sternly. "Nothing happening? Are you aware that Fred Rose has bought a town-house on Capitol Hill? Did you know he told Tabby at the gala that he was thinking of opening a D.C. branch of Rose Realty?"

"He...?" I regrouped. "Of course I knew."

Andy, helpful as a wrecking ball, offered, "Johnston said he tried to tell you, but you just yelled at him."

"With all the drivel that guy spouts, how am I supposed to know what's useful from the crap?"

Fourth sat up sharply, startling me. "Because it's your job to know."

"All right. Calm down. I'll be back in D.C. on Monday."

"Oh, no," Fourth said. "That's not all."

God. Of course it wasn't all. If someone had ordered me a cup of hemlock like Socrates, I would have drunk it down gladly. "Go on," I said grimly.

"It has come to our attention," Fourth said, "that you have cheated on a bet."

"Oh, come on!" My anger burst out of me. "That was between me and Frank."

Nicholas gave me his most evil grin. "As I understand it, when I asked Frank on a date, you lost the bet. That's right, isn't it?"

"That bet had nothing to do with you!" I rose to my feet, my hands forming into fists. "Or any of you!"

Out of the corner of my eye, I caught movement. Emmett was unfolding from the couch.

"Regina says what you did was unfair," he said in his low

voice. "Regina is the legal department. What she says is the truth."

I didn't think he'd actually punch me, but I was glad for the seven or eight feet between us. "Look," I sneered. "It speaks. It's like watching an Easter Island head talk."

Emmett's expression never changed. "When people annoy Gina, I break their fingers."

He flexed his own fist, larger than mine and with obvious battle scars over the knuckles. I swallowed.

Fourth saved me from further indignity. "I don't think we need to resort to violence. Both of you, please sit down. Emmett, Timothy. Sit."

Watching each other, we slowly sat. I relaxed my fist and saw him do the same.

Shit.

Fourth inhaled. Like hitting Return on the keyboard. He was setting up the next paragraph. "That's Emmett heard from. Benjamin, do you have anything to add?"

Ben was a hell of a nice guy and dedicated to my cousin Suzanne and her son Skip. He liked me. I knew he did. There was no way he wanted to break my fingers.

"Actually," he said, "I guess I do have something to say."

Crap. "Go ahead," I sighed. "Let's get this over with."

He thought for a moment and then looked up. "I know you love your nephew."

This line of reasoning made me uncomfortable. "He's my second cousin. Or my cousin twice removed, I can't remember which. Suzanne is my cousin."

Benjamin ignored this perfectly reasonable diversion into genealogy. "I know you love Skip."

I scoffed. "What, are you going to deny me visitation rights or something?"

Ben still wore a look of compassion and concern. "That wouldn't be my right. I couldn't do that. But you've been so good about helping Skip understand right from wrong. You're a really great uncle."

"Second cousin," I tried halfheartedly, but I knew where he was going with this.

"So, I know you wouldn't want Skip to learn that it was okay to break your word. I mean…would you?"

Trapped by his earnestness, I glared at him and shifted my attention to the final male in the room. "Okay, Vaughn. You're not a Babcock, but speak your peace."

He laughed. "I'll do my talking with my fists if Emmett doesn't get there first. You fucked with Frank, and I have adored her since before you ever thought about someone so great. You've got to treat her right. She deserves that. If you hurt her, then…then you and I are not friends anymore."

"Oh, Christ. What the hell. Is this the We Love Frank club?"

"If we started one," Fourth said calmly, "Tabby would be its charter member. We like Frank, Timothy. And right now, we don't like you very much."

"Oh, thanks a lot."

"Certainly. On to the final issue."

I gagged. "The *final* issue? There's more?"

"One more thing, and it's been a long time coming." Fourth steepled his fingers on his desk and looked into the middle distance soulfully. "I can remember prepping to be the first of the Portfolio to take the Babcock exams." Jesus, he was going back into ancient history. "I suppose I was eighteen. The rest of you were at least ten years younger. Timothy, you were eight, and Nicholas was seven."

"For eight months of the year," Nicholas added quickly. "For a third of the year, we were the same age."

"I was always older than you," I sneered, mostly because I knew it would drive him up the wall.

Fourth's hand slapped down on his desk, halting the childish fight before we could really get into it. "At that time, I would look out of my bedroom window at Ten Acre and wish that I was sailing, or on the beach, or, hell, even playing with you kids."

This perspective shut me up. Fourth had wanted to play with us? He was already an adult when we were growing up.

He went on. "There were a passel of you by then. Regina and Quinn and Joanna, all running around, sunburned and happy. But the one thing I saw that really stuck with me was you two." He looked from me to Nicholas.

"Us?" Nicholas asked.

"Yes. The two of you. Inseparable. How I envied that. What must it be like to have a friend so close? You were in lockstep. If one inhaled, the other exhaled. You were totally in sync with each other. Best friends from the cradle on. Remember that?"

I glanced quickly at Nicholas. He, too, sat with his head down. Was he remembering too? "Um," I said.

"What happened?" Fourth asked simply.

I shrugged. "We grew apart."

Fourth shook his head. "No. That isn't enough. You were best friends until suddenly, it was all rivalry and competition. So what happened?"

I looked away, uneasy. Unsure of what to say.

Nicholas broke first. His hand shot out, finger pointing. "*He* happened."

I turned, surprised to see Nicholas pointing at Vaughn. "Cox?"

"Me?" Vaughn squeaked.

I ignored Vaughn to focus on Nicholas. "Cox happened? What does that mean?"

Nicholas shrugged, but Fourth prodded him until he spoke. "You were always hanging around with Vaughn. You had no time for me anymore."

I stomped on the ground. "My ass! Why did I even *need* to find a new friend, did you ever ask yourself that? Huh?"

I just knew all the eyes in the room were following this exchange like a ping-pong match. The butler was probably peering through some butler peephole, desperate not to miss a word.

"What are you talking about?" Nicholas challenged.

"You!" I surged up to pace the room, veering away from Emmett when I got too close. "You're suddenly in my grade, and then you're ahead of me? You're leapfrogging grades like a jumping bean, and you have no time for *me* at your fancy new school! Did you think I was going to sit at the moron school and wait for you to come home? To grace me with your revered and brilliant presence?"

"Moron school?" Vaughn was perplexed. "We went to the moron school?"

Ben patted him consolingly.

"Well, what about me?" Nicholas was standing, turning to keep his face to me as I paced. "How do you think I felt, always being the littlest kid in the class? You're off breaking laws and having wild adventures with Cox here while I'm at Harvard at age fifteen. Do you have any fucking idea how lonely that was? My god. You are so selfish."

"Me?! I'm selfish?"

"All right." Fourth's voice cut through our anger. "You're either going to fight it out or hug it out. I'll leave it for the two of you to decide. But before we end this, let me ask you: Did either of you mean to lose your best friend? Well? Did you?"

I was silent. So was Nicholas.

Fourth tried again. "Please remember that you're not teenagers anymore. You're in your thirties. Take a breath. Apply your rational minds. Answer the question. Did you mean to lose your best friend?"

"No," I said.

Nicholas looked at me. "Of course not."

Fourth leaned back. "Then that's a start. Maybe this rivalry between you can begin to heal. Sit down, please, Nicholas. Timothy, you've heard from all of us on the questions of honor and of keeping your word. I don't doubt that you have some reason for reneging on your bet with Frank, but I ask you now to use your adult brain, as you just did, and decide what matters to you. Know that we are all here to help you. If no one has anything to add, shall we have a cocktail before dinner?"

Yes. Because what this evening needed was a little demon alcohol.

I supposed it was a step up from hemlock, given what I needed to do next.

42

THE COMING OF SPRING

FRANK

Swan was shaggy.

It wasn't the horse's fault. Although we hadn't gotten to warm weather yet, her winter coat was slowly giving up its will to live.

Slowly.

Using a shedding tool on a horse was a fierce mess. I was about to end up with more horsehair on me than there was on the horse, but nothing worked as well as the toothed saw. She'd stomp and shiver as I went along, but she'd love it too. Horsehair that thick must be itchy. She'd love having the irritation soothed.

I could use a little soothing of the irritation myself. I'd been out of sorts, off-balance, grumpy as hell for the more than a week since I got back from...from New York City.

No one actually liked dealing with a horse's thick winter coat. It was more like thatching a lawn than brushing. But even if Swan didn't know it, I knew that this would be the last time I cared for her this way.

After the summer season, Cal and Maria were packing up and moving to Florida. Some asshole was taking over, and that asshole had bought the livestock as well as the acreage.

Swan now belonged to...some asshole.

If this was my last time with the horse I thought of as mine, then she was going to get the most luxurious shed she'd ever been through.

I pulled the shedding tool off the shelf in the tack room and was heading back to where she waited by the paddock when I saw the truck coming up the long drive.

Oh.

Shit.

I was brought to a standstill, swamped by anger and sorrow and guilt and longing. How dare...some asshole show up here? Had he come to look at the land he was going to destroy? Count his filthy gains?

Yes, he now owned the place. He could come whenever he wanted. But...

But...

This was *my* place.

"Honey," Maria called, "you want to come in here to the office? I can keep him out."

Given the number of times she'd found me crying over the last week, her concern was understandable. I shot her a grateful look but shook my head. I wasn't going to hide from anyone.

Not standing on this land where I grew up. Where I worked. Where I was important.

I stiffened my spine and turned to track the truck when it pulled into the yard.

When it parked.

When he got out.

"Cal," Maria called into the barn. "Bring the boys."

I wondered if she wanted the stable hands nearby to stop the new owner from hurting me—or to stop me from hurting the new owner.

Timothy walked around the back of his truck slowly. I focused on details as if they mattered. Hiking boots. In good shape. Tall enough to thwart normal levels of mud.

Dark blue jeans. Terrible for a trail ride in this season. Fit well over trim hips.

Blue shirt. On anyone else, it would have been a workman-like chambray. Probably for the billionaire, it was a silk blend with a high cotton count that would feel supple and smooth under the palm. In the backcountry, one thorn or deadfall branch and it would be rags.

A neck. Well-muscled. Too thick to throttle with my hands. I could use a rope. Or a shedding tool.

The jawline. Ginger stubble sparking red in the sunlight. Groomed to look manly without actually threatening anything as uncouth as turning into a beard.

That mouth. Fuck. Turned down in concern.

I couldn't quite bring myself to get to the eyes. If he was looking at me, I might burst into tears.

If he wasn't looking at me, I would definitely burst into tears. He represented the ruination I dreaded most.

He was waiting by the tailgate. Was he waiting for a sign from me?

Maria broke the stalemate. "Young man, we're renting this property good and legal through August. You need to get gone now."

The muscles of his neck flexed as he turned to look at her. "Maria," he said, his voice sending shivers along my ribs. "I'm sorry. I forgot your chocolates."

I could hear the sneer in her voice. "Sure. You got what you wanted. Now it's back to business as usual."

"No," he protested. "I'll get them for you."

"Typical." She walked to me. "Frank, you want us to run this guy off?"

My palms were sweaty when I took her hand in mine, but I shook my head. "This is his place now. It's up to him."

"We're standing with you, Frank." Cal was now on my other side. I could feel their warmth. Two old people who just wanted a peaceful retirement. I took his hand, too, and gave them both a grateful squeeze.

"I'll see what he wants," I said. "Thanks, though."

I stepped away from them, toward Timothy. I couldn't look much higher than his chest, but my back stayed straight. "What are you doing here, Timothy?"

"I just need a few minutes to talk to you."

I nodded on a neck that felt frozen. "Go ahead, then."

"Here? Can we go, um, somewhere?"

He sounded nervous. I didn't care. "Anywhere you want. You own the place now." I was proud that my voice remained neutral. That my eyes stayed clear.

He sighed. "Here, then. Here's the thing..."

Glib, talkative Timothy was at a loss for words. *Something you don't want to say? Don't look to me for help.* I left him hanging. I said nothing. Just stared at one pearly-white button.

"I realized," he said at last, "that when I was supposed to be apologizing?" He could wait for me to acknowledge his words until the sun went down. I wasn't budging. "Well, I never did say I was sorry, did I?"

My agitation came out in my hands. The shedding tool bent back and forward like the flat of a saw.

"Um," he said, "what is that?"

I looked down at my hand. "Shedding tool. I was going to work on Swan's coat."

"Oh. Huh. Could you...would you mind putting it down?"

"Can you get on with this, please?" I wasn't sure my fists would open. Could I have dropped the handle if I'd wanted to make him feel better? Unclear. But if the tool made him envision a mini version of a two-man cross-cut saw, then all the better.

"Right. Okay. So, I came here to tell you that I *was* sorry. That I *am* sorry."

Too little. Too fucking late. "Okay. We done?"

"Hang on. Four things." The forefinger of his right hand touched the pinkie of his left. He was counting. "I'm sorry I didn't listen to you. You were right. I was acting like I owned you, and I had no right. Especially when you told me."

My forehead hurt from frowning. I hadn't expected him to apply logic to his apology. Even as late as it was, he was expressing remorse for the right reason. I didn't like that. He was violating my righteousness.

His finger flipped to the next finger. "I'm sorry that I, um, groped you at the gala."

Behind me, Maria murmured. "Come on, Cal. Back into the barn. You, too, boys. Give them some time."

"But—"

"Cal, into the barn."

I shook my head, fighting the affection for them that was distracting me. Timothy must have been watching them go because it took a moment before he spoke again.

"I wasn't thinking about what you wanted. I was just thinking of what turned me on. And you do turn me on. Every inch of you. But that's no excuse for pushing you beyond your comfort level. I sincerely regret that."

I offered him a stilted nod, watching the fingers. He got to number three.

"I'm really sorry that I ruined the relationship between us." He paused, and I heard him swallow. "The friendship. The more-than-friendship. We built it up so slowly, but it felt so strong. I ripped it apart because I was lazy and careless. The loss is shredding me. I'm really sorry. I regret what I did."

I couldn't look at those hands anymore. I had to turn to stare up the mountain to the peak where I set off fireworks every New Year's Eve. Who would set them off next year?

"And lastly, I'm sorry that I caused you pain. Or anger. Or— or concern. That I didn't fly you home myself. That I wouldn't even give you a ride to the airport. That Max had to help out. That you had to rescue yourself. It shatters me. If anyone else had done that to you, Frank, I would have ripped them apart with my bare hands. I can't bear what I did to you. I am sorry. So very sorry."

I could hear the tears in his voice, and that made me cry. But I would not let him see.

He sniffed wetly and took a breath. "So, that's the apology part. Now let's talk business."

Oh, thank god for the bolt of anger *that* sent through me. I wiped the tears from my cheeks and whirled to face him. "Business? Yes. Let's talk business. You bastard."

Those blue eyes were shiny. The pale skin was wet. He nodded. "Yes. Business. Our deal was that you would take me into the backcountry and I would pay for two semesters of engineering school at the University of Colorado. But you left the credit card behind, so I had my comptroller arrange the payments. You're set for the fall and spring semesters, and student housing is assigning you a dorm room. You've got the meal plan, and I put five thousand on an account at the bookstore. Let me know when you need more."

How like him, I thought, *to turn this into money*. I was struggling to remain angry. Fighting to not be touched by his words. His thoughtfulness. What had he done that any decent person wouldn't have? "Fine," I said shortly.

He took a step closer to me, and I winced and backed up. That stopped him, his hands coming up, palms out, telling me I was safe. "I do have one piece of bad news to share with you, though."

My scoff was watery. I was fighting hard to remain unmoved. "What more can you do to me, Timothy?"

He bit his lip and spoke. "I said I'd thought I owned you, and that was a mistake."

"Yes. Yes, it was."

"I know. But unfortunately, like it or not, I'm afraid you've got a problem. I don't own you, but it turns out you own me."

I stared at him, astonished. The strength ran out of my jaw, and my mouth fell open.

He saw my reaction and nodded. "I know. It's a mess. Not what you want. And I'm going to try really hard not to stalk you. But it's going to be hard. Because you didn't want this, but I fell in love with you."

I stopped being able to see because my eyes filled with tears. But I could hear, and what I heard was a "Yeep!" from the barn.

"You've known me for a month," I rasped through a clogged throat. "You can't be in love with me."

"I've known you for forty-eight days," he said with perfect assurance. "And the length of time doesn't matter. I fell anyway. I've discovered that I was a shit before I knew you. You made me a better person. And once you were gone, I was a wreck. I made Johnston cry. I nearly started fistfights with Vaughn *and* Nicholas. Although you'll be glad to know that I gave Max a raise."

That surprised a laugh out of me. "Good."

"Yeah. He really showed me the right way to behave. So, my point is that I'm sorry for you. I know you don't want me. But I'm afraid you do have me. I am in love with you."

My last instinct for self-preservation wilted. I dropped the tool and stepped forward, wishing I could see more than a blur of the man. My reaching hands found his chest. He pulled me in and I buried my face in his shirt, arms around his neck. "You can't be in love with me. It's impossible."

"I know it's terrible," he crooned. "I'm sorry. I'll do my best to behave."

"Goddamn it," I said, pushing back far enough to wipe my tears on something other than his shirt. "I hate what you're doing. I hate it. But I can't help it. I'm in love with you too."

"You are? Truly?" He held me back so he could peer into my eyes. "Are you tormenting me?"

"You're tormenting me! But yes. I hate your money. I hate your plans. But I can't resist anymore. I'm in love with you."

He kissed me, and I kissed him back. I clung to him like he was the last stable thing in a reeling world. He made me feel safe, this man who had destroyed everything I loved. I was adrift.

But at least he was with me.

He pulled back to wipe the tears from my eyes with his thumbs. Laughing, I did the same to him. His forehead was still creased. "You can hate my money, but you don't have to hate my plans anymore. I'm not doing it."

I froze, my palms shaping the angles of his cheekbones. "Not doing what?"

"The mining. The molybdenum."

I pulled back. "Wait. What? What are you saying?" The adrenaline racing through me was like acid eating at my veins.

"I'm not," he said. "I decided I have enough money. The Circle B means more to me. No mining."

Panic twisted in my chest, hope warring with disbelief. "No...no mining? The grotto? Daughtry Lake?"

"Safe."

It was too much. My knees got weak, and the world grayed out briefly. He caught me back to his chest with a gasp, and then I was pressing kisses across every surface I could reach—

chest, neck, jaw, ear, laughing mouth. "You're really—really? Really?"

"Really."

"What are you going to do with all the land?"

He smiled down at me. "Ride it? Get to know it? Hope I can find a good trail guide. Know of anyone?"

I looked up at him, overwhelmed. Then I drew him down for a kiss—a kiss that blistered my soul and summed up the love and excitement I was feeling. His arms came around me. Tight. But not tight enough. I pressed my belly into the growing cock. The cock I'd missed.

He groaned and backed up. "I promised I wouldn't fondle you in public." He grinned.

"Maria," I called to the barn as I took him by the hand, "I'm going to need your office for a moment."

She was laughing. I could hear it. "It's *his* office. Go ahead. Next time bring chocolate, though."

"Promise," he said, laughing.

Once I got him behind a closed door, I grabbed him. I reached around his waist to fondle his ass but felt a surprising crinkle of paper. "What's in your pocket?" I asked.

"Oh! Oh yeah. Here." He pulled out a thick envelope and handed it to me.

"What's this?" I turned it over, but it was blank save for the Babcock Holdings letterhead.

"Well, you won the bet."

"The bet?"

"Nicholas asked you out. He hasn't shut up about it for a week. Open that."

I unsealed the flap and pulled out a heavy sheaf of legal-sized papers, folded in half and then again. "What is this? What am I holding?" I squinted at the dense sea of words confusing me until I focused on the heading. Perplexed, I looked up at him. "What is this?"

"A deed," he said simply.

"A deed? Why—what— huh?"

"I subdivided the land. You now own the seven hundred acres around Daughtry Lake, plus a permanent easement to the road if you want more than a trail." I was blinking at him in astonishment as he went on talking as if this was nothing. "It's actually seven hundred and forty-three acres. We used topographic maps to establish the sight line around Daughtry." He saw I wasn't processing. "It's yours now. The lake. The grotto. Yours."

The words weren't processing. "You can't just give someone that much land."

"Why not? You won the bet."

"The bet...?"

"Didn't you tell me your great-great-whatever lost Daughtry Lake in a poker game or something? He made a bet and lost the land. You made a bet and won it back. What's the difference?"

I gaped at the papers in my hand. "It's—it's mine? Really?"

"Says so right there. If you decided to mine molybdenum, you'll become a billionaire yourself. Which might not be a bad idea, as you'll have to pay some taxes on that property. Not much, of course, and I can loan it to you until you see profits."

"No! No mining!"

"All right, all right." He laughed. "We'll figure something out. I do still need a trail guide."

I pushed him backward until he landed on Maria's desk. Her papers were about to be mussed up. He caught me to him as I climbed on the desk to straddle him.

I filled my hands with his shirt collar and tugged him up to my mouth. Once I'd steamed us both up, I let him go long enough to growl in his ear. "I need to buy one of your horses. Maybe a mule or two."

"Anything you want. Now and forever."

I kissed that man senseless.

43

EPILOGUE

TIMOTHY

Denver's Ritz-Carlton had a more Western flare than the original in Manhattan, but the thread count of the sheets still felt delicious against naked skin. Afternoon sun filtered in through the partially closed drapes, and Frank sat cross-legged and naked where she belonged—on the bed at my side. I was scrolling through the multiple listing service for homes and condos near the university, and Frank was sketching in a notepad.

"Are you really going to buy another home? Just to be here a few weekends a year?"

"A few weekends? Beg your pardon. Didn't I tell you I quit?"

She looked up, astonished. "You what?"

"Oh yes. I realized just how much I hate holding the hands of overprivileged public servants. I'm ditching the D.C. scene, and it feels like liberation day, I'm telling you."

Her eyes were huge. "You're...what? You're retiring?"

"Oh. No. I'm taking my dad's job. Director of sales. That

puts me in charge of residential, commercial, and govern-
mental sales. He's thrilled—he gets to sit on the board and
order people around without having to do any work. And I get
to telecommute from anywhere I want. So what's wrong with
Denver until you get your degree?"

Frank was grinning. "You really are full of tricks, Timothy
Babcock."

A cocky response occurred to me, but I took her hand and
kissed it instead. "I'm just so grateful that you've forgiven me."

"Twice this afternoon alone." She winked at me. "And I
suspect we're not done yet."

"Hell no."

"Then go back to your real estate listings. I'm working on
something."

Since she was working in the nude, I had no trouble
agreeing to her plan. We worked together companionably. I
found a mountainside mansion that looked interesting, and a
duplex condo in the city. One foot in the country, one in the
city. Worth looking into.

I was just wondering if I wanted to put in my own private
airstrip at the Circle B when Frank finished drawing. "Here,"
she said, holding up her concept. "Since we no longer have to
hide the grotto from anyone at Daughtry Lake, I'd like to
rebuild the front wall of the cabin. That view is amazing at
sunrise. I'd love to see it from the inside. What about adding
windows like this? See? Would this destroy the nature of the
place?"

I smiled to see her rendering. She knew that particular cave
so well that the drawing might as well have been a photo. "I
think that would be amazing. You could also add a railing
around the ledge. Protect from the drop."

She scoffed as she took back the pad. "Railing? Please.
Anyone who falls off that cliff deserves to fall."

I laughed at her calm, bloodthirsty response. "You don't worry about other people?"

"What other people?" She was still suspicious of the idea of sharing the space. "We're not inviting anyone up there, are we?"

"Up to you. It's your place. But...what if there was, like...I don't know, um, a toddler?"

She looked at me sharply. "Are you talking about your nephew?"

"Oh. Um, sure. My nephew."

"You weren't!" She Frisbeed the pad off the bed and landed on me bodily. "Are you saying you want children? Timothy!"

She didn't seem opposed to the idea, so I admitted my small yearning. "I'm certainly not saying no to kids. I really like hanging out with Skip. I'm just thinking, wouldn't it be fun for you and me to—"

"Yes!" She bounced up and down on me, which made me grunt and then groan with pleasure. "I'd love to have kids! More than one. No only children. Did you only want one? Because I think three is a good number."

"I'm one of three myself." I grinned. "And I'm not saying we should get the horse before the cart, but since you're on top of me anyway—"

My phone rang. Frank grinned at me and hopped agilely off my boner. She retrieved her notepad. "Go ahead. Talk to whoever that is. I need to think about the grotto if there's a child or three who will join us there."

She left for the living room, and I checked my phone.

Ah. Aleister Darling. The man wasn't going to like my news.

"Alice," I said. "I'm afraid I have a little news for you."

"Oh no, no, no," he said, his voice even fussier than before. "I'm afraid I have news for you. I'm about to be arrested!"

I sat up. "Excuse me?"

"Arrested! I'm about to be arrested! My stars and garters!"

He even swore like a fictional British character. "What happened?"

"What happened? My god, *what happened*?" He sputtered and raged.

It took far too long to uncover the truth, which was that my quietly larcenous Alice had decided to expand his profit-making opportunities by breathing the news of the molybdenum battery not just to me. In fact, he had four other entrepreneurs looking for ways to scam money off the exceedingly illegal sharing of a patent application.

"All four of them discovered each other, and now they've bollixed up the entire opportunity! They're accusing each other, and now the source has come back to me! Mr. Babcock, you're the only one who hasn't made me absolutely miserable!"

I ran through the implications. "If you're about to be arrested, Alice, then why are you calling me? This time, your phone really might be bugged."

"And that is why I am calling you from the last working pay phone in Anacostia! So let us proceed, Mr. Babcock, before my car is relieved of its tires!"

"All right, Alice. Tell me. What do you want to keep me out of this?"

"A lawyer!" he shrieked. "The best lawyer money can buy! You do this and your name will never, ever come up! You have to rescue me!"

It was a small price to pay. He'd already sent me thirty-something thousand dollars to invest in a molybdenum processing plant. That would be a good start. "I'll do the research, Alice, and start you with a hundred-thousand dollar retainer at a top firm. Someone will call you tomorrow at your home. Will that do it?"

"Mr. Babcock, you're a scholar and a gentleman. I knew you could be counted on."

Aleister was going to prison. No doubt about it. But a good

lawyer would get him into a country-club facility and shorten his time. And I'd be left out of the whole mess.

I hung up with him and looked through the suite to where Frank was doing an impromptu dance, holding up her pad in delight.

Good karma. I got really, really lucky. I was never going to be so stupid again.

"Oh, Frank," I called to her as I left the bedroom. "I want to talk to you about who you're going to Quinn's engagement ball with. It's going to be the event of the season, you know."

She turned to me with a grin.

God, I was a lucky man.

The End. (And turn the page for info on the next in the series, URSULA. Thanks!)

A LITTLE FOR ME, A LITTLE FOR YOU

HEY! Will you rate me on Amazon, please? Just click the number of stars (five is best, hint hint) if you don't want to leave a review. It really makes a difference for an indie author like me. I'll be doing the happy dance when I see it!

And ALSO HEY! Sign up for my newsletter, whyncha? I'll write you sporadically when something strikes me as entertaining and tell you when a new book is coming out—plus you'll have access to subscriber-only page on my website where you'll be able to download all the epilogues. There's a novella there, plus the ebook prequel to the CUPID's QUEST series, free to subscribers and ONLY to subscribers.

Nice, huh? You betcha! You can subscribe on my website at https://www.pruwarren.com/

Thanks, cookie!

NEXT IN THE SERIES: URSULA

Ever seen a millionaire scrub his own toilet? Or do her own laundry? You're about to!

"Millionaire Culture Clash" is the hottest new reality TV show, pitting wealthy and privileged young people against each other to determine who really is the best at simple tasks like cooking, interior design, fashion, fine arts, or gardening. And why would they participate in a two-month competition without servants? Ursula Babcock knows the answer: Because they're bored out of their minds. Life has become so tedious lately. Prove to the world I'm the best interior decorator? Sure—I'll do that.

Lord Geordie, Marquess of Newcastle Upon Tyne, isn't bored so much as in need of a public make-over. A TV show to determine which millionaire can tend the most beautiful garden has potential—enough to leave England to join nine other young millionaires from around the world in search of respect, purpose, and plenty of air time.

Book five of the romcom Bad-Attitude Billionaires, URSULA is the spicy, laugh-out-loud sequel to QUINN, REGINA, SUZANNE, and TIMOTHY.

ABOUT THE AUTHOR

Pru Warren (who is writing this in the third person as if simply too modest to toot her own horn) bores easily and thus has been a daydreamer since roughly the Bronze Age.

She is addicted to writing because in a novel, you can make things come out the *right* way. Life and karma really ought to take note. There are *better solutions* to these pesky daily annoyances!

Besides her in-the-laptop God complex, Pru laughs often and easily, loathes cooking, and plays way too much solitaire. She's plotting world domination even as you read this, as long as she doesn't have to wake up too early to accomplish it.

The Pru Warren website is an action-packed laff riot. (Well, it ought to be, anyway.) You can explore at https://www.pruwarren.com/

facebook

ALSO BY PRU WARREN

The Bad-Attitude Billionaires Series

Quinn

Regina

Suzanne

Timothy

Ursula

Joanna

Nicholas

Q, R, and S also sold as a Bundle of three books

T, U, and J also sold as a Bundle of three books

The Aftermath Series

Happily Ever Aftermath

The Morning Aftermath

Before and Aftermath

Also sold as a bundle of three books

Cupid's Quest:

Cupid's Quest Season One

Cupid's Quest Season Two

Cupid's Question Season Three

Also sold as a bundle of three books

Cupid's Quest The Prequel (Paperback only)

(Newsletter subscribers get the Prequel ebook as a benefit of membership)

The Muse Books

City Muse

History's Muse

Untamed Muse

Also sold as a bundle of three books

The Ampersand Series:

Cyn & the Peanut Butter Cup

Dash & the Moonglow Mystic

Ellyn & the Would-Be Gigolo

Farrah & the Court-Appointed Boss

Also sold as a bundle of four books

The Surprise Heiress Series:

Breath of Fresh Heiress

Full of Hot Heiress

Vanished Into Thin Heiress

Also sold as a bundle of three books

You Decide Books:

Emma's Mission

A Spirit Guide for Anna Maria

The Christmas Pageant:

The Christmas Pageant

Return of the Christmas Pageant

Bride of the Christmas Pageant

.

Joan's Journal (Love Gone Viral) (out of print, alas, but available free in
ebook form to newsletter subscribers) (hint, hint)

www.ingramcontent.com/pod-product-compliance
Lightning Source LLC
Chambersburg PA
CBHW072130250626
47159CB00007B/2638